PILATE'S FAITH

Book Eight in the
John Pilate Mystery Series

BY
J. ALEXANDER GREENWOOD

A Caroline Street Press Book

Cover designed by Jason McIntyre TheFarthestReaches.com

Portions of this book were previously published in the novella *Pilate's Shadow.*

Books by J. Alexander Greenwood

Fiction:

Pilate's Cross

Pilate's Cross: The Audiobook

Pilate's Key

Pilate's Ghost

Pilate's Blood

Pilate's 7

Pilate's Rose

Pilate's Shadow

Pilate's Faith

Big Cabin & Dispatches from the West

(with Robert E. Trevathan)

On Kindle Vella:

The Sign

Non-Fiction

Kickstarter Success Secrets

Kickstarter Success Secrets: The Audiobook

The Podcast Option

The Podcast Option: The Audiobook

Visit MGOPod.com

for updates, merchandise,

and the

Mysterious Goings On podcast.

For the faithful readers.

"But when you ask, you must believe and not doubt, because the one who doubts is like a wave of the sea, blown and tossed by the wind."

James 1:6 NIV

Chapter One

"I made you something." John Pilate's eyes fluttered open.

"Guess what? I'm going to open the little door to give it to you. If you will be nice-nice, you get more nice things."

"Nice-nice? Who are you?" Pilate said, propping himself up on one elbow. "Why are you doing this?"

"We've been through that, sir," his captor said with a petulant sigh. "Now, do you want this or not?"

He didn't care what it was. An open access panel door meant some cool air could get in. That was worth more than gold.

"Okay, okay," Pilate said, rolling on his side and sitting up, the relative coolness of the atmosphere on the floor obliterated by the heat layer hanging in the stultifying darkness two feet above the concrete. He flagged as nausea briefly overwhelmed him, and his gorge began to rise until he willed it back down, swallowing intensely and painfully in his parched throat.

"Okay, sir, now you be nice-nice here and I will open the panel. Okay?"

Pilate tried to place the accent. It wasn't foreign, exactly, but there was something odd about the speech pattern. It was oddly flat most of the time, but when he was excited it became an off-kilter approximation of the giddiness of a child. It was a staccato, honking vocal gyration, the aftertones of which unfailingly lasted about two seconds after each excited sentence.

"Okay, sir? Nice-Nice?"

Pilate gasped, realizing he had not answered verbally, instead he had sputtered, *Okay, mother—* in his mind, cut off by his captor.

"Okay, okay," Pilate said. "Nice-nice."

"So stand back, okay sir?"

"Yeah, yeah," Pilate said, a lone bead of sweat trickling down his forehead into his eyes, like at the gym. He felt itchy and dazed; the one-liter plastic bottle of lukewarm water he had been given last night was nearly drained. It was hot in here, not quite like an oven right before the frozen pizza goes in, but damn close.

The panel door slid back, a sliver of light cut through the soupy black cloud, accompanied by a gust of air – cool in comparison to the dead heat of his cage, but not refrigerator cold. With the panel open, he could hear the faintest roar in the distance – the sound of a highway not too far away – but he could not spare attention to that right now, not with fresh air playing on his face.

"Jesus," Pilate whispered. "Thank you, Jesus."

"Oh, so NOW you're into Jesus?" Pilate's old friend Simon teased from inside his head.

"Shut up, Simon," Pilate rasped. *Wouldn't want Mr. Nice-Nice to think I'm crazy. That goes for you, too, Jesus.*

Taking advantage of the momentary light from the doorway, he turned to peer into the dim shadows of the room. A worn and rickety wheelchair rested on its side in the corner, where Pilate had previously kicked it, the bucket to piss in unused in the opposite corner.

Not much liquid left in me.

The urge to move his bowels or vomit had mostly subsided, though the cramp in his gut—a fun feature of heat sickness—was ever-present, a perpetual, hateful kick in the balls.

The panel door was four feet off the ground, a rough rectangle about a foot tall and eight inches wide. A three-inch deep ledge was set inside; Pilate made out the lumpy welds around the ledge he had previously sensed by touch.

"Hey," Pilate said. "Hot in here."

"Now sir, you're trying to lose some weight," the voice said, then the honking laugh.

"Ha, ha," Pilate said. "Seriously, I've had heat stroke before, and it's not good, okay? This could kill me—"

"Do you want what I made for you, sir?"

"If it's an air conditioner," Simon said. *"Or a goddamned Glock. Or maybe a bazooka, even."*

"Sure. But wait, what's your name, pal?" Pilate said, switching gears.

"I am trying to give you something, sir," the voice was dull and flat again, signifying...impatience?

"Okay," Pilate said, rising to his feet and moving closer to the panel and the blessing of a breeze.

"That's close enough, sir. Stop there, okay? Nice-nice!" Pilate winced at the suddenly-loud, pestilential honking.

"Okay," Pilate said, luxuriating in the relatively cool breeze from outside the box – he was pretty sure it was a shipping container—he called home for...how many hours, now?

"Now you wait there," the honking laugh again. "You're going to love this, sir."

Pilate was intrigued, but more than anything, he wanted to keep this guy talking and that cool breeze blowing.

"Why are you keeping me here?" he said, trying to sound curious rather than outraged.

"Please, sir, it is now the effervescent moment. I made it for you."

"What?"

"Shhh." A black nitrile-gloved hand, at the business end of a long-sleeved white shirt, darted into the panel, a single index finger making the "one moment" gesture, then darting back out like the tongue of some alien lizard.

"*Oh for fuck's sake,*" Simon said...his voice strangely outside Pilate's head now...almost as if he were perched in a shadowy corner, observing.

Pilate ran a hand through his sweaty hair and breathed the welcome fresh air in deeply. Besides being cool, it didn't smell as dank and metallic as this makeshift cell. An oddly familiar *chokka* sound filtered inside the room along with the cool air, chased by silence.

"*Oh, come on. It can't be,*" Simon said.

"Ta-da!" The hand reappeared, holding a glass containing a clear liquid cold enough to make it glisten with sweat. Pilate chuckled at the thought of a glass sweating as much as he was.

With a flourish, the gloved hand placed the glass on the ledge and withdrew.

"Somewhere between a martini glass and a coupe, the Nick and Nora glass, named after the cinematic husband-and-wife detective team," the man said, apparently reading. "It brings back the suave sophistication of 1930s high life." He broke out into more honking.

"Oh my God," Pilate said. It was indeed a martini glass. It was also his favorite style, the Nick and Nora model, featured in the *Thin*

Man series with William Powell and the sexiest woman who ever lived, Myrna Loy.

"Please, drink, sir!" this time with the honking punctuated by nitrile-skinned hand claps.

"What is it?"

"Martini, sir. Of course!" *Honk, honk, honk.* "I made you a special treat."

"Umm, thanks. But the last drink I had from you made me sick and got me stuck in this box. Pass," he coughed. "What I could really use is a gallon or so of ice water."

"You'll please drink this special thing I made," he cleared his throat. "Drink it or you will not like the consequences, sir."

"It rubs the lotion on its skin," Simon intoned sardonically.

"I already don't like the damn consequences," Pilate said. "My name is John. Not sir. Now, I have been patient with you, but hear this, Mister Nice-Nice. Listening? People will be looking for me. Important people who are often tempted to violence. Get me? So you have a choice. You can let me out now and I will forget about this—"

"Like hell," Simon said.

"Or you leave me in here and my friends at Key West PD find you and kick your ass from here to the Dry Tortugas."

"You drink my special thing or I will close this door and leave you here in the hot all day tomorrow." The voice was detached, flat and soft.

"What do you want from me?" Pilate screamed, his voice echoing painfully off the room's scorching metal walls, his face filling the open panel. He looked through the opening but saw only a bright set of work lights in what looked to be a hallway.

Hmm. Not outside.

"Special drink," two hand claps, one after each word, punctuating the way annoying people do when texting. "Getting warm."

"Fine," Pilate said, snatching the Nick and Nora from the ledge, swallowing half of the drink without hesitation. It was vodka, perhaps some gin and a hint of Lillet Blanc and lemon.

"It's actually a passable Vesper martini," Simon said.

"You like?"

Pilate put the glass back on the ledge. "It's fine."

"Your favorite, right?"

"Yes," Pilate's voice barely above a whisper.

"Finish it?"

Pilate picked up the glass. "Maybe later. I'll hang on to it."

"You should finish it before it gets warm," the man said.

"What do you want with me?" Pilate said again, his naked irritability waning with the cool air and the drink.

"Want?"

"Yes," he said. "Why did you abduct me?"

"We are friends now, right?"

"Who?" Pilate asked.

"You and me. We are friends now."

"If you say so, chief," Pilate said. "Is this what you do with your friends? Lock them in a hot box?"

"I want something only a friend can provide," he said.

"Oh shit, does he want you to write a book for him?" Simon said.

"Well, tell me what it is, and maybe I can help and we can be better friends," Pilate said.

"I'm…I'm shy."

"Don't be shy, my friend," Pilate said, trying to smooth out the ragged syllables, his face hovering close to the panel again. "Tell me what you need."

The panel slid shut, cutting off the sounds of the distant roadway, the harsh slamming sound painfully reverberating in Pilate's ears in the sudden silence.

"Maybe later."

Pilate screamed, shattering the glass against the wall.

Interlude: 40 Years Ago

"I made you something," Johnny said, presenting a piece of cardboard in his shaking hands, his towhead mop falling into wide, dark eyes.

The woman didn't look away from the television. "Shhh, I'm watching this."

"Oh, well, I made it to say sorry for—"

"Shut up. I'm trying to watch this," she jerked her head towards him, then back to the TV. "Well, never mind, it went to commercial and I missed it. Thanks."

"I'm sorry," the boy said, his hands trembling.

"What is that?" She looked at his hands.

He brightened. "It's a card I made to say I was sorry for breaking the knob on the radio."

Her eyes darted at the cardboard. "You're getting glitter everywhere. And that's not going to get you out of being grounded. Now go to your room."

"Okay," he placed the card beside her on the sofa.

She reached for a pack of cigarettes, knocking the card with glue and loose glitter and crayons spelling "Sorry" on the floor.

"Dammit, Johnny, get back in here and clean up this stupid mess."

Interlude: A Week Ago

The fist crossed his jaw, forcing his head back an inch, jolting him into a strangely calm, split-second silence. His impulse was to turn away, to flee, but that would expose a defenseless flank. Instead, he kept his fists up, blocking his face from his attacker, leaving his ribs open for the stabbing left hook that knocked the air from his lungs.

"Oof," Pilate gasped, staggering back on his left foot.

"Come on, ya bum. Get in there," Simon said, ringing a bell in his head.

Pilate reset his stance and fired off a jab with his left. It was a random and desperate blow, a mile off target, but he had to do something to try and slow down the incoming onslaught of punches.

Another fusillade of hooks pounded Pilate's ribs, driving him into the ropes, where he hung like a half-deflated Mylar balloon entangled on a fence.

"Is this all you got?" Simon growled.

Pilate inhaled and pulled away from the ropes. He hopped on the balls of his feet, keeping his distance, breathing as deeply as he could through his mouthpiece and nostrils. He was having a tough time getting his lungs to fully inflate.

His opponent closed the distance in three steps, firing off a jab that glanced off Pilate's headgear. Pilate took the opportunity and landed a right hook, forcing his opponent to retreat. He followed up with a simple jab cross combo to the head.

"Get after it!" Simon bellowed.

Seizing the momentum, Pilate strode forward, firing off a sloppy left jab, right hook combo that landed, but with little force.

"Don't get cute, Rock!" Simon said. Pilate imagined Simon wearing a beanie and an old school hearing aid, cursing from ringside.

Pilate's opponent pivoted, ducking a cross he hadn't thrown and punching him in the solar plexus. Pilate groaned, dropped to one knee and covered his face with both gloved fists until the bell rang. Pilate hauled himself to his feet, the rip of Velcro signaling his opponent removing gloves with the help of a trainer.

"Nice hits, guys," Felix the trainer said, tipping his hat to a lanky, greasy-haired guy behind him. "Nick, one: don't stand so close to me. Two: get them towels." Nick nodded like a squirrel working a hugely juicy nut and scooted away.

Pilate nodded, breathing heavily in the swampy gym atmosphere. The gym's website bragged about this being an authentic, straight out of *Rocky* boxing gym with no air conditioning. Pilate had thought that was somehow a plus at the time. Now he needed an inhaler to get through most bouts, his exercise-induced asthma more acute these days.

Felix pulled Pilate's gloves off. Hands free, Pilate removed his headgear.

"Nice work, John," Val said, removing hers. "I thought you had me there for a second."

"Right," Pilate said, his wrapped fist bumping hers, sliding through the ropes and stepping down from the ring. "I was lucky to get out of there on my feet."

Val climbed down, adjusting a black sports bra underneath her red tank top. "Technically, one foot, one knee. But you held your own."

Pilate made a face, eyes heavenward.

"Let's get our miles in and then you can go."

Pilate nodded grimly.

"Oh, stop pouting," Val said, swigging an orange concoction from her sports bottle. "You're the one who wants to lose fifteen pounds."

"Yeah, yeah," Pilate said, gulping from his bottle, then taking a pull off his inhaler. The lanky, greasy-haired man offered him a towel. Pilate shook his head dismissively. "No thanks." The man nodded and loped after Felix, who brought him to heel with a whistle.

Val shoved their boxing gear in a locker and tapped a few times on the screen of her sports watch. "You okay?"

Pilate nodded. "Yeah, my lungs are a little challenged these days. Mostly allergies, and exercise makes it worse. The inhaler helps."

She nodded. "Alright. Ready? I'll take it easy on you. Here to Knight Pier and back. No stopping, no walking. Go." Val's athletic frame bounded out the door, her ponytail bouncing with each step.

"Hey, you're the one who wanted to go this whole 'Spencer for Hire' route. So get a move on, John. Simon says."

Pilate sighed and hit the street.

After the run and a pokey bicycle ride home, he straightened the "For Sale" sign hanging from the old Trevathan place's porch. Pilate hated to let it go, as Trevathan had left it to the Pilate family, but things had not worked out the way the old man had hoped. The little cottage wasn't a haven for his family to escape to; it was instead the epicenter of mayhem, misadventure, and marital distrust. If he truly wanted to get his family back, the entire island of Key West was a distraction he could no longer afford.

Pilate stepped gingerly from the small galley kitchen, chugging a Yeti Rambler brimming with ice water in one hand, a gallon freezer baggie of ice in the other. His old friend Trevathan's lounge chair groaned predictably under his weight. He placed the bag of ice on the top of his left foot, which pulsed with a stubborn case of tendonitis.

He set the ice water on the end table and reached for his MacBook. He opened his email and was met with thirty-six new messages. He quickly deleted the come-ons to buy something and scanned a few others asking him to speak at the local Rotary club or donate autographed books to charity auctions before he marked them *unread* to deal with later.

A message from his mother and father remained in cyber purgatory, unopened days after it had arrived. Another email from someone calling himself "Harold Strong" had a subject line that caught his eye: "Boxing Fan." Strong said he loved Pilate's book and heard he liked to box. He wanted to buy him "a nice drink" and have a chat about his ideas of "why friendships are ordained by the universe" whenever Pilate "had an hour or two of free time." Pilate chuckled and wrote back: **"Maybe one of these days. Glad you liked the book, friend."**

A reporter with the *Miami Herald*, doing a story on leaders and powerful people suspected of having narcissistic personality disorder, wanted to interview Pilate about his long-dead nemesis, Jack Lindstrom. He typed a reply.

"Thank you for your interest in my thoughts. Jack Lindstrom was a damned nightmare for nearly everyone who knew him. So, I hope you understand I don't want to spend one more minute of my life thinking about him. Good luck with your story (Yes, you can print this.)"

Sending the message from the *Herald* reporter brought another e-mail scrolling onto the page, and the name "Kate Nathaniel" in the sender field made him catch his breath and sit up straight. It wasn't from her work account at Cross College, the one she usually used, even for non-business matters. This one was her old personal account, which she hadn't used much since they married. Or perhaps he didn't get email from her much, until lately.

Kate and John had not been in touch - no calls, no texts, no instant messages, no e-mails, never mind an actual letter, God forbid, in the two weeks since she asked—no, *demanded*—her space and he gave it to her. He missed her and the kids both, truth be told, but he was trying to respect her wishes, as in, "I wish you would get your shit together."

"Shit coming together, babe," Simon said.

Pilate mentally waved off his inner voice and read the email. She asked for money for the kids' school clothes and to finish repairing the damage to their living room, still messed up from a home invasion a couple of years ago.

Kate didn't specify an amount. He toggled over to his bank account online and transferred $10,000. For once, he had plenty of money. His recently recovered book royalties made him more or less liquid, and the pay from the occasional teaching or writing gig, as well as living in his deceased pal's "fishing shack" rent-free, helped make ends meet, while Kate's income was adequate to keep her and the kids afloat in relatively low-rent Cross Township. The most he spent on himself was on personal training fees and vodka...and he was trying to cut back on the potato juice.

Pilate read on.

"And since we are taking a break here I wanted you to know that Grant Fielding from the history department asked me out to coffee. I'm going to go. He's a friend—that's all, but I wanted to let you know because you know you can't do anything in this town without the gossips--"

Pilate felt his guts spasm, his breath became choppy, chest tightening, accompanied by a tinny, piercing whine in his ears.

"Mother..." he muttered. He breathed deep after a few staccato breaths, starting the anxiety attack protocol Dr. Sandberg taught him.

"Where's the threat?" he asked himself. This began the calming process.

"Anxiety attacks can be headed off relatively quickly with practice, John." Sandberg had said. Pilate worked silently, breathing steadily, adjusting. Adjusting.

"Steady, John," Simon said. *"Where's that inhaler?"*

Pilate's eyes focused back on the screen.

"...gossips mouthing off. I need a friend. You understand that, right?"

Pilate slammed the laptop closed and kicked the ice pack off his foot; it hit the wall and burst open, spraying half-moon-shaped pieces of ice across the room. "Take my damned money and go. I don't care."

Hot tears stung his eyes. He prowled the room, then went into the galley, jerked open the old fridge door and scooped up a bottle of Tanqueray vodka in one rough gesture.

"John," Simon whispered.

He snatched a rocks glass from the cabinet over the sink and poured it halfway full.

"John," Simon whispered again.

Pilate slammed down a swallow.

"John," Simon whispered.

"What?" he growled.

"There's Lillet in the fridge and half a lemon in cling wrap in the door."

Pilate downed the remnants of his glass and strode out to the porch. He swung his hips into a round kick that sent the "For Sale" sign to the street below.

Interlude: 6 Days Ago

"Wow. You look like shit," Val said the next morning, looking up from wrapping her hands.

Pilate grunted and dropped his bag. His head throbbed; his eyes felt like they had been rolled in fresh-mown grass clippings and jammed back in his skull backwards.

"Hey sunny, this one of those days?" Val said, her dark green eyes dancing under sculptured brows, ponytail dancing as she bobbed her head for comic effect.

He nodded, digging in his bag for hand wraps.

"Seriously," Val said, standing up. "Have you eaten anything?"

"No," he said. His chest felt as if it was bandaged tightly, the same feeling he'd had years ago, when he was shot in Cross Township.

She searched his red-rimmed eyes. "Yo, John?"

He glanced up at her a second, then went back to fishing for his wraps.

The bell clanged; two people sparred in the ring. Pilate stopped a moment, watching the clumsy ballet as the pair bobbed, weaved, and punched—mostly striking the almost visible, humid air.

"We're, uhhhh, not boxing today," Val said. "As much as I think you want to hit something, we're going to do something else."

Pilate didn't argue as she stripped off her wraps and dropped them in her bag. "Come on."

The coffee's aroma dazed him for a second; John detected traces of hazelnut wafting past as he sat on the deck outside, idly watching Val through the window as she ordered their coffee at Frenchie's Cafe, a tiny bistro housed in a white cottage with blue trim, next door to the

Southernmost Inn, in turn, not far from the iconic Southernmost Point buoy.

Val's tanned, compact, muscular frame moved efficiently past two other customers, through the tiny cafe out to the porch overlooking United Street. Pilate pegged her at about thirty, though with her rich brown hair and vibrant bronze skin, she could easily pass for younger. He rarely saw her wear makeup at the gym, of course. And she didn't need it. Pilate admired her pragmatic approach to life and even tolerated her taste for playing country music during workouts. She was getting over a breakup with a cop.

"Total jerkface," he remembered her saying once in passing. "Turned out to be a real lunk on a power trip. Officer Asshole."

Asshole or not, Pilate couldn't comprehend how a guy could allow himself to lose a woman like Val. *She's the total package.*

"Kate loves a hazelnut blend," Simon ventured from the recesses of his mind.

Val brought him a large coffee and sat across from him. "Croque Madames coming out in a minute."

"Nice." He nodded and picked up the coffee. "Thanks. I need sugar."

"I think so, too," she said as he took the coffee to the cream and sugar station inside. He dumped a few packets of the brown raw stuff in and gave it a cursory stir before returning to the porch.

Val sipped her coffee, looking up as several scooters, tiny engines cutting through the thick Florida Keys air like wheeled buzz saws, whipped down the street towards the Southernmost Point buoy.

"Thanks, Val."

"You look better already," she said, her smile revealing dimples and impossibly straight white teeth.

"Yeah, but in about fifteen minutes I'm gonna need to poop," he smirked.

"There's an alley," she said, jerking her head over her shoulder and returning to her cup, eyes on the street.

He nodded; his eyes joining her gaze on the horizon, looking south towards the end of America.

"I…had kind of a rough night," he said.

"No kidding?" Val's smile flashed a perfunctory verbal jab.

"I uh, well, I think my marriage may be in trouble," his voice broke. He wiped his eyes on his sleeve self-consciously.

"Oh," she said. "How do you…I mean…what happened?"

"Got an email. She's apparently seeing somebody else."

"Oh my God," Val said, turning over the coldness of a "Dear John" email in her mind.

"Yeah, I mean, she said that she was going to go for coffee with a guy."

"I'm confused," Val said, cocking her head. "Coffee. Like you and I are having now?"

Pilate stopped, slowly shook his head. "Well, I mean, it's different…here. What we are…doing. We're friends."

She nodded. "And this guy…he's not her friend?" She made air quotes.

Pilate sighed, then shrugged, exasperated at himself. "If you are expecting me to be consistent and logical about things, can I remind you that last night I probably killed the last two or three remaining neurons that I had assigned to those jobs?"

"Okay. Let's put a pin in the question of who is cheating and how for a minute," she reached for her coffee cup, then stopped herself. "How long have you been separated? You never said."

"About six months. I haven't seen her or the kids in three," he said, thinking back to a quick visit to Cross, where he picked up clothes and spent some time with his children. Kate had all her defenses up, full armor and prickly defensive from head to toe, but he felt some progress. They'd slept in separate rooms; their energy and conversation was focused on the kids, but still. Progress.

And he had ratcheted up his visits with Dr. Sandberg.

"Shit, man, I'm sorry," Val said, her green eyes downcast.

He nodded. "I was…careless."

"Oh," she said, inferring something she wasn't sure he meant.

"Any idea what you're going to do?" she said.

"No," Pilate said. "I mean, I don't want to move back to that hellhole in Nebraska, but she doesn't want to leave. I miss my kids and was gearing up to move back when this hit. Even put the shack on the market." He looked out at the street at a flock of tourists walking past. "Now I guess I could still move back. Just be Mister Weekend Dad in a hellhole."

"Hmmm." Val sat back in her chair. "Maybe I should've let you punch something. I don't know much about family, John, and what I do know isn't happy knowledge. My own childhood…I learned that lots of promises get made in families, but the person making them rarely means it. Or even tries to mean it." Her features softened and she gazed at the wall behind Pilate's head, lost in memory. She shook her head and returned to the present. "John…your wife is a grown woman. She can take care of herself, and if she can't that's not your fault. What your marriage means to you and what it means to her, that's all you guys' business. But your kids, John. If you're making promises to them that you don't mean to keep, well, I like you. I like you a lot."

She blushed, then her features went cold. "But I will beat you into the dirt of Key West at high noon if you're jerking little kids' hearts around." She sighed. "That's the longest speech I've given to a man since I told Officer Asshole to get his sagging butt out of my house."

Their joint peal of laughter filled the little cafe, and the tightness weighing down Pilate's heart since he read Kate's email began to loosen, ever so slightly, at the unexpected warmth.

Interlude: 5 Days Ago

"How did it feel physically?"

"What?"

"When you read what Kate said about the coffee date?" Dr. Sandberg said, shifting in his chair, yellow legal pad and pen in hand.

"Like I was having a heart attack, you know?"

Sandberg nodded.

"Well," Pilate cleared his throat. "I saw red. Like I could barely think. My pulse was probably racing, too."

"So was there a sensation in your chest or your stomach?" His open hand hovered over his chest.

Pilate leaned back in his chair. "Both, I guess. Not pleasant."

"Was it a radiating pain or—"

"Stabbing, then a tightness."

"In your chest?" Sandberg said, his hand dropping back to his lap.

Pilate nodded.

"And you couldn't think?"

"No, not really. Not for a few seconds. I got mad. I kicked a bag of ice across the room."

"A bag of ice?" Sandberg looked confused.

"I was icing my foot after a workout. Trust me, better the ice bag than my laptop."

The therapist nodded. "What were you feeling in your gut?"

"Nausea. I wanted to throw up."

Sandberg nodded again. "How long, the nausea?"

"Probably the better part of twenty minutes. I drank some vodka to calm it down," Pilate said, looking away.

"Careful John, you tell him too much about drinking and you may not get to drink anymore," Simon chimed in.

Sandberg made a quick note on the pad. "Did the drinking help the sensation go away?"

"I think it started to go away before the booze kicked in," Pilate said. "I felt short of breath. Sick, you know? And my chest was tight. Almost like when I got the wind knocked out of me trying to do a double play in little league. Not fun."

Sandberg nodded, standing up to close the blinds behind Pilate, then returning to his seat. "Then what?"

"What?"

"Once the feeling faded away, and you started drinking, what happened?"

"I don't remember."

"Do you drink every day?"

"Used to. Until this happened I was working out instead. It helped. I wanted to lose weight. Vodka is empty calories."

"You want to lose weight—is that the main reason you started working out?"

Pilate twisted his mouth a bit. "Well, I mean, I guess I wanted to look better."

"Better?"

"For when I went back to Cross."

Sandberg looked up from his notes. "You were going to visit?"

"No, I was going to move back home to fix my marriage. I can fix it."

Sandberg looked at Pilate impassively.

"At least I thought I could. But that's not going to happen now." Pilate's hands trembled, his eyes watered. "I blew it. Stupid."

"I'm sorry." After a moment, he said, "You know, you say that often."

"What?"

"Stupid. You call yourself 'stupid' pretty often in our sessions," Sandberg said.

Pilate shrugged. "I guess 'cause I am."

He raised an eyebrow and thrust his head forward. "Really? Okay. Why do you think that?"

"Have you been listening to me the past few God only knows how many years?" Pilate said, raising his voice, trying to play off his frustration as a joke.

"Come on, man. You're a bestselling writer, a teacher, and a community leader. You've done some extraordinary shit—I mean you helped take down a drug cartel, for Pete's sake. I deal with lots of people day-in, day-out. I see what stupid looks like. You're far from stupid."

"I do stupid things," Pilate said, waving him away.

"I locked my keys in the car the other day—while it was running. Had to have my wife come home from work to help me. Does that make me stupid?"

"No, you made a mistake. Probably had your mind on other things."

Sandberg nodded. "You told me you got called stupid a lot when you were a child."

Pilate looked at his balled-up hands in his lap. "Yeah, there was some teasing."

"Teasing?"

"I did stupid things sometimes. What does this have to do with Kate?"

"It's not about Kate. It's about you, and how you react to certain things. You're very judgmental of yourself. So they weren't teasing?"

"What?"

"Growing up. You just said you were teased…called you stupid. Then you said that you actually did do stupid things. Which was it?"

"They did the best they could," Pilate said, softly, looking at the shelf of autographed baseballs behind Sandberg. "She wasn't well," he said, rubbing his neck, eyes still on the baseballs. "Is that a Marlins ball?"

Sandberg nodded.

"I like the Royals."

"Mom wasn't well?" Sandberg said.

"She's better now," Pilate said. "You know."

"You have two kids," he said, looking at his notes. "Kara and—"

"Peter. You know that, come on."

"Do they do stupid things?" Sandberg raised his eyebrows, his eyes vaguely innocent. Pilate had seen this look before, when he was setting a small trap in therapy.

"They're kids."

"Do they misbehave?" he said.

"Yeah. All kids do," Pilate said, shrugging. "But they're good kids."

"Does Peter do stuff that makes you mad?" Sandberg said.

"Mad? No. Irritated, sure. He spills stuff a lot. But he's barely out of diapers, so—"

"Ever call him stupid?" Sandberg cut in.

"No," Pilate said, flatly, his breathing shallow.

"Ever hit him?"

"No," Pilate growled, glaring up from the fists in his lap.

"Would you want Kara or Peter to spend a week living in the environment you lived in as a child?"

"Stop pushing my buttons, God damn it. Don't talk about my kids, man." Pilate's chest ached, his vision clouded, his breath coming in short sips. He stood up. "I gotta go."

Sandberg rose to his feet. "John, are you okay?"

Pilate looked past him, hands raised, palms open. "Let me go," he said, voice breaking.

"Hey, let's sit back down and let you calm down for a minute," Sandberg said, his voice soothing. "We don't have to talk, okay?"

"I feel sick," Pilate said, easing back into his chair. The room was swimming, his breath coming in short, ragged sips.

"Just breathe," Sandberg said. "Where's the threat? Breathe. Let me get you some water."

Sandberg opened the door, went out into the anteroom and brought back a paper cup of cold water. He handed it to Pilate.

Pilate drank it and started to breathe deeply.

They sat in silence.

"I have never hit my kids. You know I would never, ever hit a kid," Pilate said, words navigating his tight lips. "And I never tell them they're stupid, or worthless or that I don't want them around. I am not like that and never will be."

"John, I know that," he said. "I wondered if you truly did."

Pilate nodded. "What's going on in here, then?" Pilate said, tapping himself on the chest with his knuckle.

"We've worked on your issues for quite some time, John, and developed ways to treat the symptoms. The panic attacks. I think we're at a point where we need to start to work on finding the roots of what happened to make you the way you are."

"The way I am?" Pilate said, wiping a tear away.

"You have a form of post-traumatic stress disorder," Sandberg said.

"Really?"

"Yes, John."

"I think we suspected that for a while now, right?" Pilate sighed deeply, leaning back in the chair and finishing off the water. "From when I nearly got killed that first winter in Cross."

The psychologist shook his head. "I think that event, as well as several others you have endured before and after, have certainly made it worse. Trauma is cumulative, and you've been dealing with some pretty serious issues since you were a child. I think you developed defense mechanisms to survive some rough stuff that happened when you were a little boy. I think because of your mother's illness, you unfortunately learned to despise yourself early and often."

"Wait just a damn minute," Simon said. *"Is he talking about me?"*

"I think this imaginary friend of yours…what's his name?"

Pilate shrugged, looking at the floor.

Sandberg flipped through his notes. "Simon."

"That's my name, don't wear it out," Simon hissed. *"I don't like him anymore. Let's steal his baseball collection and go on the run."*

"John, part of the issues you're having with PTSD, with your anxiety attacks, is that you are quite self-aware. You feel them coming on and you get disgusted with yourself for having them."

"Well, I don't think…. I mean, it's not like I…" he trailed off.

"What?"

"PTSD is for people in combat, or firemen or cops. It's not like I've…I don't know," Pilate said.

"Earned it?" Sandberg said. "Most of my patients with PTSD got it when they were kids. Dad was a drunk, Aunt Edna was a toucher. Mom burned the house down falling asleep with a joint and the dog died in the fire but everyone blamed little David. I see a fair number of vets and first responders, John, but even for them the initial trauma, the root trauma, its childhood or domestic stuff. People who were abused as kids, or people abused by a spouse. Most of them think they don't have PTSD because they don't wear a uniform. The ones who do blame the day of some horrible incident or attack as the cause, but all it did was poke the old wound and get it bleeding again."

Pilate sat back in his chair a moment; his temples throbbed.

"So, you don't fully accept the attacks, John. You get mad at yourself. You despise it as some sort of inborn weakness. Over the years it got worse and worse."

"But I have worked on it," Pilate pointed at Sandberg. "With you."

Sandberg nodded, and put his notes aside, leaning forward with his elbows on his knees. "But we've hit a spot where you understand it, and you know how to calm down until the attacks pass, but you still press the ejector seat button and don't get at the full issue. Understand?"

"Dunno," Pilate said, taking a deep breath, then clearing his lungs noisily.

"It's a lot like Chinese finger traps," he said. "You know what those are?" He rose up and put his index fingers together, tip to tip.

"Yeah. Got a pair at the State Fair when I was a kid. Chinese handcuffs."

"Okay, me too. Well, you know how they work. You put these on some unsuspecting person's fingers, and they get excited—"

"They panic."

"Well…sort of. Panic isn't quite the word--but okay. So they get excited and pull their fingers apart. But that does what?" He continued to act it out. "It only makes them tighter. The way to escape is simple. Just push the ends toward the middle. That opens up the ends a bit and frees the fingers."

"Yeah," Pilate said.

"Okay. So, your way of dealing with these attacks has been like that. You get so upset about having the attacks, that instead of relaxing and fully dealing with the situation, you get angry at yourself, and that only makes the trap worse. You almost literally beat yourself up for having an anxiety attack."

"Makes me feel helpless," he said, crossing his arms over his chest.

"And helpless is something that abused children feel above all else, John. There's nowhere to turn, usually nobody to appeal to. They just have to cope. Lots of kids create imaginary friends to help them get through it. Then, as they get older, they react to emotional stimuli like this in the same way they did as a child. It helps them survive, but that doesn't always square with being an adult."

"Says you," Simon said.

"And from what you've told me, Simon isn't always all that much comfort. He's your friend in some ways, but he's also a tormentor. He's reminding you of all the things you grew up believing about yourself: that you lack worth, that you're a bad person. This janiform existence isn't healthy."

"So I need to get rid of Simon?" Pilate said.

27

"Perish the thought," Simon said.

"No, not at all!" the psychologist shook his head almost violently. "He's YOU, John. You can't get rid of yourself, try as you might with vodka and fighting drug lords."

"I've changed my mind, this guy's okay again. Cancel the ball heist." Simon purred.

Sandburg, not privy to his readmission to the kingdom, continued. "You need him to be in his proper place. When an anxiety attack hits, you have to say hi to it, acknowledge that it's happening and work your way through it."

"I have been." Pilate said, exasperated.

"Yes, but you also have to tell Simon that you're okay. That *he* is okay. Simon is that little boy, dressed up in a big boy costume. You need to tell him that you see him, but his help is not required in dealing with adult John Pilate stuff at the present time. You need to be kind to him, but hand him an imaginary iPad and let him be a little boy while you handle stuff."

"Could I give him a martini, a smoke, and a copy of Playboy from 1983 instead?"

Sandberg smiled and nodded. "Whatever he needs to occupy himself. Hand that stuff to him and tell him you got this. And maybe he'll stop with the nasty comments."

Simon blew a raspberry. *"Psychological double talk. You need me, John. You always will. Maybe not today, but the next time the shit hits the fan, you'll be crying for your old pal Simon."*

Interlude: 4 Days Ago

Pilate cruised down U.S. 1, eyes drifting from the road to the azure waves being whitecapped by the high winds. His mind raced, helpfully picturing lurid scenarios centered on Kate. Was she already seeing Grant, and the email was a formality to let him get used to the idea? Or was she sincerely having coffee?

"Oh, Grant. You are so erudite and funny. I love the patches on your elbows!" Simon said.

"Shut up, Simon," Pilate said aloud.

"It doesn't help that he's better looking and smarter than you," Simon said. *"He's like Ryan Reynolds with a PhD."*

"I know. Shut the fuck up, okay?" Pilate growled internally. If Grant is so great, why is he teaching history in a tiny backwater like Cross College? Then again, legendary author Harley Cordwainer taught there, too.

"And your old pal Trevathan did, too. He was a solid guy," Simon said. *"And you nearly got him killed. John, have you considered that you aren't good enough for Kate? That you aren't good FOR Kate? That you got lucky and she married you before she figured it out? You have it all wrong. She doesn't want to leave you. She wants you to leave."*

Pilate winced. Simon hadn't been quite that hard on him in a long time. Apparently, Sandberg had hit a nerve. He thumbed the radio volume up and rolled down the windows of the bullet-ridden old Saab. He wished he had put the top down before he hit the highway, feeling the wind in his ears and the sun on his face as he barreled past Big Pine Key back to Key West.

He had taken the day to run up to Key Largo for lunch with a friend of a friend.

"Hey there, landlubber," Ron said, his dark face nearly occluded by his floppy straw hat. He sprawled in a lawn chair outside his cabin not far from the docks, one hand working pincer pliers, the other holding a garish green fishing lure. Static-riddled Junkanoo music, pulled from a station in the Bahamas, played at low volume.

"Captain Ron," Pilate said, nodding at the lure. "Whatcha got there?"

"Green machine," he said, squinting. "Got bent by a perturbed Cobia awhile back." Ron grimaced, squeezing the pliers, then grunted. "There." He took off his hat, mopping his brow with a faded red bandanna. "Have a seat," he said, gesturing at another chair. "Move my stuff over."

Pilate complied and sat.

Ron eyed Pilate, then put his hat back on. "How you doing?"

Pilate shrugged. "Okay. How about you?"

"Well," he lay a finger across his chin in an affected gesture. "The esteemed Union of Concerned Scientists say that by the year 2100, more than ninety-four percent of Key West's inhabitable land will be under water, so I am also concerned."

"What about up here?"

"I imagine the scientists are concerned about Key Largo in a similar fashion," he said, laughing and shaking his head. "Ain't that a bitch?"

"It is, sorry I'll miss that."

"Shit yeah. There's an upside to being old, huh? You hungry?"

"I could eat."

He grunted and smiled. "Let's hit the Fish House," he said.

"Let's," Pilate said. "I'm buying."

"Indeed you are," Ron said, chuckling.

* * *

After gorging on yellowtail and clam strips, the pair enjoyed a beer in relative silence. Pilate glanced around the restaurant's dining room, festooned with twinkling party lights hanging from the ceiling, fishing knick-knacks, nets, and pictures jamming the walls.

The waitress collected their plates and dropped the check on the table. Pilate slid it in front of himself as Ron drained the last of his beer.

"Seen him lately?" Ron asked, eyes low, elbows on the table.

"No," Pilate said, fishing a credit card from his wallet. "You?"

Ron nodded. "Yup, he was touching up the paint on the *TenFortyEZ*. I think he plans to start taking charters again real soon."

"He's okay?" Pilate asked.

"He's full of piss and vinegar as usual but moving awful slow. That Jamaican affair was pretty tough on him."

"I know it was," he trailed off, his voice losing energy.

"The wife has him on a short leash," Ron added.

Pilate nodded. The last words he had with Jordan were more perfunctory than usual, and not kind. He brought the *TenFortyEZ* back to her from Jamaica, and asked to see Taters, who had recently arrived back home to recuperate from the heart condition that Pilate's last adventure had exacerbated. She told Pilate he was no longer welcome in their home, on their boat, or in their lives.

Pilate respected that, but he missed his friend.

"You should call him," Ron said, watching Pilate scrawl a tip and his signature on the check. "Jordan has probably cooled off by now."

"Yeah, well, I don't think I'm allowed to," Pilate said. "She said not to."

"Who gives a shit? She your mother? She's not fucking *you*, she can't cut you off." He rolled his head around on his shoulders, as if trying to work out a kink, then faced Pilate. "Look man, you didn't drive all the way out here to buy me lunch 'cause you missed me. For chrissake, you and I only know each other through Taters Malley."

Pilate shook his head slowly, his eyes on a Christmas light bulb flickering above the table. "I want to know he's all right."

Ron stood, crumpling a napkin at his place setting, shaking his head; heavy-lidded eyes pondering Pilate. "Makes me no difference, but life's pretty short as it is, never mind having a bum ticker."

Pilate looked up at Ron. "Is it that bad?"

He shrugged. "Could be. Could be not. I'm just sayin' you gotta bury that hatchet. This is between you and him—not you and Jordan. Now, thanks for the lunch, amigo, but I gotta go see Rosarita about knocking the BBs off my neck."

"What?" Pilate said, rising to his feet.

He pointed at his dome before putting his hat on. "She gives me a nice shave on my head and neck."

"Oh," Pilate said, extending a hand. "Thanks, Ron. If uh, if you talk to him?"

Ron sighed, resting one hand on his hip and stroking his chin with the other. "I ain't your messenger service, JP, but tell you what, just this once, I'll let him know you asked after him." He nodded and winked.

"Thanks Ron, thanks a lot."

Ron nodded, slipping a toothpick in his mouth and easing away from the table. Two steps past John, he stopped and said, without turning, "Call him soon. I mean it."

Interlude: 40 Years Ago

Johnny lay in a ball on top of his bunk bed, his finger drawing an outline around the cartoony James Bond on his *Thunderball* sheets. He had cleaned up the glitter as quickly as he could, choking back yet another "sorry" before retreating to the room he shared with his brother.

Johnny felt a lump under his Adam's apple, a hardness like a gobstopper had gotten stuck there.

He held his eight-inch Scotty doll from *Star Trek* in one hand, imagining Scotty in command of the Enterprise while Kirk and Spock were adventuring on the planet below. Scotty seemed like a nice man, though he had a weird way of talking, and he was really funny when he had too much of what his dad called "the hard stuff." In his other hand Johnny held a *Star Wars* action figure, smaller than Scotty—a beat-up Grand Moff Tarkin his older brother had once tied a tissue paper parachute to and tossed from the tallest tree in the backyard.

"You make things worse every time," the voice said, emanating from Tarkin's glowering countenance. It sounded like Tarkin's voice. Johnny thought Tarkin was a smart but mean guy, who also had a strange accent. "I know," he whispered.

"Quite stupid."

"I know," Johnny Pilate said. "I got to quit messing things up and making her mad."

"You probably won't," the voice chided. *"Like she says, you're stupid, and you shouldn't even be here."*

"I can fix it," Johnny said.

"You always say that," the voice said.

"Leave me alone," Johnny rolled over on the electronic memory game he got for Christmas from his grandparents. It hummed and lit up different colored panels in succession, beckoning him to repeat the beeping sequence.

Johnny didn't play with it much as a game, instead pretending it was Scotty's engine room on the *Enterprise*. It began the sequence, lights flashing, tones beeping.

"Be quiet, Simon. Hush up."

Today

Pilate roughed his dried-out, jerky-like tongue over cracked lips. The cruel headache that had set in hours ago, driven by gin and dehydration, pulsed behind his eyes. He sprawled on two thin beach towels between him and the floor, his Aloha-style shirt rolled up as a pathetic pillow.

"This particular finger trap is an absolute bitch." Simon said. *"You have to get out of here. And pardon me for saying so, but I already read this Joan Collins issue of* Playboy *and I'm fresh out of smokes."*

Pilate lay almost motionless except for a scant shiver running through his overheated body.

"Listen up, man. That froot loop thinks he's Annie Wilkes and doesn't have the brains to see he'll kill you if he leaves you in this box."

"Remember my bunk bed? I was on the top bed so Kyle could have his Kristy McNichol poster taped to the bottom of my bunk?"

"If your brother only knew…"

"It was hot up there sometimes, by the ceiling," Pilate said.

"Yes. But harder to reach you up there," Simon said.

"Unless the belt," Pilate said aloud.

"John, let's focus on getting out of here," Simon said.

You look like Peter Cushing again, Pilate said in his head, though chuckling aloud.

"Not a good look. Don't be a silly ass. I look like you, not the Grand Muff. I'm a much better looking, younger you, remember?"

Pilate lay there a moment, panting in the humidity.

"Simon, you gotta get me out of here. Go figure it out."

"Wait a minute, you aren't seriously suggesting that if I get through the wire…"

"I am the cooler king," Pilate groaned, sighing and rolling over, a sharp stabbing sensation in his left arm. "Ow!" He felt a shard of broken glass in his arm, and gently carefully pulled it out. "Thanks, Nora."

He gently padded on all fours, fumbling in the dark, finding the largest pieces of glass. Besides the bloody shard, he found the base of the glass, stem intact and about two inches of sharp shard at the end. He carefully put it aside, against the wall of the container.

"Not all wounds are meant to harm," Simon said.

"Not all wounds are intentional, you mean," Pilate said aloud. "Some people can't help hurting people."

"You really believe that?" Simon said.

"Some people are just screwed up. They can't help themselves. They hurt or have some crazy itch inside that they can't scratch and they hurt other people dealing with it."

"You think that's what your admirer is doing?" Simon said, retreating to his corner.

"Who says I'm talking about him?"

Interlude: Fever Dream

Pilate signed a book, his childish scrawl marring the cream-colored paper, smiled, and handed it to the woman who stood before him.

"I hope you find it interesting," Pilate said.

The woman accepted the book from him and made a face. "Oh, I don't read that true crime stuff, it's too depressing. This is for my granddaughter."

"Oh," Pilate said, pausing in the act of capping his pen. "Well, would you like me to inscribe it to her?"

She shook her head. "No, that's alright. She likes to sell these online after she reads them. It's best if it's not to one person."

"Gotcha," Pilate said, glancing over her shoulder.

"Well, I will move along," the lady said.

"Thanks again," Pilate said, looking over at the stack of books that was hardly dwindling next to his cup of cold coffee and a half-eaten brownie, courtesy of the bookstore staff.

"Cheer up, you miserable bastard."

Pilate looked up and saw a face he hadn't seen in years. Steel-grey hair and an off-center eye, clothed in a flannel shirt.

"Peter Trevathan?" Pilate stood up, knocking over his chair as he skirted the small signing table. Elated, he opened his arms to give the old man a hug.

"Can't do that," Trevathan said, recoiling.

"Why?"

"Because I'm gone," Trevathan winked, smiled, and faded away.

Pilate opened his eyes. "Oh."

"You must be delirious if you'd rather have an old dead fart visit you instead of me," Simon said.

"I gotta get out of here," Pilate rasped, his words tumbling onto the dirty, hot floor.

Interlude: Pretty Sure This Was Yesterday

"Meet me at the Hog's Snout. Six o'clock."

"That would be great, man," Pilate said, looking at himself in the nautical rope-framed mirror in his den as he spoke on the old rotary phone. His hand gripped the avocado-colored handset so tightly that his knuckles were white. Trevathan had never upgraded the phone, and Pilate liked it that way.

"Jordan's out at bunco 'til at least nine," Taters said. "I reckon that's plenty of time for you and me to murder a Modelo or two."

Pilate's eyes watered, a hardness in his throat made it difficult for him to speak. "I'm so glad. I…I didn't think, ummm…"

"What? Thinking you and me are through?" he snorted. "Not hardly. But we do have some serious shit to discuss, moving forward. Least of which is you owe me for some boat repairs. Jeebus, man, did you bring the boat home from Jamaica in second gear the whole way?" Taters chuckled.

"Oops. We'll talk. Six o'clock at the Snout. I'll be the guy in the Panama hat."

"Then you'll be the guy sitting alone all night. Wear your usual hangdog expression, mister. I'll see you there."

"Deal."

"And John?" his voice mellowed.

"Yeah man?"

"If you get there first, order some conch fritters and a—"

"Modelo Especiale. Got it."

"Good man."

"Let's not go overboard. I did kind of mess up your boat."

* * *

It was only three o'clock, and Pilate had a little time to squeeze in a workout. He texted Val, who just had a cancellation. She could fit him in at four. Pilate sniffed his gym clothes, decided they weren't too nasty, double-checked his bag and headed for the gym.

Val was stretching when he arrived, her powerful legs accentuated by dark blue leggings, a pink Susan G. Komen t-shirt tied up to expose her midriff.

"Hey mister," she said, flashing a quick smile. "Ready to mix it up?"

He smiled back. "I'd like that."

"Well, no mercy today. No more nice guy, got it?" she elbowed his arm.

"I'm in," he said.

They sparred for the better part of a half hour, then switched to a circuit of light weights and exercises. Pilate's lungs didn't love the humidity, but he kept going, sweat running down his face, his shirt and shorts nearly soaked.

"Okay, man," she said, toweling off. "Excellent workout. You pushed yourself today."

"Needed to," he said, in between chugs of his Yeti. He looked at his watch. "I better get home and get a shower."

She looked up from her gym bag. "Oh? What's up?"

"Gonna meet a friend for a drink," he said.

She raised an eyebrow, smiling, then wrinkling her nose. "A girl?"

He was surprised at the question, considering he had unloaded on her about his faltering marriage and his determination to "fix it."

His face registered confusion and perhaps irritation.

"Oh shit," she said, herself looking confused now. "I don't know why I said that."

"It's okay," he said. "Really."

She blushed. "I just, oh man. You always seem like a guy going to meet a girl. I mean. Crap. Never mind."

"Hey, it's fine. And no, not a girl. Just a buddy I need to catch up with. Going to the Hog's Snout around six. Won't be out too long, he's on a short leash."

She nodded, absently checking her ponytail, eyes fixed on the empty boxing ring. "Well, have fun."

Pilate sensed an odd unease with Val but wasn't clear what brought it on. "Okay."

Val scooped up her bag, flung it over her shoulder and jogged out the door. She never really walked anywhere.

"Interesting," Simon said.

* * *

Clusters of bright orange blooms adorned the Geiger trees near the entrance of the Hog's Snout, swaying in the humid breeze that wafted the scent of conch fritters, burgers and fries. There weren't as many trees and bushes these days; development had started to spoil the "outpost" feel of Key West's venerable Old Town. However, the booze still flowed, cocks still crowed, and music still played.

Pilate had blanched when his friend suggested they meet there; years ago he had walked in on a dying man in the Hog's Snout men's room, after all. That bloody mess on the floor was always with him, and going to the Snout could make him uneasy until the drinks kicked in. Pilate was pretty sure it was yet another PTSD moment.

"Feeling triggered?" Simon said as Pilate looked past the restroom area and took a seat at the open-air bar. Pilate distracted himself, checking out

the hundreds of stickers, coasters, post cards and antique banknotes affixed to the walls and ceiling.

"Where's the threat? Not on the wall."

"Don't help right now, Simon."

He was early; even if Taters was on time, Pilate would have half an hour to himself, sharing the place with a few dozen people eating and drinking. This satellite bar had attracted only a few old conchs and a loud group of tourists congregated at a tallboy in the corner.

"What can I get you?" the bartender asked, wiping down the bar and dropping a laminated menu.

"Pina Colada," he said. "Kidding. Can I get a Stoli rocks with lime and an order of fritters?"

She smirked and nodded, peering at the other side of the room. "Coming up."

Pilate looked around, self-consciously patting the breast pocket of his red *Magnum, P.I.*-style Hawaiian shirt, as if looking for cigarettes. An old habit when he sat at bars, even though he quit smoking years ago.

When his drink appeared, Pilate downed a healthy mouthful. He scanned the menu. Oysters looked tasty, despite his reservations about the effects of several recent Gulf oil spills. He sighed and put down the menu, deciding the fritters would do until Taters arrived.

He checked his cell for texts. Nothing. Pilate chewed his lip a bit, then typed

"Hey Val, thanks again for the great workout.
Looking forward to our next bout."

"Oh my God, seriously?" Simon said. *"She threatened to turn us into more dirt for the Key. Admittedly, in a kind of arousing way."*

He sipped more of his drink, startled when his phone vibrated on the bar.

"I am so damn sorry man, Jordan staying home. Can't make it. Will call you soon."

Pilate felt hollow in his gut, as if he had been caught doing something wrong. He forced himself to breathe deeply a moment, then responded with a quick **"No worries, Taters, lmk when you get some time."**

He dropped the phone on the bar with a clunk and pointed at his glass when the bartender slid the basket of conch fritters and a tumbler of ice water to him. His phone vibrated again, with a thumbs up emoji from Taters. Pilate finished his first drink, moved it closer to the bartender's side of the bar, and nibbled a fritter.

After finishing off the second drink and destroying the basket of fritters, he needed to answer a call of nature. "I'll be right back," he said to the bartender. "Can we do this again?" he said, holding up his drink.

"Want more water?" she asked.

"Never touch the stuff," he said as he excused himself, stopped and looked back at her. "Hey, is there a different restroom—that one's not good for me."

She looked at him, uncomprehendingly. A tall, lanky man with greasy black hair haphazardly tucked under a sweaty Jimmy Buffet trucker cap leaning on the bar a few feet away volunteered that there was one on the other side of the restaurant. Pilate nodded in gratitude and headed towards it.

At the urinal, Pilate felt the back pocket of his shorts vibrate. After he washed up, he checked to see a text reply notification from Val.

"No worries, man. had a brain fart. got embarrassed."

He leaned against the wall and texted a reply.

"Oh. I probably acted like I was bothered by it when I wasn't. Let me make it up to you with a drink. Come on over to the Snout."

Pilate strode past the other diners as the restaurant started to fill up. When he got back to his seat at the bar, there was now only a few seats left open. His drink was waiting, the empty fritters basket collected. He took a quick sip and looked at his phone.

"I'd love to, but you have your friend there and u don't need a 3rd wheel."

The drink had him feeling cheerful, further amped up by the prospect of hanging out with Val somewhere that didn't smell like Rocky Balboa's armpit. He thumbed his screen and typed: **"Actually, he canceled. Come on out. Don't make me drink alone."**

Pilate scanned the bar, looking for a pair of seats together should Val accept his invitation. More people had trickled in, and this section was no longer as empty as before. Everyone seemed paired up, conchs and tourists alike, though the lanky man under the sweat-stained Jimmy Buffet trucker cap nursed a Bud by his lonesome.

Pilate's phone vibrated again. **"Ok. Tell me again where u are."**

He texted the info.

"Be there in 20 mins or so. SEE...U R DRINKING WITH A GIRL TONIGHT."

Pilate chuckled and texted back a laughing face emoji, then put his phone down and drank more vodka. He felt excited about seeing Val socially like this but didn't have any assumptions it was anything more than two friends having a drink. He also felt a little guilty, but the vodka was doing an excellent job of translating that directly and immediately into a protective layer of self-righteousness. *If she can have coffee with Deadpool McDreamy, I can have a drink with my personal trainer.*

A few moments later, he felt a mild wave of nausea roll over him. *Ugh, not now*, he thought as his bowels cramped up.

"Maybe you should have had the oysters after all," Simon said.

The cramps came faster and more forcefully; sweat broke out on his forehead. Pilate signaled the bartender. "Hey, I have a friend joining me, can you hold my place here while I go comb my hair?"

The bartender looked annoyed. "What?"

"Please hold my seat while I go to the can, okay? You have my credit card. My friend, her name is Val. She's on the way."

She made a face like she wanted to let an exasperated "Okay!" escape her but feared for her tip; instead she gave a quick nod and moved on to another customer.

Pilate made a beeline for the restroom of death he wanted to avoid; he could tell that he needed to hurry if he didn't want to make a mess of himself and the bar. He made it inside; it took only an instant to realize the restroom had been repainted and perhaps even remodeled after the murder there a few years ago. Sure, it was still kind of run-down, but it lacked any sign of the bloodletting.

Blessed with an empty stall, he got there in time to lower his shorts and sit, only to realize he needed to throw up even more. Pilate managed to get back on his feet, pull up his shorts, turn around and vomit. Over and over, his gut spasmed, sending the drinks, fritters, and bile into the toilet.

The sweating and cramps started to subside, but he felt woozy and placed a hand on the cinder block wall. He heard a man's voice, oddly nasal.

"Hey sir, are you okay?"

"Hmm?" he said, losing his balance a little, trying to exit the stall but his feet kept wanting to twist underneath him. His chest tightened; a roar filled his ears.

"I think I'm—"

All went black.

Interlude: Almost Today

"Wake up, Mister Pilate."

With great effort, Pilate opened one eye halfway. It was dark and he felt sour, hot breath on his face.

A mild slap on the cheek. "Wake up or it's strike one."

Pilate forced his eyes open, taking in a silhouette of a tall figure standing in a doorway.

"Jack? Lindstrom?" he stammered, raising his head off the floor. "You're dead. I'm not playing this game again. I saw you die."

"Is that so?"

"I'm not spending one more minute of my life thinking of you, bad hooch or no," Pilate said. "You're not real."

"There's water in a bottle there, sir," the voice said. "It's not Parry-air but it will do." *Honk honk.* "We'll talk later. Get some rest." The figure stepped back from the doorway and slammed shut a steel door.

Chapter Two

From his perspective lying on the floor, the metal room was pitch black, save for a few stray pinholes of light coming through tiny holes drilled in the massive door. The holes were large enough to let in the dim, shadowy light, but not enough air to feel any breeze. He felt clammy; the atmosphere was again oppressive since his captor had slammed the access panel shut a few hours ago. He wished for a pull on his inhaler.

"You need to work on keeping that guy happy so he doesn't close that panel in a huff," Simon said from the corner. Pilate imagined his old friend sitting placidly in the wheelchair, legs crossed, Joan Collins issue of *Playboy* on his lap, cigarette in his lips, his face in shadow.

"Definitely wish I had finished that drink instead of painting the wall with it," Pilate croaked. He had reluctantly finished the water in the small plastic bottle hours ago,

"Yes, and now there's the broken glass to contend with," Simon said.

Pilate sat up on his elbow, one hand finding the large shard.

"That's probably as big a piece as is left," Simon said.

Pilate agreed silently and placed the glass at the head of his sweaty beach towel bed. He tried to make that end of the bed more pillow-like, manipulating the damp fabric into a bump when his hand connected with something that wasn't broken glass. *What the hell?* It was a smooth, familiar rectangle, about four and half inches long and a few centimeters in diameter. He scooped it up.

"No fucking way. My cell phone."

Pilate instinctively felt for the iPhone home button, and pressed. The screen came to life, a photo of his children beaming at him, along with the date and time: 2:02 AM. He pressed his thumb into the button, dismissing the lock screen and bringing up his familiar home screen.

"Yes!" Pilate said, dialing 911. The words "No Service" appeared at the top of the screen, and he felt the hope that had begun to break out die a lonely death in his heart.

"Damn it. Of course, there's no way a signal will get out of this steel box," he said.

"Yes, well, that seems to be the direction we're all going," Simon added. *"I guess he did hang on to your wallet though. Maybe he dropped it somewhere nearby too."*

Pilate ignored him and went to his text messages, thanking God he had set the font size larger only last week so that he could make out the text without his readers, which were sitting on his nightstand at the Trevathan cottage. He had five messages. A text from Taters arrived about ten minutes after his last text from Val:

"Hey man, I was out of line. I told Jordan that I want to see you I'm not a damn child and she can't tell me who I can play with. See you in a few. Order me a Modelo. I'm fired up."

The next was from Val: **"Hey, where are you? I'm here."**

She had followed up in five minutes with: **"John, are you around? Asked bartender. She said u not tabbed out. Where R U?"**

Ten minutes later, Taters chimed in again: **"I'm chatting with your girlfriend, buddy. She's pretty cool. Better come back soon before I tell her about your wife. LOL Seriously where you at?"**

A final text came through from Val twenty minutes later: **"You're not home. Not at the bar. U okay? You have 10 mins or I'm calling Officer Asshole."**

"Oh, I hope you did, Val," Pilate said. He thumbed his keyboard and typed a response to Taters and Val:

"Big trouble! Kidnapped! Locked in steel container I think - really hot in here. Crazy guy locked me in no water REALLY HOT. NOT A JOKE. Need HELP NOW. Don't know where I am. He's nuts he may abandon me. Please don't let me die in here"

Pilate hit send. In a moment, he received the response: **"Message Send failure. Please check your network connection and try again."**

"Oh God damn it," Pilate said. "Damn it. Damn it!" he shouted.

"Don't give up, John. This guy isn't so smart, leaving you your phone," Simon soothed.

"He probably didn't notice it," Pilate muttered. "I bet it fell out of my pocket when he dumped me in this goddamned steel sweat lodge."

"All the same, he's not careful. And he's crazy," Simon said. *"The guy likes Buffet and Bud light, after all. We need to be prepared when he returns.*

"Prepared how?" Pilate rolled over on his back.

"Check the battery on the phone, John."

Forty-two percent.

"More than enough. Turn on the flashlight app."

Pilate found the app and turned it on. The light shocked his eyes. He swung the beam around the container's grey, corrugated steel walls. Hanging from the ceiling was a cord and a broken light bulb. The floor was clean, save a few dust bunnies in one corner, a sad spider's web the one sign of even potential optimism, and tiny bits of broken glass from his martini just about everywhere. The wheelchair, despite the evidence of his conversation, was empty. It had served its purpose, to quickly spirit a helpless John Pilate from the Hog's Snout restaurant to the tall man's car, then to…wherever the hell this was. The bucket in the other corner was untouched. He looked at every inch of his prison, searching for a way out.

"Nothing," he said. "Empty steel box. I'm in bad shape."

Pilate got off his knees and stood up, shining the light at the walls again, checking out the door and the ledge by the access panel. Again, nothing. He hopped up to reach for the broken light bulb, managing to brush it with his fingertips. He stood underneath, shining the light on it, wondering if there might be a way to weaponize it. He traced the cord from the center of the room to the back where the cord disappeared into a hole.

"What the…" Pilate glimpsed a faded stencil spray painted on the wall beneath the hole.

* * *

Xtra Keys Self Storage
5027 Suncrest Road
Key West, FL

* * *

DO NOT STORE PERISHABLES
RENT DUE 5th of Month

* * *

"Oh my God," Pilate rasped. He was locked in a self-storage unit. "Clearly not climate controlled."

"Okay, you're a perishable. Still, this is good news," Simon said. *"You're not in an empty warehouse somewhere. Somebody is bound to show up and you can make noise and get out."*

"Yeah," Pilate said falling back on his haunches, then sitting on the floor. "Except this might be one of the storage businesses that got flooded out and closed in the hurricane last year. Some of them use old shipping containers as units. Smells like it."

"Well, that's depressing."

His mood plummeting, Pilate felt his energy going the same way. He lay on his back, the hard, burning floor adding to his misery.

* * *

A buzzing sound jarred him awake.

"John?"

Another buzz.

"Johnny? Wake up."

His hand uncurled on the sheet, and the Tarkin figure, loosed from his grip, fell over the side of the bunk bed. He rolled off the Simon game, which went silent without his childhood weight pressing all the buttons at once.

* * *

"Daddy, where are you?" a little boy's voice broke the silence.

"Pete? Pete, honey?" Pilate said.

"You're never home," said a girl. It was Kara, his stepdaughter.

"I'm coming home kids, I promise," he said, inexplicably wet tears in the corners of his eyes.

Pilate awoke alone on the floor, clammy, cramping, and miserable.

"Poor Kara. To lose one father is tragic, but to lose a second one, well that's just carelessness," Simon said. *"As for Peter, well… you aren't exactly around much, anyway."*

Pilate shook him off.

"I promise. I promise," he muttered. "I'll fix this."

The aura of heat before his eyes made every move an effort; his energy lower than the thirty percent left on his phone. The clock read 5:02 a.m. He went to his contacts, found Kate's number, and tapped the text messaging icon:

"Not sure you will get this but wanted you to know I spent these last hours thinking of you and the kids. Hard to explain. Just can't always be present. Even when I'm in the next room. Sometimes takes all I have to be patient with anything. But I do love you all am so very sorry I made a mess of everything. No matter what happens if I survive I want to be a better person. Even if you don't love me anymore I want you to know I will always love you and Kara & Pete are everything to me."

He pressed send, and soon received the hateful error message in return. A thought struck his sluggish brain, and he went to one of the pencil-sized holes drilled in the front of the unit. He aimed the phone at the outside world, and tried to send the text again, only to receive another error message.

His head pounded like he had a massive hangover, with a sunburn and a bonus icepick in his guts. He sat back down and resolved to try again, swatting away a mosquito who had no problems getting inside the cage and biting him.

"Maybe you should try and reach somebody who can help you. You'll only panic Kate even if by some miracle that signal gets out," Simon cooed.

Pilate nodded, wiping sweat from his eyes and choking out a raspy, dry cough. He thumbed out a group message to Taters and Val.

"John Pilate. Locked in a unit I think at Xtra Keys Self Storage. Suncrest Road on Stock Island I think. Very hot. Not sure kidnapper will return. Has been gone for several hours. I need help. I am dying."

A loud clanking sound startled him. He looked up to see the access panel open an inch.

"Sir?"

Pilate had grown to loathe that voice, but now he was ecstatic to hear it. He rose up on his elbow, summoning the strength to move closer to the access panel and the cool breeze.

"Sir?"

Pilate remained quiet.

"Sir? If you are awake, don't think I am foolish enough to open the big door. You need to tell me you're still with us."

Pilate sighed. "I'm too weak to do any harm, anyway." His throat protested with every word. "Have water?"

"Yes."

"Can I have some?"

"I think not," *honk, honk.*

"Fuck you then," Pilate said, words slurred with exhaustion.

"Sir, not nice. You know something, you are not a nice-nice friend."

"I'm not your friend. How the hell do you know anything about me anyway?"

"Saw you at the bookstore. You signed my book and did not smile with grace and favor. You emailed and said we could be friends.

And at the gym. I tried to be nice and give you a towel while you were talking to that woman who is not your wife. That's not nice."

Pilate searched his mind, fighting to remember if he had encountered anyone with a towel at the gym. "That woman is my trainer."

"You want to sweat with her?" his kidnapper said, honking.

"And you emailed and said to come meet you for a drink."

"What? I never did that," he sounded unsure.

"Well, it's obvious you did."

"John, this loon is about ready to check in for his flight to fucking Planet Mongo," Simon said.

Pilate gasped for a moment, trying to catch some cool air from the small gap. "Please tell me. What do you want?" Pilate's hand swept the ground seeking the large glass shard.

"I want you to be nice," he said. "I want you to not act so big. Be nice-nice to the little people."

"Jesus man, I *am* little people," Pilate rasped, his fingers finding and curling around the shard of glass. "Can I have some water, please?"

"I made you something."

"Can I please have some water? I can't handle another martini. On the wagon."

"No, this is morning. I made you coffee. Like you drink with your girlfriend at Frenchie's. Nice and hot. With cream and sugar. Here." The panel slid open all the way; the black nitrile-gloved hand slid a cup of coffee on a saucer on the ledge. "Come get it."

"No energy," Pilate said, slowly raising himself up.

"I think you will get the energy. It would not be nice-nice if you did not take this nice coffee."

Pilate heaved himself to his feet, a slight breeze from outside reviving him some. "How do I know you didn't poison it?"

The man honked. "Oh, that's silly. Why would I poison you, my friend? Not nice-nice."

"Yeah, and you can leave me in here to rot, I suppose," he palmed the ruined martini glass.

"Drink the coffee sir," he said in monotone. "We can chat like nice friends over coffee."

Pilate staggered to the panel, one hand grasping the shard, the other his iPhone. He reached the ledge and peered out. It wasn't bright, there was no work light illuminating the hallway this time. Must be daylight out. He saw the outline of the tall, skinny man, with shoulder-length hair, slouching a foot or so from the panel.

"So you're a Jimmy Buffet fan? I like 'Fins.' What's your name, is it...Nick? No--Strong?" Pilate said, pressing the screen on his phone at his side. The send button glimmered in the half-darkness, tempting him. He had to be certain. There would be only one chance.

"Oh, now you want to be friends. Drink your coffee."

"Where's yours? It wouldn't be nice-nice to drink coffee in front of you," Pilate said. "Anyway you said we were friends having coffee--"

"I had mine," he said. "Now drink yours."

"Here's something for you, fucker," Pilate thrust his arm through the panel, the glass shard like the tip of a spear aimed at the lanky man. The man yelped, honked and parried; his thrust with the makeshift glass dagger had missed, not unlike Pilate's impotent punches at Val in the ring. Pilate shouted, cursing, his arm flailing helplessly at the man who had backed out of reach. The coffee cup fell inside his prison cell and shattered, steaming liquid splattering his legs.

"Sir! Pull your arm back in now. Do it or I will have to hurt you," his monotone now that of a pimply high school junior, breaking comically with every other syllable.

"Fuck you," Pilate growled, his arm flailing like a dropped fire hose, whipping the air with menace. He realized he wasn't going to hit the guy, but every second of his bare arm in the relative cool of the hallway made his struggle worth it. Pilate pulled his arm back, keyed send and thrust his other arm out into the hallway, the iPhone mostly concealed in his fist.

The man pulled something from his pocket. He held it high where Pilate could see it. "I will tase you," he said, without the honking laughter.

"Come and try," Pilate said, arm still exposed, though no longer flailing. Instead, he held it high, as if trying to play keep-away with a child.

"This is your last warning," the man said. "I mean it."

Pilate jerked his arm back inside but kept the phone as close to the portal as he dared. "Alright, alright. Fine."

"Step away. Go to the back," the man ordered.

"Why? What are you going to do? Come in here and tase me, bro?" Pilate said, snickering bitterly but standing his ground. It was a standoff; the kidnapper couldn't tase him without coming close enough to risk being stabbed with the glass.

"Do it or I will forget to give you water."

"I don't have any water now," Pilate said.

"Step back and I will place a bottle of cool water on this ledge. After you imbibe, we can discuss the future."

"How do I know you won't shut that panel and leave me here?"

"You don't. But that would not be nice."

"I have two children," Pilate said. "Please."

"Big man," his tormentor replied.

"Fuck off and die, you worthless piece of shit," Pilate said, sagging against the opening in the panel, filling his lungs.

"Move away, sir, or I will tase you in the face."

Pilate felt a fresh chill go through his body; his guts seized in a painful spasm. "I'm asking you one more time. Let me out. Please? Let me out. I miss my kids," his lungs reviving with each gasp of the cooler air.

Pilate felt the phone vibrate. He read the message notification:

"ON THE WAY. DON'T LOSE HOPE. MODELOS CHILLING. STAY STRONG. – TM"

"I will count to three," the man said. "One."

"The cops will be the least of your worries if I die in here, you know."

"Two."

"Taters may be a little low right now, but he's pretty mean when somebody messes with his friends. And Kate? Ever hear about her aim with a shotgun?"

"Three."

Pilate jerked away from the panel, but before the kidnapper could slam it shut a new sound came faintly in the distance – the wail of police sirens.

"Do you hear that, asshole? That's the cops. They know where I am. You left me my cell phone, you...you amateur!"

The panel slammed shut and the kidnapper's voice came one last time, cold and angry but somehow not entirely disappointed.

"I am sorry you could not be nice. We have somewhere else to be now."

Pilate heard the man's footfalls receding rapidly as he ran down the hallway. The sirens grew louder but were still far away.

"Have a nice-nice day, you creepy fucking nutjob," Pilate whispered, falling to his knees, his eyes greedily reading and rereading the message from Taters.

The sirens were louder still as he slipped further down to the floor, laying on his side, looking at the photo of Peter and Kara.

"Hold on, Johnny. Hold on," Simon said.

"I'm good," he rasped. "I'm coming home, kids. Gonna fix it."

"Stay awake," Simon said. *"They need to be able to find you fast. Bang on the door."*

"Okay. But you have to go now, Simon," Pilate whispered.

"Not until you're alright, Johnny. Not until then."

Chapter Three

"I'm coming home, Kate," Pilate said, standing on the small balcony, his eyes vacantly scanning the boats moving through the bay. Late in the day, the green flash would be manifest soon.

"Okay," she said. "You up to it? You've only been out of that freak's clutches for two weeks."

"Like you care," Simon sneered in Pilate's skull.

"Yeah," Pilate said. "Yeah, I'm fine. In the hospital a week." He paused a second, to let it sink in. "They got my fluids back up. I feel much better."

He heard her breathing. "You there?" he asked.

"Yes. Thinking about what you said."

"When?" Pilate said.

"When you reminded me you were in the hospital," she said. "I know you were in the hospital."

"Is that why you came to see me? You know, your half-dead husband?" His voice turned acid so fast he surprised himself. He nearly died, and she could not be bothered to visit. His throat tightened; his chest started to ache.

"John, we've been through this. I couldn't get away. And what was I supposed to do with the kids? They have school."

"Good Christ, Kate," Pilate sighed. "Their father was nearly killed."

"And there it is, in a nutshell. Yet again," Kate said, her voice flat. "John, you're a disaster magnet. The whole reason we aren't together now is because everything you touch leads to somebody I love getting hurt or nearly killed."

"That include me?" he said, his eyes watering.

She paused a few seconds. "Yes, jackass. You too. You know damn well I love you."

He felt the red veil falling over his eyes begin to dissipate. "But?"

"But, we have to work on some things," she said, treading lightly.

"I know that Kate. That's why I need to come home," he said.

"You can come back to Cross, John, but you shouldn't stay here at the house," she said, matter of fact, as if she had practiced it.

"What the fuck are you talking about? You are not going to keep me from seeing my kids, Kate."

She sighed, exasperated. "No, calm down. Listen. Listen to me for a minute, would you? I am not keeping the kids from you. I want you to stay somewhere else in town. We have a routine here now, and the kids will get confused if you are suddenly back after months of being away."

"A routine?" He swallowed hard. "No. We're a family. You can't do this," he said, his jaw clenched.

"Just until we work this out. You can stay at Cusack's place," she said.

"I don't want to stay there. I want to stay at home. My home. That I help pay for. With my wife and my goddamned kids."

"Your what? Your 'goddamned' kids? Did you really say that?" Kate said, her voice rising.

"You know what I meant," Pilate said, scrubbing his fist through his hair. "Kate, why? Why are you doing this? Is there someone? Someone else?"

Pilate leaned over, grasping the rickety balcony railing for support.

"John, stay somewhere else and we can talk about it."

"That's not an answer," he said. "I can fix it. Let me fix it, Kate."

Kate said nothing.

"Kate? Are you seeing that professor guy? Have you?"

She swallowed, then inhaled and exhaled audibly. "It's complicated."

"Fuck you," Pilate said. He threw the cordless handset against the wall, exploding it in a shower of plastic.

* * *

"What you gonna do, bud?" Taters Malley said, absently scratching at his salt and pepper chin hairs, then adjusting his ball cap as his eyes darted around the cabin.

Pilate picked up the shot of tequila. "Gonna drink this." He licked salt off his hand, knocked back the shot and bit into a wedge of lime.

"Easy, tiger, you ain't exactly in fighting trim right now," Taters advised. "When's the last time you had booze?"

Pilate shrugged. "Couple weeks ago if you include my time in solitary."

Taters reached across the small table below deck in the *TenFortyEZ*. The old Connie swayed gently, tied to the dock.

"Leave it be, Taters," Pilate said. "You either drink with me or kick me off the boat, but you aren't taking my booze. Not tonight."

Taters shrugged. "Okay, okay," he sighed. "Guess I'm drinking with you, then. We can both feed the fish before morning. Jordan's still pissed anyway." Taters stood up and opened a cabinet door, retrieving a shot glass as he lowered himself to the table.

"This guy's growing on me, John," Simon said.

Pilate nodded, pouring them a round.

They downed their shots, though Taters passed on the salt. He poked himself in the chest. "Ticker don't need any more sodium."

Pilate stared out the window at the dock.

"So," Taters said, looking at the table top, then up to Pilate's face.

"So," Pilate said, looking at the glass.

"Well," Taters said.

"That's a deep subject," Pilate broke into a mirthless laugh.

Taters regarded the empty shot glasses a moment. "What you gonna do—"

Pilate held up the bottle of tequila.

"Yeah, yeah, after you get done with Jose Cuervo," Taters said.

"Casamigos." Pilate put the bottle down. Though tempted, he didn't pour another shot. "I'm going home. Back to Cross."

Taters nodded. "About damn time, John."

"Hell, I've faced down worse than getting frozen out by my own family," Pilate said. "I guess I'll see if I can get my old faculty apartment back. Maybe be weekend Dad to the kids. Yeah, that sounds right."

"You think she's…I mean, is Kate absolutely?"

"Done with me?" Pilate nodded. "Sure as hell seems like it."

"Because you had all these run-ins and stuff?" Taters said.

"Run-ins? Jesus, I nearly got you killed, Taters. Nearly got her killed. The kids…" he said.

"Wasn't your fault. And even if it was, I've forgiven you. Shit, even Jordan, the least forgiving woman I ever met, let alone married, has forgiven you. Don't tell her I told you, she'd never forgive us."

"Thank you. Kate's just...looking after the kids. And herself. Her first husband got murdered, you know. She's seen so much ugly. Maybe I represent more ugly."

"That's not a correct theory," Taters said. "You are the best thing that ever happened to her."

"You know, laying on the floor of that steel hell, baking like a piece of jerky, I begged the universe to let me see my kids again. I thought if I could get out of that cage, get away from that Mister Nice-Nice creep, I would get home to my kids and never leave them. Then I got out, thanks to you," Pilate cleared his throat. "Kinda thought Kate would come running to the hospital to see me and I could make everything right. But she stayed away. And now I'm finally able to travel again, she says not to come."

"She didn't say not to come," Taters said. "She said not to stay in the house. There's still a chance, man."

"No, I'd say it's probably over."

"You don't mean that."

Pilate contemplated swigging straight from the bottle for a second. "I know what it feels like when a woman I love has turned on me," he said, looking into Taters' face. Since I was a kid I know what that's like. You see it in their eyes."

"You drunk yet?" Taters said, just above a whisper.

"No, not yet," Pilate said, his eyes watery.

Taters poured them both a double shot. "Get drinking."

* * *

"So they have no idea who he is or where he went?" Val said, talking loudly over a Western swing band playing Lyle Lovett covers at Sloppy Joe's.

Pilate shook his head and shrugged, looking over Val's tanned shoulder at Greene Street, pulsating with a mass of tourists undulating past, then back at her. "You want another?" He held up a plastic cup with the Sloppy Joe's logo, shaking the ice.

"Get me a Key West lemonade, would you?" she said. "Need some cash?"

"No, I'm good." Pilate ambled back up to the bar, where Marlene gabbed with a busboy.

"Yo," Pilate said.

"Hey again, John," she adjusted her t-shirt, tied at the waist. "What can I get you and your lovely new bit of stuff?"

He shook his head and chuckled. "It's not like that. She's my trainer."

"Kinky." She laughed. "Take it easy, I won't tell the wife. What can I get you?"

"Couple of lemonades," he said.

With a wink she produced the drinks. "Hey. You have never come out on the *RickRoll*. Make me the happiest gal in the Keys and say you will soon?"

"If my wife, and the trainer, will let me," Pilate said, winking back. He put a twenty on the bar and scooped up the drinks.

Back at the table, Val raised an eyebrow. "So, is Miss Big Boobs a friend of yours?"

"Who? Marlene? Yeah. We go way back to before I had a place here. She's good people. Should I take it you have insecurity about yours?"

"My what?"

Pilate made a comical leer from her eyes to her chest, eyebrows waggling wildly.

She looked down a second, blushed, then laughed. "My girls are fine. More than a mouthful is a waste."

Pilate's mouth gaped a second before he broke into a chuckle. The rush of the booze made it challenging to tamp down his attraction to Val. He willed himself to cool it.

"No truer words ever said," Pilate said. "How's the drink?"

Val sipped from the white plastic tumbler. "Ooh, I like this better than that Sloppy Rita."

Pilate shrugged. "Gets the job done."

"So, this creep who abducted you, he, what, disappeared?" Val said, her voice suddenly too loud as the band finished the song halfway through her sentence.

"Yeah, Key West PD, FBI—they're all flummoxed. No idea who he is, or where he went. That grainy dark video from the Hog's Snout wasn't very helpful, and he had a cap pulled low. I remember he's tall and skinny with weird, stringy, longish hair. Shit, it could've been a wig for all I know."

"And he," Val leaned forward, her face puckering like she smelled something bad. "Kept saying for you to be nice?"

"Nice-nice." Pilate swigged more of his drink. "In a creepy voice."

"I don't get it, he drugs you, kidnaps you, and puts you in a freaking oven for days and nearly kills you? And he expected you to be nice?"

"Nice-nice."

"That's messed up."

"All the nuts roll downhill to Florida," Pilate chuckled.

"What's that make us?" Val raised an eyebrow. He noted her dimples, and how her eyes smiled even bigger than her mouth.

"Good point. Anyway, the law says to be careful. He could be anywhere, including here," Pilate jerked a thumb at the iconic Key West bar.

Val looked over her shoulder and back at Pilate, shivering. "That's creepy."

"No shit. But I imagine he's in the wind. Probably smart enough to know Key West will be too hot for him now," Pilate said. "Even so, this guy knows about you, so please be aware of your surroundings."

"Oh I am, and I can take care of myself," Val said, playfully flexing a muscular bicep.

"I know that's right," Pilate said. "You kicked my ass in the boxing ring plenty."

She smiled, sipping more of her lemonade. "So, how are things on the home front?"

Pilate adjusted in his chair and coughed, looking back at the street.

"Sorry. I just wondered." Val said.

"No, it's fine. Things are...not so good," he took a healthy swallow of his drink. "I mean, I'm going home in a couple of days, but I won't be staying with her and the kids. She thinks it would be kind of disruptive."

"I don't understand," she said. "You're their father."

"It's complicated," Pilate said. "It will be okay. I can fix it."

"Are you sure?"

"Not really," Pilate said. "But I have to try."

The band leader announced a break.

"Great band," Val said. "Want to wait for the next set?"

"If you want. It's not a school night for me. But I bet you have clients first thing in the morning at the gym."

Val tilted her head to one side as if pondering a serious question. "Actually no. My regular six a.m. is on vacation, my seven canceled and you're my eight."

"Oh, good," he chuckled. "I may not be able to get out of bed by then."

She looked into his eyes, leaned forward, her tanned, toned arms folded, pushing up modest but shapely breasts framed by a hot pink halter top. "So you need help getting up? Should I call you or nudge you?"

* * *

Pilate slipped out of Val's bed, his head pounding from too many Technicolor drinks served in plastic, his heart aching with guilt; his subscription to the self-righteousness conversion had apparently been a limited-time offer. He grasped the bedpost, brushing his hand against some old leather boxing gloves hanging there. Pilate flipped on the light in Val's bathroom, avoiding even a glance at his sallow face in the mirror. He drank from the faucet, urinated, and turned off the light, standing in the darkness.

"Don't get me started, John," Simon whispered.

I'm not talking to you, Simon. Pilate hissed in his thoughts. *I'm tired of being judged. By you, by her, and by the whole damn world.*

"Pity poor Pilate. Can't get his shit together. Can't stay out of strange beds," Simon tsk-tsked.

Pilate opened the door, finding his bearings in the morning light through the open window. He stood, shifting his weight from foot to foot.

"Get your naked ass back in bed," Val whispered, "Close the curtains first. I bet we put on a quite a show for the neighbors last night. No need for a matinee."

"Nice," Simon said.

Pilate yanked the curtains closed and slid into the sheets next to her. He avoided touching her. She rolled on her side, resting her head on her elbow. "Don't get all awkward on me now, okay?"

"Okay."

"I always thought you were a bit of a panty-dropper, John. And what we did, we did. I don't regret it, and neither should you," she said, her hand resting lightly on his chest.

"But I don't regret it, Val. That's the problem."

"Oh," she said. "What does that mean?"

"I wonder if this means something," he said.

"Well, I hope it did, John," she said.

"No, no," he said, taking her hand. "I'm saying that I have feelings for you, and I, well, I...dunno."

"And your feelings for her have changed?"

"Yes. Yes, they have. And I hate myself for it, but not as much as I thought I would. Does that make any sense at all?"

"I guess," she lay in the gloom a moment, biting her upper lip in thought. "What I think it means is you have some unfinished business, and you need to go."

"Oh," he sat up. "Okay."

"No, dork, not now," she pulled him bodily onto the bed and straddled him, her soft flesh sheathing muscled thighs. "You need to go in a few hours and figure out what you want. Take your time."

"What do you want, Val?"

"I want something nice." She leaned down and brushed his lips with hers. She bit Pilate's lip, gently. Then enough to hurt.

* * *

Pilate rarely drove in Key West. Besides the packed streets, his old Saab convertible, elegant even with the acne of hastily-repaired bullet and buckshot holes—was too attractive a candidate for the knackers, boosters, and parts specialists who also made the islands their home. Taters shook his head the first time he saw Pilate in another old Saab, warning Pilate not to get sentimental about cars, especially ones that nobody made anymore.

"Is that the Taters Mulley theory on that?" Pilate had asked.

"It is," he said.

"So, that should apply to old boats nobody makes anymore, as well?"

Taters had said, "Shit," and shook his head as he walked back down the pier to the *TenFortyEZ*.

Sentiment aside, Pilate had to agree that a bullet-ridden Saab is hardly anybody's idea of a great ride but he figured the old whip would get him across the country one more time as he set out for the impending seventeen hundred miles to Cross Township.

He stopped at an oil and lube joint, replacing fluids, wiper blades, and everything else the sad-eyed mechanic brought to his attention while Pilate sipped burned coffee in the customer lounge. He even sprang for the overpriced air filter and got a wash and quick detail.

Pilate cruised to the marina to find the *TenFortyEZ* had set off for the Gulf, so he went on to get a solo brunch at Pepe's Cafe. His belly full of steak and eggs, he wasted little time going home to pack. Closing in on autumn, he reminded himself. The shorts, t-shirts and boat shoe wardrobe wouldn't cut it back in Cross Township, Nebraska, even in the good months. He dug out a heavier jacket, long-sleeved shirts, boots, and other necessaries, shoving them into a weekend jump bag. He dumped toiletries in his dopp kit, along with his statin prescription, pills for acid reflux, and the Wellbutrin that allegedly kept him level. He shook the bottle, noting he had enough for about two weeks.

Pilate slid the dopp into the larger bag and wandered around the house, making sure he picked up the presents he had bought for Peter and Kara, silently questioning if they would even like what he picked out.

He checked the fridge for perishables, downed most of what remained of a half-gallon of one percent milk, then poured the rest down the sink. He tossed takeout boxes and a few leftovers into a trash bag, Tupperware and all. He collected all the trash can contents, stacks of magazines, and the big trash bag and took it all to a dumpster owned by a cafe one block over.

"Anything else you want to throw in there, John?" Simon asked as Pilate closed the lid.

"Yeah, you," he said aloud.

"That's not nice-nice," Simon said.

Pilate froze, his hand on the scalding steel of the dumpster, the scent of rust, rot, and trash conspired with the texture of the dumpster surface to freeze him in place. His chest rang like bells, his throat tightened. He thought of the man who had abducted him, all straggly hair and gangly frame; the man's insistence that John be *nice-nice,* no matter what indignity or damage the stranger inflicted on him. The way the steel walls felt as he banged on them and begged God he be let out.

"Ouch," Pilate said, drawing his hand back from the scorching surface, shaking it, snapping himself out of the microseconds-long agony of an anxiety attack.

"You okay, John?" Simon said, chastened.

Pilate breathed in, then out, deeply, to reset his mood, dissipating the panic.

"Where's the threat?" he said to himself. "You're okay. You're outside, taking out the trash. Mister Nice-Nice isn't here. You're fine, pal." He blinked, remembering something his therapist had said. "You're okay too, Simon. It's all right. I'm not mad. Nobody is mad." His inner voice was silent for once but did not seem displeased.

He breathed purposefully a moment longer, then walked slowly back to his place, his fingertips brushing the trunks of palm trees he encountered on the way.

* * *

Rolling out of Key West, Pilate looked in the rear-view mirror, catching the blue tides, the garish paint of the island's buildings, and the eyes of his constant companion in the backseat, clad in an Aloha shirt, quietly filing his nails.

After an uneventful day of tedious driving, Pilate spent the night in a hotel near Marietta, Georgia. He soaked his aching back in a surprisingly nice tub and caught up on email with his phone. He wasn't up for a conversation with Kate, so he texted her that he would arrive the next day, and would find accommodations elsewhere. He did, however, insist on seeing the kids right away. He kept the message civil, even apologizing for hanging up on her.

He put the phone down on the toilet beside the bathtub and closed his eyes. A moment later it vibrated with a text he assumed would be from Kate.

Instead Val wrote him on her way home from the gym. **"Hope your trip is going ok. Do me one solid so I don't worry? Let me know you got to Cross, saw your kids, saw the wife, and aren't suicidal or trapped in a shipping container? Thinking about you but will respect your privacy."**

She punctuated it with a boxing glove emoji. The actual word Pilate had used was "boundary," but he appreciated her thoughtfulness. He texted her back a quick update and a heart emoji, then deleted the heart in favor of an agreement that he would call or text her after he saw his family again.

"You're a suave bastard, that's what you are. Send the eggplant." Simon drawled. Pilate went with two boxing gloves side by side instead.

The next day he stopped in Kentucky at the J-Mack BBQ in a wide spot in the road called Gilbertsville. The pig in the chef outfit on the sign was all the encouragement he needed, coupled with the powerfully sweet odor of barbecue wafting into the car.

He ordered a pulled pork sandwich crowned with slaw on the bun. The smoke flavor was sweet and the meat moist enough that he chose to forgo adding sauce. After he wolfed it down, he contemplated a chili dog, but decided against it, considering he wouldn't have Val to work it off him in the gym or elsewhere anytime soon.

Back in the car, his mind wandered to the Tin Roof Rib Shack in Cross, where barbecue had served as a strangely literal smokescreen for criminal behavior. He hoped it would be under new management when he got back, perhaps run by people who have no desire to get involved in drugs or killing.

That evening, about two hours from his destination as he cruised I-29 through Kansas City, his stomach growled. He rationalized that nothing would be open by the time he got to Cross, so may as well eat in KC. Besides, he had always wanted to try the legendary Z-Man sandwich at Joe's KC BBQ. Named Zagat's Best BBQ Sandwich in Kansas, and a favorite of Anthony Bourdain, it featured sliced smoked brisket, smoked provolone cheese, two onion rings, and some barbecue sauce on a Kaiser roll.

The twenty-minute wait outside in a line of BBQ fans that snaked around the gas station-turned-restaurant was more than worth it. He wolfed the jumbo sandwich down with a side of cole slaw and a Boulevard Pale Ale. His mood brightened as he ambled out past the line of new customers to his car.

A billboard for a bank affiliated with the Kansas City Chiefs caught his eye, and momentarily, he considered finding a place to stay the night so he could take in more of the City of Fountains, but decided against it as he made his way out of the tight parking lot.

"You have music to face," Simon said. *"Get going."*

Outside of St. Joseph, Missouri, he received a text from Kate. **"You here yet?"**

He responded that he would be there in an hour or so. She replied that the kids could see him after school tomorrow, if he wanted to pick them up. It would be a surprise.

Overjoyed, he texted: **"Can't wait! Will pick them up and take them for a snack, then bring them home, ok?"**

She replied that it would be great and asked where he planned to stay.

Pilate tossed the phone down on the passenger seat and glowered at the sunset, hands tight on the wheel.

* * *

"You could use a wee bit of the Jameson, I reckon," Cusack said after hearty back claps and handshakes, gesturing for Pilate to have a seat at the small bar in the Irishman's bed and breakfast. He poured each of them a couple of fingers. "Slainte'."

Cusack and Marcy had moved to the county a few years ago and purchased the Carlson mansion, a thirty-room structure built in 1866 by the Carlson family, on the edge of downtown Cross. By the late sixties, a string of new buyers had purchased the mansion and converted it to a B&B. The Cusacks were now the owners of the Cross and Cork, running it like an Irish pub and rustic bed-and-breakfast.

"So, how are 'tings? What's the craic?" Cusack said, his eye twinkling as the pair clinked glasses and drank.

"Oh great. I haven't seen the fam for a while, you know. I miss them, so I thought I'd stay here with you and drink."

Cusack chuckled. "Rough patches happen, my friend," he said, pouring Pilate another.

Pilate nodded. "Yeah, I seem to get my share."

"Well, it's merely a wee dalliance, I reckon."

"Dalliance? How do you know?" Pilate said, sitting up in his chair. Cusack blanched, screwing up his face a second.

"Oh, I used the wrong word, sorry," Cusack turned to polish a glass. "Stay as long as you need. On the house. We owe you."

"No, no, I can't take up valuable real estate for free," Pilate said, trying to smile.

"Not at all, not at all," he said, dismissing Pilate's objection with a wave. "You saved my life, remember?" He examined the clean glass in the light, then placed it on the shelf. "So, what's next for you?"

Pilate sighed. "Get some sleep. Tomorrow I get to see my kids."

* * *

Pilate had an entire day to kill in the smallest town in the world, but he couldn't force himself to sleep in. He arose, showered, and went downstairs. Cusack's wife Marcy made him a proper Irish fry up of two eggs, mushrooms, tomatoes, baked beans, and blood sausage with Irish soda bread and butter.

Pilate finished most of it, with a notable exception, eliciting a raised eyebrow from Cusack as he cleared the table.

"Sorry, the blood sausage is a bit of an acquired taste," Pilate said, shrugging.

"No worries," Cusack said. "More for me in the back."

Pilate walked out onto the wraparound porch with the last of his coffee in a to-go cup, sipping it as he heard the Cross College quad clarion bells ring. His heartbeat quickened as he flashed back to that brutal blizzard on the night he holed up in the library tower to avoid Jack Lindstrom's thugs intent on "eliminating" him. He had narrowly survived, saving Kara's, Dean Trevathan's, and Kate's lives.

"And you got shot in the face for your trouble!" Simon bellowed.

Pilate dropped the coffee cup in the trash bin and set out on foot towards campus. He passed the rows of old houses, some on the historic places register, some modest, some ready for the wrecking ball. An occasional pickup truck blew past, drivers waving as they did to everyone in this tightly knit and sometimes tightly wound community. As he rounded a corner, he spotted a familiar figure wandering through her garden.

"Hey, Lanie. Remember me?"

The woman turned. Lanie Hansen had been the most beautiful woman in Cross forty years ago. Her glory days were behind her now, as she tended old gardens and a husband whose accident had cut short a happy and vibrant marriage. Pilate could still see the spectacular woman she had once been, though denim had replaced silk and work boots crowded high heels out of her closets. "Well of course I remember you, Sheriff Scovill. Have you come to say hello to Marvin? I think he's out driving around somewhere."

Pilate stopped in his tracks. He'd heard that the strain of caring for her invalid husband had made the slow onset of dementia somewhat less slow and, as impossible as it seemed, somewhat less kind. Marvin, he knew, was inside the house, unable to move from his bed and certainly not driving anywhere. And he himself looked little like the former sheriff of Cross, Morgan Scovill.

"She's nuttier than you are, John. Nobody home," Simon opined with his customary kindness and consideration for the mentally troubled. Pilate hushed Simon, then gave Lanie his best authentic fake smile.

"No Lanie, I saw your beautiful flowers and wanted to compliment you on them. But I'm not Morgan, honey, I'm..."

"I know you're not Morgan. I wouldn't give that toad the time of day! You're Morgan's daddy." She blinked. "How long ago was that? Seems like such a long time ago. You were *such* a good sheriff. We were safe then. Not like it is today."

Pilate winced. Long before his time, the elder sheriff Scovill still served as a kind of touchstone for the older residents of Cross, the ones who remembered the times that strong and honest men protected them from the predators that circled places even as small and seemingly innocent as Cross. Morgan, the son of the older Scovill, had his own turn as sheriff but could make no progress against drugs, much less against the corruption that had come to the college.

"Are you going to be sheriff again, Sheriff Scovill? We need you so much." As sad as it was that Lanie did not remember him at all and was apparently had one foot in the current day and one in the much happier times of 30 years ago or more, his heart broke anew at the innocent, helpless hope in her eyes. He touched her arm gently, made some reassuring noise but no promises (*"Like she'd remember,"* Simon muttered) and resumed his walk to the campus of Cross College.

He made it in five minutes of casual strolling, musing at how much smaller the town seemed, even compared with tiny Key West. So much had transpired here; though Cross was nothing more than a wide spot in the road, it had grown larger in his memories. He had an impact on the world when he was here.

The memory was not comfortable. He hadn't been home for...*back*. He hadn't been *back* for more than an hour past breakfast, and already the dead generations crowding Cross Township were making demands of him.

Pilate heard the bells signifying eight-thirty as he stepped on campus, passed the President's residence and then the hall where his late friend Peter Trevathan once served as a cantankerous dean. Pilate smiled at the memory of Trevathan's wild glass eye and disapproving grunts upon their first meeting.

"Never thought you'd miss that guy, did you?" Simon said.

"No," Pilate said, aloud, softly.

His reverie broken by a gaggle of students, mostly girls, chatting and laughing as they passed him by, evaporated. He thought of Derek Krall, who could never let an opportunity pass to rate a coed's ass. Dead as Trevathan, but it wasn't cancer that took Derek Krall off campus permanently. In a way, he got off lucky.

Thinking of the former college librarian, Pilate turned towards that old building, thinking he might roost there a while, reading magazines and doing a little people watching. Across the quad he saw a familiar face, walking with her satchel over her shoulder, looking into her smartphone. His wife. Kate. Mother of his son. His heart melted in his chest and his breath caught, adrenaline rushing through him. Her hair was different; strange to his eyes, but he liked it. He quickened his pace to try to intercept her before she made it to the fine arts building.

"Might as well say hello now," he thought, smiling, and lengthening his stride further. "Surprise her with a hug before I see the kids."

A rush of emotion seized him; elation at seeing her, guilt for betraying her, a surge of remembered love from having won her. But he would make it right again. He would fix it. He could do it this time.

Twenty yards from her and closing fast, he cleared his throat to call to her and raised his hand to wave. The syllable died in his throat as a man walked up to Kate, hugging her quickly but intensely and kissing her on the mouth before they proceeded into the fine arts building together, arm in arm.

Pilate stopped cold. His head felt as though the entire Gulf of Mexico was pounding through it. An iron band straitjacketed his chest, his eyes locked on his idiot hand hanging stupidly in the air, immobile, short-circuited by the sight of his wife and her boyfriend.

Chapter Four

Guts roiled, skin clammy, he turned away from where he saw his wife and started to run. He didn't jog, instead bolting at full speed off the quad and into the middle of the street. His feet pounded painfully, shod in the casual boat shoes that provided no support or cushioning. His breath came out in gusts through his nose, fists churning at his sides. He ran several blocks before he slowed down, exhausted, and staggered to a light pole. Pilate leaned and tried to keep his breakfast.

"Hey, need a ride?" Pilate heard over his shoulder. He breathed deeply, trying to reset, ignoring the question.

"I say, do you need a ride, John?" He turned to see the lean face of Jeremy Ryder, county commissioner and acting sheriff. Ryder was driving behind him slowly, pacing him in a late model Dodge Ram pickup.

"Yeah, I guess I do," Pilate said, opening the door and climbing in.

* * *

"Didn't expect to see you strolling down the fair streets of Cross," Ryder said as the pair looked over cups of coffee at newly renamed and garishly painted Chatty Kathy diner downtown. Pilate stared vacantly ahead, "John?"

Pilate roused himself, willing his mind to pull itself from the well he had dropped into. "Hmm?"

"I said I didn't…"

"I heard you," Pilate snapped, meeting the man's pale blue eyes, which responded to Pilate's exhortation with an infinitesimal widening, then settled back into the customary squint. "Sorry."

"When'd you get into town?" he asked.

"Last night," Pilate said.

"Okay. Good."

"Good?"

"You fly into Omaha?"

"Drove in from Florida to see my family. We have…some issues."

Ryder looked out the diner window. The bank facade across the street needed a coat of paint, just as the diner did. "So, I guess you found out?" he said, uncharacteristically softly.

Pilate nodded. "I just don't know how to fix it."

"Fix it?" Ryder said.

"Yeah. I can't believe she's serious about that guy. I mean, I know things got distant, but I didn't think…" he trailed off, eyes pointed at but not truly seeing the coffee mug before him. "Kate's tired of the drama with me. It's always some scary situation. Always some joker trying to hurt us. She wants to protect the kids. I do, too. I came back to tell her I can do whatever it takes to save our family. Show her I want to fix the situation."

Ryder reached under his Stetson to scratch his steel gray forelock, exercising his jaw muscles a second. "You know, I have found that fixing situations can often be only a temporary solution. When I break up a domestic or a bar fight, I'm fixing the situation in the moment. Typically, those same people are back to their usual idiocy by Saturday night."

Pilate's stomach rolled. He muttered, "That's…really not helpful."

"Reality often isn't, John. What the hell did you expect?" Ryder shrugged. "You've been gone for months. Any momma worth her salt is wired to protect her babies. If the daddy runs off, she finds a new one."

Pilate sat in silence.

"And just like us useless men, women have needs," Ryder said.

"I know you're the sheriff and county commissioner here and all," Pilate said, his jaw tight. "Had no fucking idea you were also a goddamned judge."

Ryder snorted. "Okay. I deserved that. There's a reason I'm a peace officer instead of a family therapist." Ryder still bore a flinty resemblance to the actor Peter Weller, albeit the AARP-friendly version. "But I'm not wrong, John."

He paused a moment, looking back out the window before turning back to Pilate. "Shit," he half-sighed, signaling the waitress for a warmup. "I'm not trying to ride your ass. Not my job and your personal life's not my business. Kate's a great lady and you have to do what you can do."

Pilate glanced at two farmers in overalls bursting through the door, laughing and seating themselves at the counter. He inhaled deeply, trying to reset his breathing.

"You know, John, we've been through our share of scrapes," Ryder said, sipping his black coffee.

"No shit," Pilate said. His mind raced through memories of the past few years in Cross Township, dealing with homicidal nut jobs, brushes with the Hillbilly mafia, and the eccentric cast of characters on staff at Cross College. "Lots of scrapes."

Ryder went silent as the waitress refilled his coffee mug. Pilate covered his mug with his hand. "Thanks, Toni," Ryder tipped his hat, then focused back on Pilate. "Well, I guess you could say we may have another one."

"We?" Pilate said, picking up his coffee, tasting it and putting it back on the table. Reaching for the sugar packets, he cocked an eyebrow at Ryder. "What do you mean?"

Ryder looked down at this ostrich boot, crossed over his knee under the table. He spat discreetly on a napkin and polished a bit of dirt off the toe. "You heard about the shooting, right?"

"Shooting?" Pilate said, leaning in. "I've been gone, remember?"

"I figured Kate might have mentioned it," he cleared his throat, backtracking at the crestfallen look slicing through Pilate's face. "Well, yeah. Night before last," Ryder cast his gaze around the diner, ensuring they were not overheard by the customers at the counter. "Damndest thing, too. You know Bob Hayes out at the airfield?"

Hayes unwittingly helped Jack Lindstrom when he "returned from the dead" and tried to kill Pilate and Kate a few years ago. Pilate shrank in his seat, his chest tightening again as he mentally confronted yet another reminder of an occasion when he nearly got his family killed.

"Uh-huh," Pilate said.

"Well, going on what we could get from Bob in between a mild cardiac arrest and shots of morphine, he was out there at the airfield by his lonesome as usual; just got through talking James Green's Cessna into the air. He closed up the door to the control tower. Piecing together the few bits of what he said to the nine-one-one operator, somebody appeared in the dark and shot him straight through the kidney."

"Is he dead?" his face contorted as he braced himself for the news.

Ryder sipped his coffee and shook his head. Swallowing, he said, "He managed to crawl to the phone. Dispatched the paramedics, Burl and Story, who got there toot suite. Been in the hospital since. They had to do surgery last night. Old' Bob lost the kidney."

"Shit. Any idea why?" Pilate said, shaking his head. "Robbery?"

"Well, as far as we can tell, robbery wasn't the motive. Didn't take his wallet. Didn't steal anything from the airport. Guy showed up, cleared his throat and shot him. I mean, Holy Christ, there was no motive. You know Bob's practically a monk since his wife passed, right? No enemies, keeps to himself. Rides that silly bicycle all over creation when he's not running the muni airport."

Pilate recalled Hayes' claim to fame was as a long-distance cyclist, participating in the Des Moines Register's Annual Great Bicycle Ride Across Iowa every year for his vacation. The RAGBRAI is a seven-day race across the width of the Hawkeye state. Riders start the ride on Iowa's western border and ride to the eastern border, stopping in numerous towns along the way. Pilate recalled the *Cross Courier* newspaper recycled a profile about the "(insert age)-year-old lone rider Bob Hayes" every year. As he recalled, last year Bob's birthday tally had reached fifty-nine.

"I mean, whatever floats your boat," Ryder chuckled. "Personally, those bike seats hurt my bony ass. Much prefer a horse."

"I find it hard to believe you ever rode a bicycle in your life, sheriff," Pilate said. "Who can ride a bike in cowboy boots? So, no motive. No enemies?"

"Don't think so, I'm going off what I know about Bob. He's been in and out of it since the shooting, and I need to grill him pretty heavily when he wakes up later today."

"Okay. You said 'we' and I know there's no mouse in your pocket, so what do you want me to do for you?"

Ryder drank more coffee, then placed the mug down to the left side of the table, leaning forward, hands clasped, he said, "Bob said something odd before they took him to surgery."

"What?"

"The guy who shot him said the bullet was a present from Jack Lindstrom."

* * *

Pilate spoke with Ryder for a few more moments, then realized the time. He had to pick up the kids from school. Actually he had a few hours, but needed as much time as possible to get his game face on.

Ryder asked Pilate if he would submit to formal questioning, if necessary, to which Pilate agreed. Then Ryder asked if he would, off the record, consult on the case.

"Given you being the world's leading expert on Jack Lindstrom, I many need your help."

"Sheriff," Pilate protested. "Jack's dead. This is just some nut."

"Agreed, but if this nut is fixated on Lindstrom, that means he's fixated on you," Ryder said. "And John, I know this is a lot to process, but that means he's fixated on your family, too."

Pilate shook his head slowly. "Damn it," he whispered.

"John, listen, I have my deputies driving by your house twice a day, showing the flag. Now that you're here, you can—"

"I can't stay at the farm," Pilate said. "She wants me to stay at Cusack's."

Ryder whistled low and leaned back, the bentwood diner chair creaking with the shift in weight from his slight frame. "Well, then you know you gotta tell her."

"Fucking great. That's exactly what she wants to hear, 'Hey hon, I know you're gonna leave me over all this bullshit I visit on you and the kids, risking your lives and all, but I need to move back in because I'm a risk to your lives again," Pilate said.

Ryder shrugged. "I can tell her if you want."

"Thanks, no. I will tell her."

"You still got that 9-millimeter?"

"Yes," Pilate said. "There's also a shotgun at the house."

"Oh, I remember. Kate is hell on wheels with that damn thing."

"Hope she doesn't use it on me," Pilate said, blowing a sigh through his cheeks.

* * *

Back in his room at Cusack's B&B, Pilate flung himself on the bed, forearm over his eyes.

"Well, it's not like you haven't done the same thing, you know," Simon said.

Pilate sat up.

"I'm referring to screwing around," Simon chimed. *"Though if you prefer, we can talk about the odds of Jack Lindstrom shambling out of his grave…again."*

Pilate thought for a moment. "Well, I'm pretty sure Jack was cremated. I can't imagine he's among the walking dead without a body. It's gotta be a nutjob of some sort."

As Pilate knew from researching the book he wrote about Lindstrom and the Cross College conspiracy, Jack Lindstrom didn't have close family besides his ex-wife. And no close friends. Pilate stared up at the ornate ceiling fan as it lazily stirred the atmosphere.

"Are you thinking what I'm thinking, John?" Simon said.

"When am I not thinking what you're thinking, Simon? We're the same person."

"That's an uncharitable thing to say. Also, if that's true, why do you miss so many of my jokes?"

"You're thinking that the shooter didn't kill Bob Hayes. Bob is slow as molasses and no threat to anybody. Got shot and lay there. The shooter didn't finish him off—he gave Hayes a message."

"To give to us," Simon said.

"Us? I thought you said we are separate."

"Again, uncharitable."

"The book. This is somebody who read my book."

"Which details the way Jack Lindstrom flew into the county to try to kill you. Or us, whichever."

"If I'm being charitable."

"Focus, John."

"This is some nut who read the book and has a weird fetish for Jack Lindstrom. There are tons of people out there who fetishize serial killers and arch criminals."

"Yes, and there are people who have written best-selling books about their experiences. Authors who end up, in self-defense, killing the object of their fetishes," Simon hissed. *"Authors who get abducted. Authors who are left to die in a steel shipping container in Key West, Florida."*

"Oh Jesus," Pilate said aloud.

"Some people are simply not very nice-nice, John."

* * *

"Daddy!" Peter's eyes widened to the size of saucers as he bolted from his teacher's side and leaped into Pilate's arms, shrieking with delight. "Where you been, Daddy! I miss you all the time!"

Pilate choked back tears, hugging the four-year-old who had grown impossibly much the past three months. "Oh baby boy, I missed you so much." They chatted and hugged for a few moments before piling into the car and driving to the elementary school to pick up Kara.

When they had signed in at the office and made their way to Kara's classroom door, Peter yelled "Kara, its Daddy!" Kara looked up from her coloring, smiled at Peter, then her mouth went slack as she saw Pilate.

Kara stopped coloring and walked over to her cubby to pick up her *Monster High* backpack. She said goodbye quietly to a few friends and her teacher, then met Pilate and Peter at the door.

"Hi, kid," Pilate said. He went down on one knee. "Do I get a hug?"

Kara tucked her chin into her chest. "Are you staying this time?"

* * *

After getting ice cream from the Dairy Queen in Goss City and opening the presents he brought them - a genuine conch shell for Kara decorated with smaller sea shells in the shape of a crude map of Florida, in Pilate's opinion it was the ugliest conceivable souvenir of the Keys but an instinct had told him that the awful thing would please her, and indeed, she seemed to think it an absolutely lovely gift, while Peter was delighted by the simple foot-long model sailboat with real sails, and had already requested and received permission to sail it in the bathtub four times before the ice cream came. Satiated and happy with one another, they headed back to Cross Township and the farmhouse.

"Your bar blew down in the backyard," Peter announced as they cruised down the state road to the Cross Township exit.

"Oh no," Pilate said. "That's awful."

"Mom said you won't be needing it anyway," Kara said.

"And Grant laughed," Peter said,

"Shut up, Pete," Kara hissed, leaning over to Peter's car seat and elbowing him in the shoulder "You're not supposed to talk about Grant."

"Ow!" he howled, rubbing his shoulder.

"Ow is right," Simon said. *"It's a double shame because I have this ominous feeling you are really going to need a drink soon."*

* * *

Kate met them in the gravel driveway, hugging the kids and sending them inside, telling them to do their homework. Peter protested "I'm just a little man" and did not have homework. He also protested his big sister's use of physical violence, and tentatively reasserted his right to begin operating his own personal bathtime navy that evening with his mother. Kate patted his butt, agreed in her capacity as harbormaster that the weather forecast for bathtime sailing were favorable, and sent him to watch *Teen Titans Go!* and have some Graham crackers.

Alone together in the farmhouse kitchen, Pilate took a step towards his wife. "I like the new hairstyle. It looks great."

Kate seemed confused, then rolled her eyes up, as if she could see her haircut. "Oh, this? I cut it shorter. Less fuss. You've lost weight," she said.

"Yeah, I've been using the sauna a lot lately, and…"

Before he could finish his weak joke, Kate closed the distance and hugged him. Hot tears leaking furiously from her eyes, she buried her face into his shirt. "I'm so glad you are okay."

Pilate gingerly put his arms around her. She too had lost some weight. Kissing her head, he said, "You have no idea how glad I am to see you."

She pulled away enough to look at his face. She wiped tears with the heels of her hands. "I promised myself if I wore mascara I would not cry."

"Me too," he said, smiling. "That's why I rarely wear it. A man has to show emotion now and then."

She touched his cheek. "You look tired."

"Long, long drive, and I guess being home made me a little wrung out. Too many bad memories."

"Plenty of good ones, too," she said. "Don't forget those."

"How could I?" He wanted to kiss her, but it felt wrong, somehow, as if they were warm but platonically intimate business colleagues rather than husband and wife.

"Mom, where's the peanut butter?" Kara called through the screen door.

"Pantry, Kara Jane. Go look," she called back.

"So where are you staying?" she said.

"Cusack's," he said, his smile fading.

"Best place in town," she said.

"If you say so. I know a better place," he said, his tone gentle, locking eyes with her.

She looked away, then cocked her head at him. "Stay for dinner?"

* * *

Pilate set the table, refereed two squabbles between Kara and Peter, and followed the smell of Kate's lasagna into the kitchen. Kate bent over, looking at the lasagna through the oven window. Pilate fondly remembered seeing her shapely rear end for the first time the day they met.

"Some things never change," Simon trilled, following up with a wolf whistle.

"Can I help with anything?" he said, leaning on the doorway.

She stood, reaching for a bottle of wine. Without facing him, she held the bottle out to him. "You can open this."

"On a school night?" he said, taking the bottle.

"Never stopped you before," she said, pulling two glasses from the cabinet.

"Well said," Pilate fished in the junk drawer for an opener. "Where's the thing?"

"Oh, here," she opened another cabinet and pulled out a fancy contraption. "Here. This is much easier to use. I mean, for me, especially since you haven't been around to open my wine for me."

Pilate fiddled with the opener a moment, figuring out how to use it. "So, nobody has helped you open the wine lately?" The cork popped, he poured the wine into a glass and handed it to Kate.

"I just said I got this because nobody. Oh," she took the wine, leaning against the counter. "Who blabbed? It was Pete, wasn't it?" She tried out a smile, but it survived only a moment before it wilted into a pathetic smirk that came and went.

"No, not really," Pilate said.

"John, it's nothing to get worked up about," she said, sipping the wine.

Pilate's chest tightened. He felt his heart start to race; strange, warped lights flooded his vision a second. He put down the wine bottle, breathing deeply.

"John, are you okay?" she placed her glass on the counter. "Hey?"

Pilate shook his head comically, as if he were a cartoon character who got walloped by an anvil. "Yeah," he said. "What's nothing to get worked up about?"

"We're just…friends. Grant is kind to me."

"So when I saw him kiss you this morning on the quad, that was just Grant exhibiting his kindness?" Pilate said it in quiet, measured tones, careful not to say anything the kids might overhear.

Kate blanched, her eyes searching the space on the floor between them. "You followed me?"

"No," Pilate said. "I was coming over to tell you I was back. And I saw you and Grant all chummy before you went into the building. At that point, I felt like I would have been intruding."

"Shit," she said, scooping up her wine glass and taking a healthy swallow. "I never meant for you to see that."

"Obviously. I know when I don't want anybody to know who I'm kissing, I go and kiss them on the god-damned quad in front of the entire world," he hissed. *"Oh, this is going really well,"* came a voice, apparently finding Sybil Danning less attention-compelling than Joan Collins.

"I knew you would fuck this up somehow," she said.

"Oh, I fucked this up? No, my dear, what is fucked up is me being in an ICU bed for a week and you never even bothering to come see me."

"Here we go again. John Pilate's latest brush with death movie, and I get the role of supporting actress. No. I can't. I will not risk our kids' lives by being around you in Key West. It's too dangerous."

"Need I remind you that this place, this lovely little burg you can't stand to be away from, is where we were both nearly killed a few weeks after we met? That my fault, too? Was it my fault this inbred, shithole town started us both down this path?"

Pilate turned away from her, glancing into the living room. Miraculously, the children appeared not to have heard, and were contentedly snuggling on the couch and laughing at Raven's tactful attempts to redirect Robin's boyhood love for her.

"You're saying your little adventure in Jamaica with your ex-girlfriend was completely innocent? You lied to me about that and God knows what else. I have let too much go. So many suspicions. Things I wrote off because of your mental health issues and the stress you are under. But please, John. Don't make me ask questions that you do not want to answer."

Pilate sighed, trying to reset his breathing. "Okay, Kate. Fine. I'm sure I have not always been the best at communicating, and I have kept secrets," he said. "There are reasons, good reasons for the things I've done. But I never, ever, wanted to hurt you or the kids. I hated being away from you."

"That's the thing, though, isn't it? You missed us so much, but you found ways to be away as often as you could. And then when you said you would try to accept Cross as our home, you did everything you could to make me regret asking you to stay here." She swallowed her wine and set the glass on the counter.

"Can we just take a look at trying to fix things?"

Kate folded her arms across her chest, looking out the window a moment. She turned back to face Pilate.

"I'm sorry, John. I didn't want to do this now, but I think we need to talk about formalizing this."

"Formalizing? What the hell does that mean?" his vision narrowed; chest aching.

She looked at Pilate with watery eyes. "Separation. I just..." she cleared her throat. "I just think we should do what is best for everybody."

"Kate, no," Pilate said. "Let me make this right."

"John, the best thing you can do right now is stay near your family."

"Yes! That's what I want, I just told you."

"Stay near. Not here. Show me you mean it."

"But I have to stay in a fucking B&B? Not in my own home? Damn it, this is bullshit," Pilate said, rustling a hand through his hair.

Kate pondered the faded linoleum.

"Oh, I get it," Pilate said. "If I'm in this house it makes dating Grant a little complicated, huh?"

"John, why don't we talk about this tomorrow, when the kids are in school?"

Simon snapped his fingers in Pilate's brain. *"Good idea, John. Cool off. You're fucking this up but it's not a train wreck. Not yet."*

Pilate rocked on his heels a moment, his eyes welling. "Kate?" He whispered. "Do you...do you still love me?"

Her voice broke, saying, "How could you ask me that? I love you. I will love you forever."

"But, are you still, you know? In love with me?" His head bowed, chin nearly on his chest.

She lifted his head, making him face her. "I don't know."

"Oh," he said, stepping away from her. "I guess I better go."

"No, please stay. Be with your kids," she wiped her eyes with a dish towel.

"Our kids," he said.

* * *

Pilate managed to hold it together as they went through the motions and shared an excruciatingly awkward dinner. He fired off his best dad jokes, earning a few groans. Kara interrogated Pilate about why he had iced tea instead of wine.

"Because I don't always have a drink with dinner," he said.

Kara laughed. "Good one, Dad."

"Daddy, are you tucking me in tonight?" Peter asked. Kara shushed him.

Pilate looked at Kate. She nodded.

"Of course I am, little man," he said.

"See, Kara? I told you Daddy would tuck me in."

"But you won't be staying over?" Kara said, looking to her mother for affirmation.

"I can't stay tonight. I have to-"

"Dad has to work across town," Kate said.

"But I will see you again tomorrow," Pilate said, leaning toward the kids, his eyes on Kate for permission. "I think mom probably says I can pick you both up from school?"

Kate nodded.

"Yay!" Peter said.

Kara picked up her fork and pushed bits of her uneaten meal around the plate, pleased but still dissatisfied deeper down. "It's dark.

Can we go out in the yard with Daddy and look for lightning bugs for a minute? Please?" Kate frowned and checked the calendar on the refrigerator.

"I don't know if there are going to be very many, honey. It's almost September. They're usually more in June."

* * *

Pilate realized he had not messaged Val to let her know he was still at large, unmurdered, and technically sort of welcome in his own home. He didn't want to talk with her on the phone when he got back to Cusack's that night; he would be too crushingly sad and vulnerable. And he didn't want to get verbal here in the house, with Kate already on the verge of filing divorce papers.

"Some quiet time in the big back yard to call Val real quick might be just the thing, champ," Simon said, surprisingly helpful.

Pilate said "Kate, why don't you let me take them out and bug hunt for a minute, and then we can put them to bed and chat about that thing we were talking about." Kate looked resigned but nodded her assent and went into the kitchen to wash up.

The steady roasting of the Nebraska summer had parched the fields and browned the grass, but also had kept the lightning bug population hanging on past their usual span. Kara and Peter were soon rushing around chasing the darting, glowing fireflies and screaming with delight. Pilate strolled along behind.

He took his phone out, gauged the distance to the house and the ambient noise from the wind and happily noisy children and decided to chance the call. He thumbed dial on Val's contact and half-listened to the ringing until Val's sleepy, warm contralto voice came across the instrument.

"Well, hello sailor. You flatter me with the return of twentieth century courtship. An actual phone call."

The kids had wandered farther, down to the small creek barely making its way across the old corn field, and Pilate saw them suddenly drop to the ground in excitement - a box turtle by the creek by the sound of it, a biological find sufficiently exciting to drive even lightning bugs off the agenda.

"Hey Val. I'm here. Alive. The kids are great. Kate...well. It could be worse, though I don't see how," and he quickly detailed the disastrous first night and the apparent return of Mr. Nice-Nice. He apologized for not being able to talk longer and promised another update in a day or two before hanging up.

He strolled closer to where the kids were seated on either side of a small but genuine box turtle, intending to tell them it was getting late and time to go back home, when he heard Kara's voice through the rustling prairie grasses.

"Peter, does Daddy love us? Does he?" Pilate's heart froze in his chest and he stopped moving, stopped breathing. Even blinking seemed impossibly loud and vulgar, revealing too much of his presence.

"Because he was gone for months and years you mean?" Peter did not seem alarmed by the query, but rather was thoughtful.

"Yes, and because...because what if mommy doesn't love him. That will make him mad and then he won't love us anymore. Is that why he went away for so long?"

A single tear ran down Pilate's cheek. His legs tensed as he thought about springing towards his sweet, kind, bright daughter, sweeping her up in his arms to tell her how no matter what, the love in his heart for her and Peter was a fire that would never burn out.

Then he heard Peter's response. It was quiet at first, but each word came fiercer than the last.

"Daddy loves us. He loves us the most. More than Grant even. He has boats and cars and houses in Florida but he comes here. He loves us the most."

Kara breathed out a sigh of acceptance and when she spoke again Pilate heard iron in her voice. "Okay. Then we have to love him too so he knows and doesn't get scared."

"Well that's easy! He knows that! He isn't scared of anything! Not bad men or goblins or...or SNAPPING turtles even!"

Pilate could stand it no longer and strode from the darkness and towards his children. "There you are! I've been looking everywhere!"

"Daddy look, a turtle!" He praised the turtle and its discoverers, commiserated with Kara and Peter both that the lightning bugs seemed to have wandered off for the night, and led his charges back to the house, hand in hand, two little and one big, and for the first time in a year his heart was at peace.

Chapter Five

Standing on the front porch after the kids were in bed, Pilate and his wife gazed at one another. She was emotionally exhausted, run ragged. He was calm but knew he still had to bring her up to speed on the newest threat to their safety and happiness.

Pilate cleared his throat. "Listen, there's something I need to tell you."

"John, we agreed to talk about it tomorrow," she said. "I'm tired. I had a tough day already."

"This can't wait," he said, touching her shoulder for a moment. She looked at his arm, not in anger, and he pulled it back.

"Focus on the part where there are killers trying to get her and her children, John."

"Okay. What?" she said.

Pilate told her everything Ryder had said, without adding in his own speculations about obsession and the ever-resurrectible Jack Lindstrom.

"Oh for cripes sake, are you serious? This!" she jabbed a finger in his face. "This is what I am talking about. This shit…this fucking drama follows you wherever you go, doesn't it?"

"I don't know what to say. I know how it looks."

"This is for real. You're not just jerking my chain to try to get back in my bed."

"Oh Jesus, Kate, yes, it's real. I'm sorry but it is. This is not some elaborate ploy so I can sleep on my own couch."

"I can take care of myself," she said.

"Never in question. I'm just asking you to double check the doors and keep the shotgun in arm's reach until we figure this out, okay?"

"It never ends," she said, jerking open the screen door and going back inside. She let it slam behind her.

"I didn't see anything at all out here earlier, but I'm going to do a quick perimeter check —make sure everything looks secure. Then I'll be at Cusack's," he called through the screen door.

"Fine. Whatever. Good night." she said in the coldest tones he had heard from her yet today and closed the oak door, the heavy deadbolt slammed into place and the lights in the living room went out.

"That went well," Simon said.

* * *

Pilate found nothing amiss outside the house, other than the wreck of his beloved Frontdoor bar, which had indeed collapsed in a storm during his absence. He texted Kate to let her know he was leaving, then drove to the B&B, where Cusack waved him over to the bar.

"You look like the dog's dinner, old son, if you'll pardon my impertinence," he said, chuckling. Cusack had the ability to tell the truth in a way that should make you take offense, rather than laugh, but you always laughed.

"I've definitely had better days," Pilate said, sliding onto a barstool.

"Jameson?" Cusack offered.

"If I asked for a martini would I get one?"

Cusack silently pulled a glass from beneath the bar and poured a double of Irish whiskey, looking over Pilate's head as he gently shoved it toward him. "This is an Irish martini. Better for you."

Pilate shrugged and drank half of it. Alcohol is alcohol.

"Slainte."

"Easy for you to say," Pilate said. "You leaving me to drink alone?"

"Aye, sorry. Marcy has me working the honey-do list right now, but I'll leave the bottle within reach." Cusack nodded and toddled into the kitchen area.

"Don't mind if I do," Pilate said, pouring himself another double. Raising the glass to his mouth, he inhaled the sweet sharpness of the whiskey, then breathed back into the glass, his eyes received a puff of his exhale and started to water. He gently placed the glass down in the dim of the empty bar area, turned his head towards the door, and wept.

Chapter Six

"Bob, how are you doing?" Ryder said, holding his hat, standing at Bob Hayes' bedside.

Hayes' eyes flickered open, taking a moment to focus on Ryder, then on Pilate, standing beside the rangy sheriff. "Oh, hey," he said above the sound of a monitor beeping.

"You're looking good," Ryder said.

"Then I evidently look better than I feel," Hayes said, wincing as he stifled a weak chuckle.

"Hurts, huh?" Ryder said.

"Strangely, it hurts but not as much as my kidney stones," Hayes said. "Doc says I got a little bonus losing my kidney. Now I only have to deal with one kidney's worth of stones." He gestured with a hand impaled by an I.V. port at the bedside table.

"Water?" Pilate said, picking up a large plastic jug with a lid and flex straw.

"Yeah," Hayes said, taking a sip and handing it back to Pilate. "You look familiar."

"John Pilate," he said, sheepish.

Hayes' face flashed with energy a second, then fell back into the flat affect of the ill. "Oh. Right. Been a while. Then you got the message, I take it?"

"I am so sorry, Bob," Pilate said.

"S'okay," Hayes said, turning his gaze back to Ryder. "What can I do for you?"

Ryder fingered the brim of his Stetson, then put it on and removed a small notebook and pen from his breast pocket. "Bob, can we go over what happened the other night?"

"Sure, sheriff," he said, gesturing for the water again.

Pilate stood, motionless.

"John?" Ryder said, elbowing him.

"Oh? Sorry," Pilate said, handing the water jug back to Bob.

Hayes sipped the water, gasping mildly. Eyes closed, he wordlessly passed the jug back to Pilate, who placed it on the bedside table.

"Just locking up the tower after I got Green's Cessna off the ground. Short hop to Lincoln to play a gig downtown or something."

"Go on," Ryder said.

"Well, it's dark on the field. I had turned off the main strip landing lights and heading over to my trailer. Going to tune up my bike for next week's ride. Damn thing's wobbling after I hit a rock over on the state highway."

"Bob?" Ryder said, gentle but firm.

"Yeah?"

"Get on with it," he said.

"Gotcha. Anyway, I noticed that the lights on the outbuildings were off."

"I thought you turned them off?" Pilate inquired.

"The landing lights. Not the lights around my office and trailer," Hayes said. "They're on a timer. Well, not a timer, a motion sensor. My motion should have made them fire up. They didn't. Stayed dark."

"Unusual, I take it?" Pilate asked.

"Yeah," Hayes sighed, grimacing. "I need a little more of that painkiller juice. I think it's close to my next dose 'cause it's starting to hurt like fire."

"Sorry," Ryder said, hitching a thumb over his shoulder. "I can get the nurse."

"No use," he said. "She'll just tut-tut and say not until time."

"Oh," Ryder said. "Well let's keep talking, maybe it will take your mind off it."

Hayes opened his eyes and looked at Ryder quizzically. "Yeah, right, sure." He closed his eyes again. "Okay, so the lights aren't working, and Jet wasn't around, either."

"Jet?" Pilate asked.

"Yeah, he's my dog. Sweet chocolate Lab. Boon companion. Had him a couple years. Had the run of the place, but when he'd hear my keys jingling he usually came running 'cause he knew dinner isn't far off. But he didn't come."

"The dog that did not bark in the night," Pilate said, low and under his breath.

"Huh?" Hayes grunted.

"Nothing. So, the lights are off, the dog's not around, and you are doing what?"

"Well, I called for Jet a couple times. Nothing," Hayes grimaced. "Bastards." He breathed in through pursed lips, exhaling as though silently whistling.

Pilate shot Ryder a look. Ryder stared at Hayes, folding his arms across his chest wordlessly.

"So I headed towards the office to see if he was up to something in there. Also wanted to see if there was a problem with the lights. It's only about twenty feet from the tower door."

"So," Hayes continued. "I whistled for Jet as I walked over. I got to the office door and opened it."

"Locked?" Pilate asked.

Hayes made a face. "Folks don't lock the doors much 'round here, John. Figure you'd know that by now."

"Well, you locked the tower door."

"That's FAA regs, man," he said. "Tower is critical infrastructure on a muni airport. After nine-eleven, everybody got worried about terrorism, even in this little burg," he guffawed, coughed, and cleared his throat. "Come to think of it, maybe they were right."

"The door was unlocked, and you stepped inside," Ryder stated.

Hayes nodded.

"What happened next?" Pilate said.

"I flicked the light switch. Nothing happened. Dark as pitch. I got a little spooked and was reaching for my phone to use the flashlight when I heard the shot. Next thing I know, I'm on the floor, my side wet. Hard to breathe. I'm gasping and trying to comprehend what happened. That's when I saw him."

"You saw his face?"

"Not exactly," Hayes said. "I'm feeling warm on my side, like I just pissed my pants. Didn't hurt yet. I guess I was in shock. But I see a shape move in the darkness. Comes right at me in a couple of silent steps and stands over me."

"What did he look like?" Pilate said, leaning closer to Hayes' bed.

"All I could conjure at first was he had longish hair, to his shoulders. Tall and thin. Face was in shadow. Stood over me a second or two. Didn't say anything."

"Too dark to see his face?" Pilate said.

"Yes. Then without saying a word, he lit a match and I could see it," he shuddered. "They say there's no devil, John, but I've seen him. Just as sure as I see you standing there."

"Devil?" Pilate said.

"He looked…demonic. Maybe some kinda high-priced mask. Looked like Old Scratch himself. You know? Or maybe the Underwood deviled ham guy. Arched eyebrows, slitted eyes, maybe a thin mustache and beard? It happened so fast."

"Okay, what happened then?"

"He said that the bullet is a present. A nice present from Jack Lindstrom. Dead Jack. Then he put out the match and stepped over me and disappeared."

Pilate grasped the handrail on Hayes' bed. Nausea washed over him.

"So I dug out my phone and called for help. Burl and Story got to me pretty quick."

"They're the best," Ryder said, nodding.

"Weird voice," he said. "I'll never forget it."

"What kind of voice?" Ryder asked. "Deep? High? Nasal?"

"Kind of a strange. It didn't seem to fit the face, such as it was. Hard to explain. But I don't get this psycho. Why would he shoot me? And Lindstrom's been dead for nigh on two years. I don't get it," he said, plaintively. "Look, John. You have a history with Lindstrom. I barely knew him. Can you tell me who might want to shoot me on his behalf?"

"No," Pilate rasped. "I can't."

"So I guess you can't tell me why this freak son of a bitch killed my dog, either?"

* * *

Pilate splashed his face after throwing up some coffee in the sink of Hayes' hospital room. He overheard Ryder telling Hayes thanks for his time. When Pilate emerged, nurse Juilie Hulsey eyed him.

"You look white as a sheet," she said. "You all right, John?"

"I'm okay, Juils," Pilate said, waving her off. "Just something I ate, I guess."

"Okay, whatever roadkill you wolfed down, don't eat it again," she brushed past them. "You guys need to scoot," she said, checking Hayes' vitals.

Ryder tipped his hat, then turned back to Hayes. "If you remember anything else, give me a call, Bob."

Hayes nodded, his eyes moving from Ryder to Pilate.

Pilate cleared his throat. "I'm sorry all this happened to you, Bob. Really sorry about Jet, too."

"Find the sick bastard," Hayes said, scrubbing a fist over his eye. He looked back at Ryder. "Then kill him."

* * *

Ryder sipped coffee in the hospital cafeteria, Stetson on his right knee, crossed over his left. "So, we got a weirdo in a satanic mask who apparently had feeling for Jack Lindstrom—"

"Dead Jack Lindstrom," Pilate added.

"You sure about that?"

"That's not funny, considering," Pilate said. Jack Lindstrom had faked his death once, but Pilate watched him die the second time—up close, and in the town cemetery, no less.

Ryder snorted. "Sorry. He's dead as the proverbial door nail, that is true. So, any thoughts?"

Pilate shrugged. "I've been up to my ass in weirdos for years. I mean, there's very little that surprises me anymore."

"Narcissists like Lindstrom tend to attract broken types," he said, absently digging a thumbnail into the lip of the Styrofoam cup. "It's how they get people to do their bidding. Remember Dick Shefler? Guy had plenty going for him but he threw in his chips with Lindstrom and bought himself personal ruin and jail time. Not to mention the others in that sorry crew you helped clean up."

Pilate bit his lip, looking around the mostly quiet cafeteria a second. "Could be a student who's off his rocker."

"Yeah, and that's why I am canvassing the instructors," Ryder said. "Hoping to see if we have any candidates for the freaky seats."

"Okay," Pilate said. "Sounds logical."

"You want to save me some trouble and ask your wife about this?" Ryder said, flinty.

"Why not? We need some interesting things to talk about."

"I don't want to pull your coat about it but—" Ryder dropped his chin to his chest a moment. He snapped his head back, scooped up his hat and put it on his head as he stood. "Okay, pard, you ask her, I'll ask a few others on campus. Maybe you could also ask your new landlord if any unusual characters with a passing resemblance to Old Scratch have passed through his establishment."

"Will do," Pilate said, standing. "I'll check back in with you in a day or two."

"Yep," Ryder said, touching two fingers to his hat brim and walking out.

Pilate absorbed sounds of the kitchen crew washing dishes a moment and felt his phone vibrate in his pocket. A missed call from Val.

He tucked the phone back in his pocket and left the hospital.

* * *

"Diabetes may turn out to be the best thing that ever happened to me," Morgan Scovill said, hobbling gingerly from the fridge with two beers. "I mean, I miss my big toe like a sumbitch, but it got me out of the hoosegow, so, fair trade."

Pilate accepted the can of Coors Light, popping the tab and slurping a geyser of foam that rushed out.

"Sorry, Mister Pilate," Scovill said, thumping the top of his can before he opened it. "Musta shook it up as I moved at Mach one to here from the fridge." He smiled, his right eye squinting like always.

"No worries," Pilate said. "Good to be out, I bet."

"True story, though this little bit of jewelry is a pain in the ass," he nodded at his ankle monitor.

"Looks like a drag."

"At least they put it on my good foot," he said, another chuckle. "The bathing process is complicated, being on my own."

"Sorry things went the way they did with your wife," Pilate said, eyes low.

"Me too. She wasn't the same after her Dad died, and then I got myself into the little jackpot with Lindstrom and Ollie and the gang. Stupid. Pure-dee stupid."

Pilate and Scovill had formed an uneasy alliance not long after Pilate had moved to Cross. In fact, the pair brought down Jack Lindstrom and a minor cartel of thugs—solving a fifty-year-old murder mystery to boot. But Scovill proved to be the slightly bent cop he is—one who started experiencing freedom for the first time in three years.

They pondered their beers a moment. "So, I guess you're wondering why I called?" He hadn't actually called Pilate directly; he had left a message on Kate's home phone explaining he would like to have a word now that he had "made it out of the hoosegow."

"Well, it's been a while, but I'm happy to see you," Pilate said, sipping the beer. "Besides, I owe you one or two."

Scovill waved Pilate off. "No, we're square," the former sheriff said. "I hear Ryder's got you advising him on this latest drama and trauma our fair community is enduring."

Pilate smiled, reminded of an old saying Kate had about Cross—you couldn't fart on one side of town without the other side smelling it.

Pilate hedged. "Yeah, he wanted my thoughts on a few things."

Scovill reached behind him and pulled his crutch to the table, leaning it beside him. "He's worried, I reckon."

"Worried?"

"He has no clue who the shooter is," Scovill said.

"Wouldn't you be, then?"

"Sure would, but Ryder's got an election coming up. He filled Welliver's unexpired term, but if he wants to keep the job he has to make sure law and order prevails here in Nebraska's best-kept secret."

Pilate nodded. "Well, there's always the town constable job if sheriff doesn't work out," Pilate said.

Scovill snorted. "Reminds me, you did good with that. Stopping that nut Gary Rich from killing those kids. Then you helped take out half of Hilmer Thurman's soldiers over at the jail. You turned into a regular action hero, John."

"Just unlucky, I guess," Pilate said.

"The drive to survive is the most powerful one we have," Scovill said. "There's a reason I'm still alive and kicking. Well," he glanced at his crutch. "Not kicking."

"True," Pilate said.

"It's why you left town?"

Pilate looked up into Scovill's face. "Couldn't take any more of it."

"You have definitely had your portion, Mister Pilate," Scovill said, draining his beer can and crushing it. "Another?"

Pilate shook his head. "But here, let me get you one," Pilate hopped up and retrieved another beer for Scovill.

"Thanks, you saved us both a half hour of travel time," Scovill said, flicking the top of the can, opening it, and taking a drink.

"So, you think Ryder's in over his head?"

"No sir, did not say that," Scovill shook his head, then wiped his beer-soaked goatee on his sleeve. "I said that he is up for re-election soon and he needs to nail things down with law and order. Jim Kolar's itching to run against him for the full term."

"I...I don't follow," Pilate said, raising an eyebrow.

"He's bringing in the celebrity crimefighter, and I suspect he is not shy about being seen around town with you."

"So? I mean, that's not...I mean, wouldn't he look weaker if it looks like he is trying to get help from a civilian?"

"Maybe. Depends on the civilian."

"I still don't follow," Pilate said, leaning forward on his elbows.

Scovill screwed up his face in mock irritation. "I thought you were supposed to be the smart guy."

Pilate shrugged.

"Hilmer Thurman is very much weakened by your efforts—intentional or not. He's laid low for a year trying to rebuild, but your jail escapade cost him more than men. It cost him cred with the people he sells hillbilly heroin for. Scary guys in Kansas City and Chicago."

"Okay, good. So?"

"Ryder is trying to draw him out, and he's using you for bait."

"Wait, what?" Pilate laughed nervously. "I don't get you."

"Think about it," Scovill said. "You're the guy who made Hilmer Thurman's life miserable. Ryder knows that. Shoot, everybody does. Ryder is drawing him out with you."

"So, Ryder thinks Thurman shot Bob Hayes?"

"Doubtful. But he is drawing you alongside to smoke Thurman out a little. Sure, you can maybe help with that mess, but I think he's trying to get Thurman to make a move on you."

"That's mighty nice of him," Pilate said. "You think so?"

Scovill shrugged. "Seems like it to me. Ryder's a loner. Bringing you in isn't on a whim or by accident. Now, don't get me wrong, he's not trying to get you killed, he's just adding a little flavor to the stew."

"Yeah, well stews are often made with dead meat," Pilate took a hard swallow of beer.

"That's why I wanted to talk to you," he said. "There's some weirdo running around with the cult of the dead college president—which is related to you. I mean, my god, there are people who see shit on the interwebs and think that there's some vast conspiracy. They start filling in the blanks. You're filling in quite a few, it would seem."

"People are crazy," Pilate said, feeling a familiar pang in his chest.

"I heard about your time in the cooler back in Key Weird. Christ on a pony, Mister Pilate. You sure know how to party."

"It was a hot time in the old town, for sure," Pilate chuckled, not smiling. "So, again, about Ryder."

Scovill nodded. "Ryder is trying to strike the death blow to Thurman. He figured he had all the time in the world; you were down in Florida drinking yourself to death, we all assumed, no offense..."

"None taken. It's still an option."

"But then you roll in, ready to win back your bride and resume your role as hero of Cross Township."

"Shit, Morgan. We both know that is one hundred percent pure grade-X bullshit."

"Doesn't matter what we know. Matters what the voters know. I was never much of a sheriff. Never lived up to my old man. But I knew what the voters wanted and I think I still know. It probably isn't you, but there's *juuust* enough of a chance that it *is* you, that Ryder is worried about it."

"Well, what about Thurman? What is he even doing these days?"

"He's been trying to rebuild his little empire. Word I hear is if he doesn't get his infrastructure repaired PDQ, he's going to go the way of the dodo. He owes the big boys a fair amount of coin—and it wasn't just the drugs. Apparently, that gold that nobody ever found was real, and Thurman thought it was gonna be his." Scovill raised his hands in air quotes. "He borrowed pretty heavy against that gold, and it's hobbled him ever since."

"The old Confederate story? Come on. An actual Confederate treasure here, in Nowhere, Nebraska?" The story was that a huge Confederate, or Union, or European, payroll or treasury shipment of some kind had gone awry near Cross in the 1860s. Whoever's gold it was, the unshakable popular belief in Cross Townships was that it was buried under Cusack's place, to be exact. Despite years of searches, effort, and the deaths of some overzealous treasure hunters, the gold had never turned up.

"You honestly can't think it's true." Pilate said.

Scovill smirked. "I know there was at least some truth to the story."

"How?"

"I just do," he said, slugging back another mouthful of beer. "You can skip the interrogation. I know because I saw it once. When I was a kid."

"You saw it?"

"I saw a piece of it, to be exact. My Daddy had a piece of it. It was beautiful. But it scared him."

"Scared him?"

Scovill's head bobbed up and down. "He brought it home and showed my mother. He held it in his palm, and his hand shook. She told him to get it out of the house. He did."

"What did he do with it?"

"Put it away somewhere for a long time, then I think he cashed it in to pay for mom's hysterectomy. Just one piece out of hundreds, from what I can glean. No idea where the rest went. Heard him tell mom that it was a piece he filched while they reburied the rest of it."

"Who's 'they'? Who got the gold?"

"That I do not know," he said. "Peculiar, is it not?"

Pilate rubbed his chin. "Yeah, damn peculiar. Thanks for the beer, sheriff."

Scovill nodded. "You watch your back, Mister Pilate. There's doings going on you want zero part of."

"No shit," Pilate said, standing. "Keep me in the loop on stuff you hear?"

"That's the plan," he said, draining the Coors and crushing the can in his fist.

"One last thing, John. I don't even know that I should say it. But you always treated me straight, even when I was crooked as an epileptic snake, and I appreciate that. So here it is. I don't know why, I don't have any reasons to offer at all. But something tells me not to trust Ryder. He looks clean as a church on Easter morning. But when I breathe in the air around him...it doesn't smell right. Watch your back, is all."

The hairs on the back of Pilate's neck stood up. He nodded his thanks and took his leave.

* * *

Pilate spent the next few days getting into a routine of spending time with the kids while simultaneously avoiding face time with Kate. She had her wall up, and he could not scale it with his usual verbal retinue of humor and bluff. Three days of her deflection brought on a weariness that made him long to return to Key West.

"That's what she's up to, my friend," Simon whispered. *"She's wearing you down so you'll leave and it's all your fault and then her Ken doll boyfriend takes your family away from you."*

Pilate swatted the thought away, eyes forward as he sat in the parking lot of the Cross Township Church of the Redeemer. A massive sculpture of two hands clasped in prayer dominated a large pool with a sputtering fountain in the circular driveway that marked the entrance to a large A-frame building.

"My god, they could baptize people in that thing," Pilate said to himself. There were only three cars in the lot this Thursday afternoon, a blue Subaru, an old Chevy and a sparkly new-looking Land Rover. "Three guesses as to who drives the Rover."

Ryder called earlier and asked Pilate to check in on the Reverend Falley, as his church ministered to most of the students who "trucked with religion" in Cross.

"Falley's right out of the Dr. Gene Scott school if you ask me, but he's got a handle on who comes and goes since he has his church and also runs the chapel at the school," Ryder had said on the phone. "Why not go meet him and see what you can find out?"

"Dr. Gene Scott?" Pilate had asked.

"You mean to tell me you never stayed up late watching that cigar-smoking guy wearing a sombrero asking for money on behalf of the Lord?"

"Usually I stayed up to watch Count Gregore's Shock Theatre."

"Figures."

"So is this guy Falley, he a nut or a flim-flam man, or both?"

"Oh, I don't know, He's odd, but he's got his virtues, I suppose. Let me know what he says."

Pilate navigated to the church on the outskirts of town, not far from the state highway exit, and he had his doubts about what good the meeting would do.

"It's not like you have anything else to do," Simon said.

* * *

Kingston Falley leapt from the massive leather chair behind the desk in his study, his stride covering the length of the large room in seconds. A large man with a Bob Ross perm, he wore a bright red with white flowers aloha-style shirt not unlike Pilate's, but much more expensive. He also sported khakis with sandals. His meaty hands, fingers festooned with gold rings, a fancy gold watch on his wrist, clasped Pilate's hand before he could get a word in.

"John Pilate, my brother. It is good to meet you in person at last," he said, his eyes bright and wide. "You are an inspiration and I dare say my flock would take great joy in having you witness one Sunday."

Startled, Pilate grasped for the words. "Umm, thanks? I don't know what to say," he sputtered.

"Say yes, of course!"

"I appreciate that, though I don't know what I would witness," he said as Falley continued to pump his hand. "I'm not sure exactly what that even means."

Falley released Pilate's hand and gestured for him to follow to a pair of chairs beside a cold fireplace. "Well, Mr. Pilate," Falley said. "It means that you are here and by the grace of God, from what I understand. You have had much tribulation in your life and it has made you stronger, I daresay."

"You can say that again," Simon said.

"So, how is it that we have you here in this house of the Lord today? I am a terrible host. My apologies. I'm happy to meet you is all. Please, have a seat."

"This guy is more excited to see you than Kate."

Pilate mentally shut Simon's commentary off.

"You know what I've always found your name fascinating. Not many Pilates out there in my experience," he said, sitting opposite. "You know, I have often wondered if you get jokes about washing your hands of this or washing your hands of that?"

Pilate chewed his lip and looked a moment at the improbable-looking pastor. "Reverend, actually most people think I'm an exercise class."

Falley gazed at him quizzically.

"Like the spin class? Pilates?"

Falley's face registered recognition and he burst into a full-body guffaw, eventually removing his round spectacles and wiping tears from his eyes with a handkerchief. "Oh my, that is too much."

"It's true," Pilate said.

"We all have our crosses to bear," he said, sighing.

Pilate eyed a large cross hanging above the fireplace. "I'll say."

Falley gazed at Pilate expectantly. "So," he slapped his thighs with both hands. "To what do I owe this visit?"

"Well reverend, it's like this," Pilate stopped a moment, hearing the unmistakable sound of island music quietly issuing from a small speaker in the ceiling. Pilate pointed at the speaker. "Is that?"

Falley's face brightened. "Tiki music? Yes. It's a passion of mine."

Pilate gestured at Falley's shirt. "Now it all comes together."

Falley nodded. "I find it comforting and it keeps me in a good mood," he said. "Besides, who doesn't love a good Mai Tai?"

"Good point," Pilate said. "I have a friend who would love your shirt. Anyway, I don't mean to monopolize your time. I just have a few questions."

"Shoot," Falley said, leaning back in his chair.

"I'm kind of an unofficial consultant to the sheriff, and you may have seen or could potentially see some new people coming through town here at the church."

Falley stroked his beard a moment. "Yes, okay, so you're talking about illegal aliens? You must understand the Lord did not know illegal aliens. Jesus Christ himself would've been an illegal alien."

Pilate held up a hand, interrupting him. "No, we're not talking about an ICE raid here. We're talking about the fact that Bob Hayes over at the airport was shot."

Falley's eyes closed as if saying a silent prayer. "Yes, so tragic. Tragic. I understand he lost a kidney. I need to go to the hospital and minister to Bob."

"Oh, I thought he was an atheist," Pilate said.

"Mister Pilate, many people consider themselves atheists until they've been shot and lost a kidney. Bob may be thinking it's probably as good a time as any to rethink that."

"Well, you got me there reverend. Anyway, the deal is we were wondering if maybe you had some new people come through your church recently, and I'm not talking about illegals or anything like that. Anybody unusual."

"How so?"

"Maybe a little offbeat."

Falley laughed for a moment and looked to the heavens, which were incidentally painted on the ceiling, then back to Pilate. "You must understand that there's plenty of gatherings in a church, starting right with me on the pulpit. My point being I'd have to search my memory and perhaps talk to my deacons because you know we do have several hundred members of this church visiting every Sunday and we do have guests come through with the college being right here in town. We get plenty of young people who are seekers."

Pilate nodded.

"However I will give it some thought."

"Well I would appreciate it sir if you did," Pilate said. "I wonder is there anyone else I should speak to here?"

Falley raised both hands in a motion as if to push the thought back into Pilate's mouth. "No, Mr. Pilate, there's no one else, you should talk to. I mean, we have a church secretary, Gloria here, but the deacons and elders aren't here right now."

"Okay," Pilate said, startled as if on cue, Gloria entered the room with a tray and two steaming mugs.

"Tea?" she asked.

"Oh, of course, thank you," Pilate said, taking a mug.

"It's Darjeeling," she said, smiling warmly, then extending the tray to Falley. "Sugar or honey?"

"Oh, no. Thank you," Pilate said.

Taking his tea, Falley said, "Let me please talk to my people and I'll get back to you about anything strange."

"Very good. Pilate glanced at Gloria, a matronly woman in her sixties. "Ma'am, may I ask you a question?"

She smiled, looking at Falley, who dropped his chin slightly, eyes on his tea. Gloria's eyes hardened back at him in response, then softened as she shifted her gaze to Pilate.

"Certainly," she said, hugging the now-empty tray to her bosom, eyes on Pilate.

"Wondering if you have had any…umm, unusual guests here at the church or in the college chapel?"

She pursed her lips, looking up and to her right a second. "Unusual how?"

"Offbeat types? Perhaps a little sketchy?" Pilate said.

"Sketchy?" Gloria said, an eyebrow raised.

"Well, someone who is perhaps a bit of a lone wolf. Maybe someone who seems...off?"

"I see," she said, again pursing her lips a moment. "Are we talking about men or women?"

"Male," Pilate said.

Gloria thought for a moment.

Falley again closed his eyes as if receiving a message from some invisible radio, then said, "Well, Gloria, if you think of anything, I can tell Mister Pilate-"

"You know there's a man who did come through to Wednesday night Bible study," she said. "Hunting for an AA meeting, but our AA meetings are on Thursday nights. Anyway, he went ahead and stayed for Bible study."

Falley leaned closer, setting his tea on a small coffee table.

"Oh yes, then he asked plenty of strange questions," Gloria said.

"What kind of strange questions?" Pilate asked, taking a sip of his tea, then setting it down.

Gloria glanced back at Falley. "Well he asked a little bit about the tragic and checkered history of Cross Township that I'm sure you're very familiar with," she said.

"I understand that completely. Specifically? He ask about the murder-suicide from fifty years ago?"

She pondered a second, a finger to her temple, "No, he asked about the former president of the college. Jack...what was his name?"

"Lindstrom," Pilate said, feeling a chill. "What was he asking about Lindstrom?"

"I remember now," Falley said. "He wanted to know if any of us knew Lindstrom. He asked if Lindstrom had a church home. I sadly had to say that I believed Dr. Lindstrom an atheist, because he professed that to me at a luncheon for the Chamber of Commerce shortly after he arrived in town. He said he'd be happy to come to church but I must understand that he was not a believer. I said of course, you know what, let me see what I can do to help you with that, and we both laughed. But yes, he never did come to church so I didn't have much to do with him. Gloria, thanks," he said, dismissing her with a gentle wave of his hand.

"Thank you for the tea," Pilate said.

She nodded and left the room.

Pilate sighed. "Well what did you tell this man at your Bible study? Did you tell him what you just told me?"

"Well no, I didn't. I told him that there was lots of information online about all that and frankly we had some members who have lost family over the years to some of these sad events and I could tell it upset them. I gently said I didn't think it was the appropriate place to discuss that stuff. He didn't seem satisfied with the answer and stood up to leave. He did say the strangest thing before he left."

"What?" Pilate asked.

"You know Mr. Pilate, he made a little disjointed speech for about thirty seconds. I'm sorry I don't remember exactly what he said. I remember how odd. Not threatening, but it was a somewhat accusatory speech that maybe this town wasn't good enough for Jack Lindstrom. Almost like we all had a hand in his death. Bizarre."

"Yes, that is weird."

"I said something along the lines of you know that not everyone is one hundred percent good or one hundred percent bad, and we all have our trials in our life, but unfortunately Mr. Lindstrom went a different way."

"What did the stranger do then?"

"He sort of shrugged and said that we're all in darkness and we contain multitudes or something like that. Then he left the sanctuary."

"Interesting," Pilate said, jotting down a note in a small notebook. "Whatever you can tell me about his appearance would be helpful."

"Yeah, we didn't get a good look at him," Falley said. "He was sitting in the very last pew at the back of the sanctuary, it was a little dark because we didn't have the main house lights on."

"Oh, so you have Bible study in the main sanctuary?" Pilate asked.

"Lately, yes, because we had so many people show up lately for we were crammed into one of the study rooms where we do the AA meetings or have fellowship and stuff like that. We're victims of our own success here," he said, smiling. "What I do recall was he was young and had kind of long hair underneath a dirty looking trucker cap. I remember the cap because I don't approve of people wearing hats in church, but didn't want to make a stink."

"I see. Did the cap have a logo or anything on it?"

He shook his head slowly. "Couldn't see him well. The brim rode low on his forehead, and it covered his face. Like I said, I didn't get a good look at him. He came in late, and nobody was near him. Tall and skinny. I think Caucasian. Yeah, pretty sure."

"How was he dressed?

"Seem to recall faded jeans and a t-shirt with a jean jacket. Kinda like Reverend Jim on *Taxi*. Loved that show. Except for the cap. Reverend Jim didn't wear a cap."

Pilate scribbled the notes down. "Okay, this helps."

"Don't forget his voice," Gloria said from the doorway where she had clearly been eavesdropping.

Falley looked put out, then said, "Yes, Gloria. Thank you."

"What about his voice?"

"It was just, well, strange."

His chest tightened.

"Can you elaborate?"

Falley closed his eyes again, tuning into his memory. "An odd cadence. If I didn't know better I would think he was putting us on with that voice. I don't know if that makes any sense."

"Oh, yeah, that makes perfect sense. Can you tell me if anybody else besides you and Gloria got a good look at him? I'm happy to make some discreet inquiries without disrupting services, of course."

"I want to help the authorities and your good self, but is there something I should know?" Falley said, lowering his voice, presumably so Gloria could not hear from the next room.

Pilate leaned close, his voice also lower. "Yeah, if this person comes back in, I want you to call the sheriff. He will deal with it. Ryder won't make a scene; we need to talk to this person. It's very important. So again, you say he has not been back. But if he does come back we definitely need to speak with him, okay?"

His head bobbing furiously, he said "Very good." Watching Pilate scribble more notes, he said, "Now, I have a question for you."

"Shoot," Pilate said, looking his notes.

"How do I get you to come back? I want you to witness and tell your story."

"Reverend Falley, you've been very kind, but I told my story. I wrote a book about it."

Mildly crestfallen, he reached over and touched Pilate's knee. "Well, what about this. Instead of having you speak to the entire congregation, we ask you to come speak to our book club. That's only about thirty people. We could read it and then you could come talk to us about it?"

"I'll give it some thought," Pilate said, standing up.

"Just so you know, we buy the books and pay full retail."

Pilate laughed. "I'll give it fair consideration, reverend, and I'm not saying no out of hand. Thank you so much for your time and the tea."

"Very good," he said, then closed his eyes a moment more, his index finger rising and pointing to the ceiling. "Do you hear that?"

"Hear what?"

"That's *The Quiet Village,* composed by Les Baxter, played by Martin Denny, who is pretty much the father of Tiki music."

Pilate's head bobbed a bit as he listened. "Cool."

Falley proffered his hand, Pilate took it. "God bless you, John Pilate."

"Thanks, I may need it."

* * *

When Pilate told him about the strange man, Ryder sat up in his chair as if a firecracker had gone off under his ass.

"Well, that is some news right there," he said. "Wonder if they have cameras going there at the church. Hmm. If not, maybe we could get a sketch artist involved. We don't have one but there's an instructor in the college art classes who could help."

"I don't know, sheriff, I mean Reverend Aloha over there didn't seem all that high on getting too deep into this," Pilate said.

Ryder chuckled. "That's too damned bad. I know a little bit about the good reverend and it's in his best interests to cooperate fully. Leave that to me."

"Fine by me, yeah. So 'Mister I Contain Multitudes' is the prime suspect right now?"

"Such as it is, yeah," Ryder said, shrugging, then putting his hands in his jean pockets. "Wonder if he's a student?"

"Nobody could get a good look at him, but it sounds like he's probably youngish at the very least," Pilate said.

Ryder clicked his tongue, looking at the corner of the office a second. "Hmph. We'll see. It's right about lunchtime. You up for some barbecue?"

"I'm always up for barbecue," Pilate said. "But where we going to go around here?"

"Oh, you didn't hear?" Ryder said, cocking his head slightly. "The ol' Tin Roof reopened, under new management."

"Really?" Pilate said. "Anybody I know?"

Chapter Seven

Nelda Foshee's lanky frame didn't so much as stride across the courtyard from the smokers to the Tin Roof Rib Shack dining area; instead she galumphed like a giraffe who had finally let gravity get the best of her.

Still thin, she nevertheless had a visible muffin top resting on her Lee jeans, due to copious amounts of beer she washed down atop the daily barbecue she sampled. Her darkly tanned skin featured the patina of a ripe banana. Nelda glanced up as Ryder's Ram truck pulled up and the two men spilled out of it, closing the doors and surveying the scene before taking steps toward Nelda.

Pilate inhaled the rich scent of cherry wood and pork smoke. He observed few signs of change at the Tin Roof, which if you didn't know better had the faux authenticity of a Bubba Gump Shrimp Co. Not so - the Tin Roof was the real deal.

Corrugated tin roof and walls accented with posts of salvaged wood and shipping pallets, sheltering paint-flecked picnic tables with vertical paper towel holders, gingham paper cloths, pink butcher paper and plastic utensils in Mason jars. A bar of reclaimed wood sprawled about twenty feet along the north wall, with Nebraska Cornhusker pride, Black Betty Imperial Stout, and Miller Hi-Life signs and tractor seat barstools bellied up, awaiting the lunch rush. A dented milk can and stuffed bobcat dominated a corner, with twinkly cheap Christmas lights strewn everywhere attempting whimsy—evidently Nelda's touch. A wagon-wheel chandelier supplied most of the light in the dining area, which comfortably seated around fifty.

Ryder regaled Pilate with the tale of how the once-popular barbecue Mecca had been closed for some time since the previous owner, Bart Robeson, was killed in the attack on the jail that nearly took his own life a year or so ago. He added that even under the less-expert new management, the smell of pork and grease still made his mouth water.

* * *

Nelda waved her hand, slender fingers grasping a cigarette, greeting Ryder, as her eyes flicked over Pilate, launching the beginnings of a sneer, then quickly papering over it with yellowing teeth curled back in a tortured smile.

"Well hello there, sheriff, how are you all doing?" she called.

Ryder tipped his hat. "Nelda, I'm fine."

Her eyes took in Pilate again as she said, "Well, y'all I guess you're here for to eat something. Come on in and we'll take your order and get you settled." She hurried into the door.

Ryder and Pilate didn't move. Pilate glanced at Ryder.

"You are fucking kidding me," Pilate said. "She's the best Hilmer Thurman can do as a front to own this business?"

Ryder shrugged. "Well you know what? We didn't leave a whole lot of hillbilly mafia to choose from when we reenacted the Alamo at the jail." He glanced around the courtyard, eyeing a lanky white man tending to the smoker near the woodpile. "'Sides, he knows he can trust Nelda.

Keeps her in booze, barbecue, cigarettes and a little bit of money and she's fat, dumb and happy. Well, not really all that fat."

"So where is Thurman these days?" Pilate asked.

Ryder spat tobacco juice near his boot. "Keeps a pretty low profile, which is fine by me. I like to show the flag a little bit and come out here to eat some decent barbecue."

The pair went inside and made their order. Soon, Nelda shuffled over with two racks of ribs, coleslaw, and potato salad with Mason jars of sweet tea, then disappeared to the back.

They dug into their food. Pilate made a face as he chewed some rib meat.

"What's the matter?" Ryder said.

"I don't know. Seems it's not as good as it used to be. It's a little tough," Pilate swigged some tea.

Ryder chuckled. "That's because you killed the best barbecue cook in the county."

"Well, it's not like I had any choice, sheriff," Pilate said, straining to chuckle but settling for a sigh as he dejectedly poked the remaining ribs. "Pass the sauce? So what do you think? Hilmer Thurman have something to do with these crazy people trying to kill me?" Pilate said, squirting the ribs with a beet-colored sauce.

Ryder shrugged. "Not his style. He's way too old school than to hire some freaks to go out all the way out to Key West and try to kill you in a bizarre fashion. And he's not gonna try to do that here, either. Right now you're in no position to hurt him. Hilmer's rebuilding his empire and praying to the lord above that those assholes from Minnesota don't come down here and take it all away from him."

"However, I will say this to you, John: stay clear. There's no reason in the world for you to go to the Brown Betty or anyplace else he might be hanging out."

"Maybe so, but what if at the very least the man knows something?"

"That's why we're here. The easiest way to find out what's on Thurman's mind is not to ask him. It's to ask his right arm woman Nelda." As if on cue, Ryder tipped his hat and signaled for Nelda to come have a seat. "Nelda, Nelda, Nelda. This is delicious. You certainly are carrying on Robey's tradition."

She chuckled, charmed by Ryder, despite her discomfort from being in the vicinity of Pilate.

"So what's new around here? How's business?"

She looked around the sparse dining area. "Take a look. It's nearly noon and there's two customers in the whole fucking joint," she said.

"Well, you just reopened, when?" Ryder asked, helpfully.

She exhaled cigarette smoke and looked heavenward. "Two months ago. I mean, we did okay the first couple of weeks, then it dried up."

"Like the ribs," Simon said, an aside in Pilate's brain.

"Well, it'll pick up during football season," Pilate said.

"What planet are you on? It is football season," she said, dismissing him with a flick of her wrist.

She sighed, composing herself. "We're making do. We do a lot of carry out. It's going all right."

"So what about the Brown Betty?" Ryder asked, scooping up a spoonful of coleslaw. "Are you doing anything over there?"

"Oh goodness no," she said. "Hilmer's got a whole crew over there. He wanted me to get out of there and get this place into shape."

"I like the Christmas lights," Pilate said.

Ryder shot him a glance that suggested he kindly shut up. "Well, I'm just keeping up with the rogue's gallery. Present company excepted."

"I'd say you're consorting with public enemy number one right here," she said, the entire table chuckled.

Ryder wiped his mouth with a paper towel he had folded in half. "Mr. Pilate here is in town helping me out on some questions about some local weirdos. I thought maybe you'd know something."

"Weirdos huh? Well definitely there's plenty but I ain't clapped eyes on anything special," she said, patting her heavily-sprayed bangs against a breeze that filtered in through the flyscreen door. "Unless you count my grill guy, Fuzzy. What you huntin'?"

"Looking for some young people who may be just a tad..." Ryder paused, looking askance.

"The term is cuckoo for cocoa puffs, sheriff," Pilate said.

Nelda raised an eyebrow, exhaling cigarette smoke not quite in the direction of Pilate, but close enough to give him a little tickle in his throat.

"You're looking for the creep who shot Bob Hayes, aren't you?"

Ryder stretched nonchalantly, eyes on a fixed point at the bar over Nelda's shoulder. He yawned.

"Maybe," he said, eyes now on hers. "Well, it's like this, Nelda. We're looking for some new people in town who may be a little offbeat, a little left of center, know what I mean?"

She looked at him, silent.

"Maybe they don't fit in around here," Ryder said, holding his hands up in a 'what are you gonna do?' gesture. "Maybe they've been showing up a lot over at Falley's Church."

Nelda guffawed. "Good lord, really? Reverend Hawaiian Punch bilking money out of these weirdoes? That's a shocker." Her head darted at the men on the last syllable, punctuating her annoyance at the thought.

"Nobody's been in here. Just pretty much the usual. I would say the only way I know if somebody is really offbeat is if they ordered the wings. I mean, you know we do a good job on the barbecue and most of the sides, but our wings are godawful. No meat on those little things, and you need three orders to fill yourself up. So I guess if somebody came in and ordered those that might be something."

Ryder folded his arms, wordless.

She fidgeted on the picnic bench seat. "Well, give me an idea of what I should keep on my radar. Maybe I can tell you something."

"Don't know much, just young age people who don't look right. Maybe don't look like they should go to the college. You'll know when you see 'em. Keep your ear to the ground for me?"

Nelda stubbed out the cigarette and hauled herself off the bench with a groan. "Don't you worry, I know where to find you if anybody really weird shows up. Though I think your Mister Pilate here's as weird as it gets."

Pilate and Ryder stood up. "Always a pleasure, Nelda," Pilate said.

She leveled her watery eyes on his, hands on her hips. "John Pilate, you can kiss my bony ass."

Ryder nudged Pilate with his boot under the table. "John, I'll meet you at the truck."

Pilate looked at Nelda, who guffawed.

"You heard him," she said.

Pilate shrugged. "Thanks for the food. Good stuff," he said, excusing himself and walking out. When Ryder got back to his truck, he slid a Styrofoam to-go carton next to Pilate and got in.

"So, what did Emily Post in there have to say?"

Ryder slipped a toothpick into his mouth. "Oh, this and that."

* * *

"You know we don't have to be like this. We can work this out. No need to be at each other's throats," Kate said, leaning against the front porch railing. "You know the kids love you. We're in a spot right now where being apart seems to be the best thing to do."

He shifted from foot to foot in the dust of the gravel driveway, a cool breeze rustling his hair and seemingly passing through his shirt. He fought a shiver and the urge to lean against the warm hood of his car. His eyes worked up from her boot-clad feet, her Levi's with the worn knees to the red buffalo plaid shirt under an old fleece jacket. Cropped dirty blonde hair framed an elegant face with a beauty that nonetheless betrayed weariness.

"Okay, I don't understand how being apart can help us come back together."

She looked down at the dust at his feet, then his face, and said, "I don't either, but I don't want to see you right now. I don't want to deal with this right now."

"Kate, I don't understand what I did to make you hate me."

Her head jerked to face him, sharply. "I don't hate you, but I do hate what I think you're becoming. I think you're very opportunistic in your decisions about how you run your life."

"What the hell does that even mean?"

"I don't think you put the children and me first," she said, folding her arms across her chest. "There, I said it. Do you feel better now?"

Pilate recoiled as if he had been hit by buckshot again, as he had been back in his early days in Cross. "Jesus Christ, Kate, I had no idea you felt that strongly about your lack of feeling for me."

She shrugged and said, "I don't have a lack of feelings for you. I have very deep feelings for you." She leaned forward, her eyes boring into his. "I feel betrayed and I don't know why. I just sense it."

Pilate's voice quavered. "Kate you know," he trailed off a bit, his chest tight, his vision tunneling. "It's pretty clear that you've had your own little situation here."

"Yeah? Well, I've earned it," her voice steely.

Pilate sucked in breath, trying to get his bearings. "My therapist says when people feel entitled to something it doesn't matter what the facts may be. So it's evident you feel entitled to closing the door on our marriage. But I will tell you this right now," he started to sputter.

"John, no," Simon said, a bystander shouting from a mile away.

"You are not closing the door on me being a parent to my kids."

She turned her back and opened the screen door, then stopped and glanced over her shoulder. "I never want you to not be their parent. But I don't know that you and I are a partnership anymore. I just don't know." She stepped inside and quietly closed the screen and wooden doors.

* * *

"Oh, Mister Pilate, why you drink so much?" Cusack said with an attempt at an Italian accent, leaning over the bar as if he were Mr. Martini in *It's a Wonderful Life* speaking to George Bailey about the obliteration of his entire life.

"Look here, Cusack, I don't need any judgment. I need a wee bit, teensy, teensy, little more of the Jameson, since you obviously cannot make a good goddamn martini," Pilate said, slurring his words.

"All right now, I'm saying this as a friend. You need to go upstairs and sleep it off. I can't have you down here scaring the customers. My lord, man you're even scaring me."

Pilate looked down at the empty tumbler in his hand, then slid it across the bar back at Cusack.

"One for the road?"

Cusack eyed him a moment then shook his head. "Then you go upstairs and don't disturb anyone, right? Get some sleep."

"Deal," Pilate said.

Cusack poured two fingers of Jameson and placed the tumbler before Pilate.

He took a sip, his eyes on Cusack over the rim, then slid the almost untouched drink back to Cusack.

"What, you done? I just poured that."

"I'm done," Pilate said. "Had to know."

"Know what?"

"If you were still my friend. That you still trusted me."

Cusack stared at him, blankly.

"And also," Pilate slurred, a bit reluctantly, "to make sure that I could give it back."

He stumbled upstairs, fumbling with the room key, cursing at his door until he gained entrance. Once inside, he vomited in the sink, then stumbled from the bathroom and lay on the rug, the vertigo so strong he couldn't climb into bed.

* * *

Kingston Falley raised a hand in the air, palm facing out, motioning in a seeming benediction, left, center, and right, his chunky gold bracelet catching the light.

"Is there anyone here who does not have a relationship with the Lord?" His other hand grasped a gold-colored microphone, his eyes clenched tight as if he were passing a righteous stone right there on the ermine-carpeted stage at the Cross Township Church of the Redeemer.

Behind Falley, a heavy-set man in a western-cut shirt with pearl snaps hit a solemn note on his keyboard, bathing the sanctuary in a soft dirge of expectation.

"My friends this church is filled; there is not a single empty seat," Falley crooned into the gold mic. "I know, and you know, that not everyone here is right with the Lord. I am offering you," he paused, inhaling deeply, then opening his eyes and exhaling, "The mystical redeeming grace of the Holy Ghost." The organ volume moved up a notch or two. "I am offering you the stern, paternal love that only the Father can give; and I am most importantly offering you the loving embrace of the Son, Jesus Christ."

A man appeared from the wings of the dais to the right of the keyboardist, sliding into the strap of an acoustic guitar. He strummed a complementary note.

Falley's hand fell to his side, the bracelet sliding down his wrist as he scanned the room. "Friends, we have only to accept that which we know we so richly deserve. Profess your faith," a murmur from the crowd interrupted his thought.

A woman with long, thick and shiny blonde hair in her early twenties, wearing torn jeans and a tank top that accented thin, colorfully tattooed arms, walked haltingly down the left aisle, her eyes down, one hand clutching the strap of a flower-patterned handbag.

Falley smiled, raising his hands in an open-palmed gesture of welcome as the organ broke into a faster tempo, a lighter key, with the guitar player adding flourishes. "Come on, up, child, and receive the love of the Lord!"

Falley turned to place the microphone in its stand beside the lectern and whirled to face the woman as she moved up the steps to mount the altar. "Child of God, what is your name?"

Her eyes flicked from the floor, then into Falley's eyes.

"Jezebel," she shouted. In a fluid motion, she dropped the bag from her shoulder as her right hand dove into it. The bag hit the floor, revealing in her hand a small pistol pointed at Falley.

"No, child!" Falley exclaimed as the gun went off. The wide-eyed keyboardist dropped behind his instrument, his hands playing foul notes as they dragged across the keys, the guitar player ducked, hugging his instrument with a yelp. The congregation erupted as two more shots exploded into Falley. The large man, suddenly diminished, crumpled to the floor, eyes wide, mouth working wordlessly in prayer.

"Pilate has washed his hands of you, false prophet!" The woman shouted as she whirled, pointing the gun at a man and woman from the congregation tentatively closing in on her. Whether they were trying to help Falley or disarm her, she was having none of it.

"Back off," she shouted, then fired a shot into the ceiling. "John Pilate prophesied the return of Dead Jack. He gave me the list of Pharisees—starting with this con artist."

She fired again at the stricken Falley, the bullet missing him and throwing up a tuft of carpet.

"Pilate made the list. I will make it right," she shouted again as she waved the gun around, her arm trembling as if the pistol were suddenly heavy. The crowd shrieked and dropped to their knees as the woman pelted past the people lying on their bellies and crouching in the aisle. In seconds, she crossed the door of the sanctuary, then disappeared into the night.

Chapter Eight

Pilate opened his eyes to the sounds of people chattering and dishes clattering downstairs. He stared up at the ceiling, blinking and wondering for a moment how he got on the floor. It felt like some kind of creature, perhaps a badger, was scraping at his eyeballs in a frenzied attempt to escape his cranium.

He took a moment, summoning the strength to roll over on his belly, then get his knees under him to rise unsteadily to his feet. He shed his shoes and pants and shirt along the way to the bathroom. He cranked up a hot shower and stepped in, forgetting to take off his underwear.

He sighed and stepped out of his soaked briefs, throwing them into a corner of the bathroom, landing with a sickening wet squelch. Pilate poured an entire bottle of hotel-sized shampoo over his head and scrubbed, creating a massive weather system of suds on his head. The rainstorm pelting the outside of his skull felt almost as painful as the badger furiously trying to escape the inside.

"Oh we're doing really well this morning aren't we?" Simon said.

Pilate nodded and swayed under the shower head until the hot water turned cold. He forced himself to stay under the icy water. He felt his genitals trying to climb into his body as his eyes burned from the shampoo that leaked down his face.

* * *

"My gosh, Marcy that smells damn good," he said.

Marcy looked up from the buffet, restocking a large tureen of white gravy over a can of sterno. "Oh John, good morning. I understand you had a bit of a bout last night."

"Yeah, I guess I did. Sorry. I hope your husband is still speaking to me."

She waved him off. "That guy has seen so much worse. Sorry you're having a rough time," she bit her lip, looking back at the buffet. "What would you like? I'll make you a plate."

Pilate shook his head. "I really need coffee at the moment. If my stomach will settle down I might try for some biscuits and gravy in a while." He felt his gut turn over at the thought of eating.

"All right, suit yourself. Here's a mug," she toddled off behind the counter.

Pilate poured the coffee, doctored it up with vanilla creamer and parked himself alone at a table for two overlooking the street through the large bay window. Marcy silently breezed past his table, leaving him a large glass and a small pitcher of ice water.

His phone vibrated. He pulled it out of his shirt front pocket. A text from Val.

"How are you holding up, my friend?"

He snorted, rubbed his eyes and put the phone down wondering if he could impose on Marcy for about half a bottle of Tylenol. He debated responding to Val when he realized that there were other texts from last night.

"Oh jeeze," he whispered to himself.

"You were quite the wounded texting creature last night," Simon said.

Pilate reviewed the text which went from him texting her to ask her what she was doing to what was she wearing to does she think of him and does she miss him.

She implored him to explain. Pilate spilled his guts, remarking he is "headed for divorce town" and then some convoluted things about his children and how he let everyone down.

Pilate scrolled through, seeing how Val kept trying to call him and saying nice things in her text responses, but it became evident that Pilate had checked out of sobriety. His numerous typos in self-pity and were probably very off-putting to say the least. Her last text: *"John go to bed and quit drinking. talk to me when you're sober."*

He drank his coffee, then half a glass of water. The badger slowed down the clawing. He typed: **"I am now sober, to a first approximation. And very sorry about last night."**

The dots danced on his phone as he realized she had read his text in a matter of seconds.

"Are you miserable with a hangover?"

"Ummm yeah"

"Good."

"I deserved that."

"Think you have it out of your system?"

"For now."

The dots danced as she formulated her reply. Then stopped. Pilate typed frantically.

"I really am sorry."

"It's okay. I have to go, my nine-fifteen is early." His gut tightened.

"Okay. XO"

Pilate scrubbed at his face with his hands, running his fingers through his damp hair. The smell of biscuits and gravy enticed him. Maybe it would settle his stomach? He ambled the buffet table and filled a bowl with three biscuits and two heaping ladles of white sausage gravy. The second ladle-full went off-center and he managed to pour a fair amount on the tablecloth of the buffet. He looked around discreetly to see if anyone noticed, then headed to his table.

He plopped himself back down and began to plow through the congealed mixture of starch and protein. *Dad used to make good biscuits and gravy*, he suddenly recalled.

He started to feel a little better. About fifteen minutes later, Marcy took away the empty bowl and refilled his coffee. Pilate stared out the window, the distant sounds of the college clarion calling students to class. Head throbbing, he resolved to go to the store and get some aspirin and get some fresh air in the process.

"You'd probably still blow a breathalyzer anyway," Simon chided.

After bussing the coffee cup from his table, he went back to his room, slipped into a jacket, combed his hair and headed outside. Three or four blocks to the store, with the weather relatively mild for Nebraska in late summer, but to his alcohol-poisoned body the sunlight felt like knives and the fresh air smelled of the grave.

How much did I put away last night?

Cars blew past him along the street but the sidewalks in his path were deserted. When he got to Mostek's store, he nodded at a bored-looking young checker and glanced around. Former Sheriff Welliver, bleeding out from a gunshot wound in the throat, had nearly been killed here.

"Clean up on aisle six. We'll need two mops," Simon said.

Pilate shook off the memory and wandered to the back for some Tylenol. He also picked up a bottle of Pedialyte, a bottle of orange juice and some water. He also scooped up some crackers and a tube of Braunschweiger. When he put it on the counter, the checker said, "Oh we've all been there before, Mister Pilate."

He avoided her gaze. "Yeah, tell me about it," he reached for his wallet. "Wait a minute, do I know you?" He thought back to the first time he shopped at the store years ago when the checker knew his identity before he had met a soul.

The checker shrugged and said, "Well, you know what they say about this town."

"Yeah, I know what they say: you can't fart here without somebody across town smelling it," he chuckled.

She wrinkled her nose in disgust. Apparently not everybody said it.

"I just meant that people talk to each other a lot. She rang up his items.

"Okay, it's sixteen eighty-seven."

"*You charmer,*" Simon said.

Pilate handed her a twenty and wordlessly accepted his change. He picked up the plastic bag and headed outside. He stopped a moment, eyeing the charred remains of the jail.

He thought about that day and how if it hadn't been for Kate he would probably be dead right now.

"*Probably the last good bit of love she had in reserve. Enough to save your life,*" Simon said. "*Enough to keep you all afloat a little bit longer. But instead of staying here to work on the marriage, you had to get away.*"

'Shut up, Simon."

"And in doing so, you made your decision in her eyes. You made your choice. Then you had your little adventure in Jamaica with that hot-assed former cop."

He texted Kate:

"I won't be picking up the kids today. I need some time."

She responded with a simple "OK."

Pilate slipped the phone back in his shirt pocket and sat heavily on the wooden bench next to the bag. A large, chipped terracotta flowerpot with some fading pansies and cigarette butts set next to the bench. He dug around for Tylenol and downed three with a generous slug of Pedialyte. He thirstily gulped the treacly drink.

Simon said, *"You know, Tylenol is hard on the liver, especially when it's trying to process an entire Irish distillery."*

Pilate watched a pickup go by, the truck bed overflowing with dozens of net bags full of sweet corn, just harvested. Dark brown cornsilk signified readiness for dinner tables countywide. Time moved forward, whether you were ready or not.

* * *

"Okay, Mister Pilate," Dean Trevathan had told him a few years ago after surprising him with a large sack of sweet corn at his faculty apartment door. Pilate protested the generosity until Trevathan said not to be flattered, there was so much extra, the entire county got some.

"Unless you're an asshole," Trevathan had allowed. "Jury's still out on you."

Trevathan pulled an ear from the bag. "Here's what you do. This should be okay, but go ahead and check the ripeness. Pull back the husk a little bit and take a look at the kernels," he said as he demonstrated. "Make sure the kernels are filled all the way from the very tip of the ear to the base. Rub your thumbnail along the kernels. Should feel tender and squirt a bit of milk out as you press against 'em.'"

Pilate roasted an ear in the oven that night and ate it with a generous scoop of butter, pepper, and a little salt. It was the best-tasting thing he had ever eaten up until that point.

He cast his thoughts back to dear old Trevathan, dead now for...how many years? That tutorial on sweet corn had occurred a month or so before the events that nearly got them all killed, and about a year before Trevathan's body succumbed to cancer.

A hopeless twinge flared through him; a hollowness in his chest which became a tightness that erupted into nausea. His stomach growled. He tried to swallow back the vile taste as he leaned over and vomited gravy, biscuits, and Pedialyte into the flowerpot.

He felt as if a fireplug in his guts had opened up; he gagged and retched further into the pot, eyes clamped shut until the urges subsided. Gasping, he opened his eyes.

"Damn it," he moaned. In the pot atop the flowers lay his phone, glistening with vomit. Without thinking, he snatched the phone from the disgusting slurry and wiped it off on his shirt tail.

"Holy shit," the checker said from inside, watching him through the painted window of the store. "Gross!"

"God. I hate you," he whispered aloud, bile dripping from his lips down his shirt front.

"Just to be clear, do you hate God or yourself?" Simon asked.

"I hate everything," Pilate hissed back, rising to his feet. He staggered to the Cross and Cork, head down in a self-imposed walk of shame.

Pilate avoided Cusack's pitying, silent gaze as he summoned a last drop of dignity, straightening his back as he walked through the dining area, working his way up the stairs and back into his room. He fell into bed.

The blessing of sleep claimed him in moments.

* * *

Pilate sat up in bed, wide awake in a dark, unfamiliar room.

"What?" he shouted, hand grasping at his pocket. The phone vibrated again.

He couldn't make out the number through the crust of dried vomit. He swallowed hard, avoiding his gag reflex and accepted the call.

"Hello?"

"Hey," Ryder said. "Can you meet me over at Falley's church? Soon as you can?"

"Yeah, I'm not feeling so good."

"We got another shooting," Ryder said, terminating the call.

* * *

Ryder stood alone outside, a cell phone pressed to his ear, speaking animatedly. A deputy bent and peered into Pilate's car as he rolled up, then waved him to a parking spot. Police tape fluttered in the breeze, attached only to one door handle of the church's main entrance.

Pilate fought a wave of nausea as he reached for the door handle in his car. He stopped, sighed, and gulped water. Both hands gripping the steering wheel, he closed his eyes and breathed deeply, as if trying to shake off the hangover through force of will.

Ambling over to Pilate's car, Ryder put his phone away and leaned down. Catching a look at Pilate, he whistled, low and slow. "Well, you sure as hell don't need me to tell you that you look like three shades of shit, do you?"

Pilate shook his head slowly, releasing his grip on the steering wheel and opening the car door.

"What the hell, man? You drink Cusack's joint dry last night?"

"Who got shot?"

"Falley," Ryder said. "Some woman came in here during services in full view of God and everybody and shot him."

Pilate blanched. "Is he?"

"Dead? Nope. Wounded. He's the only one. Only other casualties are the wits of the congregation and the guitar player's pants. Looks like our dear reverend is going to get the room Bob Hayes just checked out of. I got off the phone with the hospital a few minutes ago," Ryder said, taking a Field Notes notebook from his hip pocket. "They said they got the bullet out of his upper right shoulder, and are closing him up. Couple other shots winged him."

"So what happened? Who is the shooter?"

"That's why I called you," he said, flipping open the notebook. Scanning his notes he started to read aloud. "Witnesses—and there were dozens of witnesses, I might add, said it was a tall, thin blonde woman, approximately twenty-five. It was during the invitation portion of the show."

"Invitation?" Pilate asked, leaning against the car.

"To come on down and be the next contestant on the big show in the sky."

Pilate's face contorted. "I don't follow."

"Probably 'cause you have a hangover that would wreck a John Deere harvester," he said. "The end, when they ask all sinners who want to become one with the Holy Spirit to come to the altar. Right before they ask for donations and such."

"Right," Pilate said, folding his arms across his chest. "Of course, I get you. I did a little time in the Southern Baptist church as a kid. So she came down?"

"Yeah, though nobody could recall seeing her during the service. She suddenly appeared in the aisle and walked right up." He looked back at his notes. "Said her name was Jezebel, then yanked a gun out of her purse and said something along the lines of 'Pilate has washed his hands of you, false prophet.'"

"Please tell me the sermon was about the Gospel of Matthew," Pilate groaned, rubbing his temples forcefully.

Ryder shook his head. "Nope, they were actually doing Luke. Prodigal son."

"That's even better," Simon said.

"Suspect went on to say that 'John Pilate prophesied the return of Dead Jack.'"

Pilate groaned.

"There's more," Ryder said, his eyes sparkling. "She continued, saying that, 'He gave me the list of Pharisees—starting with this con artist.' Then she fired again at Falley, laying there in a pool of his own blood. Missed his vitals. I'm pretty sure that's when the guitar player crapped his pants."

"He crapped his pants? Nevermind. Nobody tried to stop her? Way more of them than her," Pilate offered.

"You've been under fire. You know what that does to people," Ryder said, looking up from his notes. "They were bewildered and terrified. A couple did start to rush her, but then she started waving the gun around."

"Understood."

Ryder thumbed through his notepad and recited more. "So, this super fan of yours shouted that 'Pilate made the list. I will make it right.' And beat feet out of the sanctuary. You can understand I am reasonably curious about this list of yours."

Pilate tasted bile. No amount of toothpaste and mouthwash would do the trick anytime soon. He shrugged. "I am innocent of this man's blood; see to it yourself."

Ryder chuckled, tucking the notebook back in his hip pocket. "I often forget you're a writer. And you evidently did do some time at church."

"Yeah, that fever broke a long time ago," Pilate said.

"Well, we have a problem," Ryder said. "This is either a copycat, or it's the same shooter who got Bob. Either way, it's a problem, and we have to fix it."

"You got a mouse in your pocket?" Pilate said automatically, patting his own pockets for the travel-sized bottle of Tylenol. He took four after reaching through the car window to pick up his bottle of water.

"Well, if you are saying you aren't in the mood to help," Ryder said, hands on hips. "I guess, hangover or no hangover, I can run you in for questioning. And I have questions about why a lunatic assassin is killing ministers - trying to kill ministers - in my town, with your name coming out of her mouth. A lot."

"Oh bullshit," Pilate said, drinking the remains of the water. "This is some nut, sheriff. I don't have a list. Jack is dead, and I have my own problems to deal with."

"I know you do," he said, raising his eyebrows and tipping his hat back a quarter inch off his brow as he leaned into Pilate's personal space. "And I'll chalk your recalcitrance up to that and your cocktail flu. But I have my own problems and lately they all seem to have something to do with you. That means you cooperate, or you can add a huge pain in the ass problem on your stack of sorrows."

Pilate sighed. "Okay, where do we start?"

"That's more like it," he said, stepping back. "First, I think you oughta go in there," he jerked a thumb over his shoulder at the church. "And say a prayer for your headache."

Pilate shook his head slowly, his eyes heavenward.

* * *

"So what do these two shootings have in common?" Ryder said as they walked into the diner. Ryder took a seat in the corner by the window, tossing a laminated menu his way. "You should eat something. Something greasy. Burger should do the trick."

Pilate's stomach turned, and almost on cue, growled. "Maybe."

"We got the airport manager, Bob. Now we got the town Holy Joe."

"Who really is holy now," Pilate said, nodding at the waitress as she put an ice water before him. He put the glass to his forehead in hopes the cool condensation would stop the mariachi band playing at full volume in his head.

Ryder looked up from the menu. "Huh?"

"He's got a new hole in him?"

Ryder nodded. "Yeah?"

"Holy."

Ryder rolled his eyes, grunted, and went back to the menu. "You're in a bad way, Pilate."

"What'll you have?" Toni said, pen and order pad ready.

"Miss Toni," Ryder sniffed the air. "What's the special?"

"Meatloaf and mashed, with green beans and a side salad," she said. "It's super good."

Ryder nodded. "That's for me."

She wrote it down, then looked at Pilate. "And you?"

Pilate sighed. "I'm good."

"Don't be silly," Ryder chirped. "He'll have," he eyed the menu. "He'll have the double burger with fried onions, cheese, mayo."

Pilate made a sound like a tortured burp. His eyes bored into the table as he willed himself not to vomit.

"Okay, hold the onions."

"And the mayo," Pilate whispered.

"Make it heavy on the grease. And a side of fries, please, Toni." As she walked to the counter, Ryder put the menus away and pulled out his Field Notes. "You're gonna feel a lot better as soon as you get that chow."

"If you say so," Pilate said.

"Okay, so Bob and the Rev both took bullets from somebody in your name," he said.

"Why do I attract all the weirdoes?"

"Everything seeks its own level? Cosmic justice? God hates you? Lots of theories," Ryder said, grimacing. "Moving on. So, tell me about your recent run-in with your biggest fan." He laced his fingers together and rested his chin on them.

"You mean Mister Nice-Nice?" Pilate asked, his chest tightening slightly. "The guy who put me in his Easy Bake Oven a little too long?"

Ryder nodded.

Pilate threw up his hands. "Not much to say. Not very nice-nice."

Ryder remained silent and dispassionate. "Okay, okay," Plate said. "This guy had been watching me for a while. He drugged my drink and kidnapped me. Put me in a steel shipping container at a self-storage place. So hot I nearly died. But I got out."

"Obviously," Ryder said as Toni slid a steaming plate of meatloaf in front of him.

"Your burger's coming right up, hon," she said.

"That may be an accurate premonition," Pilate said, under his breath.

"So that's it? Just some flake locked you up and left you to die?" Ryder said, forking into his meatloaf.

"No, it was a couple of days and he kept visiting to bring me a drink," Pilate said as Toni placed the plate of burger and fries on the paper placemat.

"Water and such?"

"Well, a little. But once a martini and once a cup of coffee."

Ryder stopped chewing. "A martini?"

"Yeah, he was all about giving me my favorite drink so we could be friends," Pilate said, with air quotes around the last two words.

"Did he ever let on why he had abducted you?"

"Not really. Kept saying shit about being nice-nice. And being friends with him. For me not to act so big or whatever," Pilate picked up the burger. It smelled great, and his stomach needed something. He bit into it.

"So big?"

"Just not to put on airs, I guess?" Pilate said around the mouthful of burger. He swallowed and wiped juice from his chin with a napkin. "This is good. I think the guy was clearly disturbed. He had read my book and saw me on TV and decided we should be friends."

"Typical stalker behavior. Locks on to a somebody and decides they know the real person better than anybody, and he should be friends with them. Most are harmless star fuckers, seeking validation from the object of their obsession," Ryder said. "Others are true narcopaths."

"Narcopaths?" Pilate took another bite of his burger and reached for the fries.

"I'm just learning about it, heard a retired FBI profiler speak in Lincoln a few months ago. It's not in the DSM. More a catchall term, but it's a convenient phrase for people who have a mixture of narcissistic personality disorder and antisocial personality disorder."

"Antisocial, all right," Pilate said, putting his burger down. "What do they do?"

"Well, mostly they fuck people over in their personal relationships without any empathy or, at their worst, they shoot John Lennon."

"Oh," Pilate said.

Ryder's phone rang. He fished it out of his jacket pocket and answered it. Nodding for a few seconds, he said, "Okay, thanks," and put it away.

"Finish your food. We have somewhere to go."

* * *

Val unwrapped her hands after the workout, sending her new client, Trevor, home. Unlike most of her older, heavier, and easily winded clients, Trevor had some game, and giving him a workout actually got her heart rate up. She didn't bother rolling her wraps—they smelled pretty ripe and she would soak them in the sink with Woolite when she got home—instead shoving them in her bag and heading to the locker room.

On her way to the locker room, she locked the main door of the gym. Felix had given her the keys to use the gym for her late customers. She flipped off the lights above the boxing ring, leaving only a small desk lamp on in the glassed-in office near the locker room door.

She adjusted her ponytail in the mirror, as several strands of hair had broken free of the rubber band. Val felt the pangs of cramps coming on; just about that time. She looked forward to getting home, having a shower, and slipping into some sweatpants. Maybe pour a glass of wine and figure out why having an affair with a most oddly charming, yet totally fucked-up, married man, is somehow a good idea.

"Stupid," she said, just above a murmur as she turned on the faucet. "You know better." She punched some soap from the dispenser and washed her hands. Rinsing the soap, she cupped her hands and leaned close to the sink, splashing her face.

At that instant she felt a hard shove, as if someone had front kicked her tailbone, launching her into the rusty faucet on the sink. Stunned into a split-second of silence, she heard the rush of the water and felt sharp pain at her temple. She grasped the hard porcelain of the sink and started to push herself away, turning her head to get a look at her assailant.

Stymied by yet another hard shove, this time definitely from a shoulder, Val was thrust back into the sink. She put her hands in the way to avoid banging her head, but still felt the air rush from her lungs. Warm blood trickled down her forehead.

Val grunted and wiped the blood from her eyes, catching a glimpse of a shape pushing her yet again—this time against the wall, punctuated by a sharp kick to her solar plexus. What little air her lungs had regained deserted her as she crumpled to her knees. She felt her sweaty wraps being looped around her neck.

As the wraps pulled taut, Val started to choke. Her mind raced.

If you pass out now, you may never wake up.

Reflexively, her hands scrabbled at her neck to try to loosen the wraps.

Summoning as much air and as much strength as she could, Val whirled and jabbed in the direction of the shape now before her, somehow connecting. Her knuckles felt a hardness—teeth?—and she heard a yelp of pain. She summoned the strength to follow up the jab with a salty left hook, this time connecting with an eye socket. Another yelp as Val struggled to one knee and used her remaining strength to loosen the wraps. Gathering them in her fist, she wiped the blood from her eyes and greedily gulped air. Her vision widened from the narrow tunnel of survival and she made out the tall, thin, person wearing a bizarre devil mask.

Screw this.

Val launched into a side kick that took the devil down to one knee. She danced forward and jabbed twice, connecting again to the hard plastic mask, eliciting a groan.

"Motherfucker, you've messed with the wrong girl," she hissed at the shape as she stepped back and wiped a fist across her eyes, clearing away the last of the blood. "Who the fuck are you?" Her adrenaline at about an eleven as she danced back a few feet in a boxing stance, she shouted, "What do you want? Some more of this? Answer me!"

The shape gracefully got to its feet as something akin to a snicker or perhaps a laugh escaped the mask. "You are not nice-nice at all. Like your boyfriend."

Val cocked her head to the left, fists still raised. "Who are you?"

"A friend," the shape said in a high, strange, watery voice. "If you'll let me be."

"You're going to get on your belly, asshole," she hissed. "With your hands behind your head while we wait for the cops. Do it. Now."

Again, the odd snicker muffled by the mask. "I don't think so." The devil reached underneath the black hoodie and pulled a blue steel revolver from his waistband, pointing it at Val.

Val recoiled, eyes darting side to side in vain for cover.

"I don't think you want to be not nice to me," the devil pulled the hammer back on the revolver. "You see, people who aren't nice-nice to me don't live very long. Sad, really. I set everything in motion, and I so wanted you to see it."

"What are you talking about, you crazy fuck?" Val shouted.

"Your boyfriend's wife is about to get hers, and I so wanted you to see it. Alas—"

"Please," Val said, trembling. "Don't do this."

"—not to be. Get on your knees," he gestured with the gun. "Do it."

Val's mind raced, sizing up her limited options.

Well, this is it. I'm damn sure not going down crying.

"Don't I get to see your face?" She stammered. "If you're going to kill me anyway?"

The devil stopped moving, as if pondering the question.

"If you're my friend don't I at least get to see your face?" Val sputtered, her fists hanging in the air, defiant and pathetically useless against a bullet.

"Okay, that is true. I should be nice so you will be nice-nice before I shoot you in the face."

Val's entire body spasmed in terror.

No, please God. Not like this.

The devil stepped back, the promise of Val's certain death outstretched in his left hand. The other hand reached for the mask, fumbling with its comically pointed chin.

He looks like devil guy from that canned stuff we ate when I was a kid. I hate that shit.

Val threw herself to the left of the gun and fired a round kick at his wrist, sending the gun flying. The devil yelped in surprise and took a swing back at her, smashing a bony fist into Val's left ear; her turn to yelp in pain as the blow disoriented her and a ringing set in. She grunted and fell back against the sink, her hand landing on something cold and metallic. She could not believe her luck. The gun had landed in the sink.

She scooped it up and whirled to face the devil. She caught only a fleeting glimpse of him darting out the door, slapping at the light switch as he fled. He was gone, and she was alone in the dark.

"Fuck you!" She fired twice at the door purely on general principle, punctuating each round with a curse. Feeling her way to the door, she found the handle, switched on the lights and barreled into the gym. The light of the office lamp revealed the gym's main door, swung wide open into the warm, dark, and above all else, empty, Key West night.

"Damn it," she muttered, reaching for the phone on the wall.

Chapter Nine

Pilate glanced down at his phone and saw that he had a text from Taters.

"You. Me. Vega$. Two weeks. Southwest having a fare sale."

Pilate shook his head as the Dodge Ram sped down the highway with Ryder at the wheel.

"Where are we going?"

Ryder looked over, then past him through the window. "Look at that. Another harvest almost done." he remarked as a huge green harvester sucked up feed corn, row by row. "Pretty soon we'll be up to our asses in snow."

"Joy of all joys," Pilate said. "You know right after I got here a few years ago I remember being astounded at how much damn snow this town gets. My God, man, I thought I landed on Hoth—that's a *Star Wars* reference. And then of course the blizzard was very nearly the instrument of my death."

"I have heard of *Star Wars*." Ryder nodded. "Yeah, it nearly killed you, young Luke, but you did okay. Look at you now," he chuckled.

"Are you still planning to keep our destination a secret?"

Ryder squinted at the road ahead. "Nope. I had to get significantly far away from town so you wouldn't try to jump out and walk home when I told you."

"I don't get it," Pilate said.

"I think it's time we both confronted a certain Mr. Hilmer Thurman."

"Oh damn it," Pilate said, theatrically reaching for the door handle. "Must we?"

Ryder drove on, wordlessly, for a few miles. "We're gonna good cop, bad cop him."

"What, like we did Nelda? That was such a winning strategy."

"Mister Pilate, are you familiar with the concept of disruption?"

"I guess?" Pilate said, eyebrow raised in consternation.

"The term refers to any innovation within an industry that radically changes the way the companies in that sector operate," he said.

"Is this from another FBI extension course?"

Ryder slid a cinnamon toothpick into the side of his thin-lipped mouth. "For example, there's several things that can cause a business disruption. Acts of God, or the weather, as in your aforementioned blizzard. Or loss of talent or skills in the workforce or technology dramatically changing—like the Internet. Or introducing a wild card into a situation."

"Okay, I'm still listening," Pilate shrugged. "Not understanding, mind you, but I am still listening."

"For better or for worse, like it or not, you are my wildcard. You're my disruption. I can bring you into the situation where I am trying to ascertain what Hilmer knows because even though he knows you, he does not know how to deal with you. That puts him off balance and makes it easier for me to make my maneuvers. Does that make more sense?"

Pilate nodded. "Sure, I get it. He thinks you're coming, he makes a plan, but suddenly the situation is not what he expected and not only does he not have a plan, he has a situation he didn't foresee. It's a headache he doesn't want to deal with. And on my own I'm a gigantic pain in the balls."

Ryder smiled at him. "You broke the code, John. You're no box of rocks, that I can tell."

"I guess former Sheriff Scovill was right, John," Simon whispered. *"And if he was right about Ryder using you against Hilmer, he might be right about everything."*

"You know, I kind of established what passed for detente with that gentleman," Pilate said thoughtfully. "I'm not sure it's a good idea to use me to poke that particular bear."

"Your opinion is noted," Ryder said, turning off the highway and onto a county road. "We'll be at the Brown Betty in about ten minutes or so. You might want to chew a few more aspirin before we pull in."

* * *

Steam rose from the mug of green tea perched on the front porch railing. Kate drank a sip, then put it aside to cool. Seated on the porch swing, a quilt around her lap, she paused from grading papers when she heard the sound of a harvester in the distance. She stared out at the farmland, the swing squeaking as she focused on the harvester and pickup out in the field she rented to a farmer.

Her smartphone dinged; she noted that this would be the second voicemail left after she fended off two missed calls from Grant. She didn't want to talk or listen as she pondered what to tell the kids.

She searched her feelings, trying to figure out when it all started to go in a different direction. Kate liked to blame it on Pilate. She alternately lied to his face or froze him out to make him feel as if it's all his fault, but it wasn't that simple. Something had changed inside her...she didn't know what. She didn't dislike him, she decided. She did still love him.

Kate simply didn't feel anymore.

Initially, she wondered if middle age had changed them. Both felt the aches and pains of gravity catching up with their bodies, but also the natural detachment that couples often experience after years together raising kids. Sex becomes pro-forma, or worse, disappears altogether. Intimacy orbited in a distant parabola around the needs of kids and work. His jokes and stories were stale to her ears, and she had little to discuss but the same-old, same-old.

But she also knew that all marriages have their downtimes, they could get through this.

Yet, the kids needed stability, and John Pilate is many things, but stability is far and away not his strong suit.

It wasn't all his fault and she knew it. She liked life with John for a time. Hell, she liked it a lot when she met him. He was exciting and sexy and a little broken, but she could deal with that. *He was worth the risk.*

But she had to wonder as time went on whether or not the real risk is what John is taking with her. She led him to believe that she wanted to move on with her life and get out of Cross, but something kept her here. It was a steady pull, a cruel magnetism that was not entirely uncomfortable, if she was being honest. As much as she said she wanted to leave, she did not.

He seems so much happier and more at peace by the ocean.

He liked his friend Taters, to fish and drink, and he liked to write. And of course, John Pilate also liked to look at women. She knew from the get-go that he had an eye for the ladies, and the ladies liked him. In fact, one of the things she noticed that women and men had a very tough time keeping up a front around John Pilate.

She had no illusions about marriage being perfect. God knows her first husband, the long dead father of Kara, was certainly a different kind of person in his own way. He had his foibles, she had hers—as much as high school sweethearts had them. But her second husband was an open person in many ways, even though he always seems to be shielding some kind of secret grief; tamping down some kind of conversation she couldn't penetrate.

In their relationship her own demons had found voice, not the least of which was an insecurity about what life was supposed to be about, where she is supposed to go, and what she's supposed to do. Kate always attracted men, strong and weak. She had her own gifts in that regard and knew she didn't want to spend the rest of her life going through a cycle of looking for a good man or having a good man find her; then getting to the tough part and everybody bailing out. Wash, rinse, repeat.

Grant exuded steadiness. On track to be dean, and probably president of a college in a few years. Certainly the current lady running the show is eyeing a larger university job.

Steadiness. That steady pull.

Grant would embrace staying in her beloved Cross, raise the kids in the atmosphere she wanted. The environment could be easily controlled compared to living in a strange place like Key West or some city somewhere. John would be all right if she decided to leave him. No matter what, she'd always want to be his friend and love him if they decided to part ways. She wanted to co-parent with him. Kate mused that after the hurt ended, if she handled it right, they could get to that point when he would realize this was what he probably wanted, too.

Her thoughts were interrupted by a rickety sound. Looking over her shoulder, she saw plumes of dust barreling down the road. In a few seconds, a white panel van emerged from the dust. She took another sip of her now cold tea, then stood up as the lanky driver pulled into the driveway, hopped out, and handed her an envelope.

"Do I need to sign for this?" she asked.

"Nope," he said, fingering a tablet. "I noted that I handed it to you. All good. Have a good day," the driver said, hopping back into the van and peeling onto the dusty gravel road.

The return address didn't give her a clue—a post office box in Florida. Her stomach dropped.

Oh my god, are these divorce papers? Jesus.

She inhaled deeply, exhaling as she ripped the strip off the top of the envelope. Inside she found an 8 x 10 black-and-white photograph of a man and a young woman, nude in shadow, clearly having sex.

Kate didn't recognize the woman's face, but the man? Her husband, John Pilate.

* * *

No matter what happens if I survive I want to be a better person.

Pilate turned the sentence over in his mind as Ryder steered off the highway. It was the sentence he uttered as a pleading prayer while locked in the oven-like cargo container, struggling to survive; the desperate words he rasped to a God he doubts.

His entire adult life, Pilate despised and simultaneously admired those who "had religion." The solemn surety of communion with a Higher Power; what he considered the smug arrogance of people who had it all figured out.

Yet, they also could end up in an aloha shirt with a hole in it, gunned down by a heretic.

"Where was your god the other night, Rev?" Pilate said, before Simon could intrude on his thoughts and plant that hateful seed.

"John, you are not being a better person right now," Simon said.

"Leave me alone," Pilate said.

"What?" Ryder said.

Pilate realized he had spoken aloud. "Nothing, sorry."

Ryder shrugged with his eyebrows. "Here we go," the Ram pulled into the parking lot of the Brown Betty. There were a few cars out front of the old roadhouse, but it is early yet. Ryder removed his aviator sunglasses and double-checked his Colt New Frontier.

"What the hell, you think you'll need that?"

"It's when you don't check your gun that you find out it's empty," Ryder said, opening the truck door and stepping out, sliding the pistol in its holster.

"What's that, some sort of cowboy wisdom?" Simon asked.

Pilate stepped out and followed Ryder inside. The pair paused inside the doorway of the dark bar, their eyes adjusting to neon and the warm glow of the jukebox. Cigarette smoke hung in the air like a dry fog. A few of the five patrons looked up from their beers a second, then went back to their conversations.

A wiry man of about thirty wiped down the bar, He greeted Ryder and Pilate. "Hey there, what can I get you?"

"Your boss," Ryder said, slipping a fresh cinnamon toothpick in his mouth.

"Oh, well," the man said, sheepishly. "He um, doesn't want to be disturbed."

Ryder grunted in amusement. "Son, I'm not asking. Get him."

The man looked pained by the order, mouth open to respond, when Hilmer Thurman's office door opened. "That's all right, Benny," Thurman said, making an "after you" gesture. "Gents, step into my office."

The tiny office presented just as Pilate remembered. An unassuming desk, a poker table with a carousel of chips, five chairs, and the strong odor of cigars.

"Had a game recently?" Ryder said, picking up a few red chips.

"No, not really," Thurman said, squeezing into his chair behind the desk.

"Kind of tough to get a game together these days, huh?" Ryder said, noisily dragging a folding chair from the table over to Thurman's desk. "Most of your poker buddies dead and all."

Thurman's face reddened at the remark, then eased as he worked a smile into his lips. He glanced at Pilate. "Mister Pilate, been a while."

Pilate pulled up a chair and sat down. "Yes, I suppose it has been a while since we've spoken face to face. Where you been keeping yourself?"

Thurman shrugged. "Here and there," he said. "Here and there."

Ryder grunted and smirked.

Thurman leaned forward; hands clasped on the Bank of Cross desk blotter. "What can I do you for, sheriff? Or is it commissioner? You seem to be running or trying to run everything these days."

Ryder crossed his legs, removing his hat and perching it on his knee, one hand resting on the butt of his Colt. He rolled the toothpick around his mouth a second before speaking. "Still both."

"Crucial election coming," Thurman said.

"It is indeed," Ryder said.

"Let me guess, you're going back to being the commissioner full time. You're running Mister Pilate here for sheriff and looking for a donation?"

Pilate smiled. "No. thanks. Sheriff is a dangerous job."

"Yeah, that's true. Last couple before the good acting sheriff here didn't end up so well. One of 'em in jail, the other eating his meals through a tube," Thurman said. "Speaking of broke-down old men, how's that buddy of yours? The skipper of the S.S. Minnow out in Key West?"

Pilate cut his eyes at Ryder, whose eye twitched once.

"He's fine," Pilate said.

"How's his ticker?"

"Good, thanks."

"Not what I heard," Thurman said, arms folded. "Apparently he had a nasty old heart attack trying to bail your ass out in Jamaica."

"Well, you know how the rumor mill is," Pilate said. "I mean, it's crazy but some people think we turned your entire poker night crew into dogfood on main street a while back."

Thurman's self-satisfied smirk faded into a humorless rictus.

Ryder shifted his weight from one skinny buttock to another. "Let's cut the bullshit, Hilmer, mmkay?"

"Suits me," Thurman said, hands raised, palm out, at his visitors.

"There's been some shots fired around here lately," Ryder said.

Thurman made a face of mock concern. "Oh, I know. Terrible. A man of the cloth and poor old Bob at the airfield."

"What do you know about it?" Ryder said.

"What I just told you," he said, smiling broadly.

"That so?" Ryder drawled.

Thurman nodded, pulling off a loose thread from his plaid shirt.

"I thought you knew every little thing that happened in this town?" Pilate said.

"I do," Thurman said, eyes on the thread as he transferred it to the wastebasket. "Not as much as him, though." He nodded at Ryder. "Ain't that right?"

Ryder snorted.

"And that's all you know about the shootings?" Pilate asked.

"It's all I'm telling you," he said.

Ryder chuckled. "Oh?"

Pilate felt his phone vibrating underneath his jacket. It wasn't a text, but the persistent vibration of a call. Pilate removed it from his pocket, glancing at the screen. Val. He silenced the call and put it away.

"Yeah," Thurman said. "And if you don't like it, you can talk to my lawyer. He's with the firm Fuck You, Your Mother, and Your Horse."

"Okay, Hilmer," Ryder said, scoffing. "If that's the way it's going. Of course, you know, this kinda makes me think you had a little something to do with all this."

He sniggered. "Give me a break, Ryder. You know this shit's not my style."

"True," Pilate said. "That recent all-out assault on the jail excepted, you usually just make people disappear. Like poor old Perry Mostek."

"Yeah, yeah," Thurman said. "Same old shit. He blew town after he shot Sheriff Welliver, and you know it."

"Amazing that the grocer of pert near the smallest town in the county successfully went all-in on being Dr. Richard Kimble and never been heard from again."

Thurman shrugged. "True. I never thought Perry had it in him."

"You ever finish the sale on his store?" Pilate said. "I'm behind on current events." Thurman had made an offer on Mostek's grocery store soon after he went missing. "I hear you made Perry's widow—or wife, if you will, an offer she couldn't refuse."

"Oh, John, you didn't hear," Ryder said standing up and putting on his hat. "Bottom fell out of the grocery store market and ol' Hilmer here withdrew his offer. Greg Bartley bought it."

Pilate nodded in an exaggerated way, throwing up his hands. "Oh! Well, that's too bad." He slapped his thighs and stood up. "Better luck next time."

Thurman slowly stood, looking at the desk blotter. "You done?"

Pilate looked at Ryder, who nodded. "Yup, I think so."

"Then listen carefully," Thurman said, eyes still on the desk. "I am not the author of every evil deed in this town." He looked up at Ryder. "However, I damn sure don't always disapprove."

Ryder grunted in amusement. "Not sure how to take that."

"I don't give a good goddamn," Thurman said. "Take it any way you want. But right now, you're gonna take it outside. Get out of my place."

Pilate felt his gut tighten as the momentary wave of bravado he surfed crashed.

"Hilmer," Ryder tipped his hat as he and Pilate squeezed past the poker table and into the bar, eyes forward as they walked outside.

"He don't know shit," Ryder said as he turned the ignition.

Pilate pulled the Ram's door closed and put on his seatbelt. "You sure? He seems like he's hiding something."

"He's always hiding something," Ryder said. "But what he was hiding a minute ago was that he don't know shit about what's happening around here anymore. I believe it has him spooked, because he has never really come back from that pasting we gave him a while back."

Pilate nodded, slipping his phone from his pocket and glancing at the screen. Val had left him a voicemail.

"Odd, she usually texts," Simon leered.

"Most of his local crew got killed and his supply chain is busted up," Ryder drawled. "He's a diminished figure, and that could be awful unfortunate for him if his masters from up north decide he's a liability or a poor earner. However, this may play in his favor."

"So, you're saying he doesn't know who's behind it, but he likes what's going on?"

"Sure. This ripe pain in the saddle horn for us gets him a little of what he needs."

"What's that?" Pilate asked, pressing the voicemail button and holding the phone to his ear.

"Disruption."

* * *

"John I have no other way to say this since you didn't answer I'm gonna leave this on your voicemail," Val said on the recording, her voice quivering slightly. "And you need to call me back now. Somebody tried to kill me and I think it's the same guy who tried to kill you—and now he wants to kill your wife. You better call me as soon as you get this—the Key West police will be calling the local sheriff up there soon. Bye."

"Jesus," Pilate said.

Ryder threw Pilate a glance as he steered the Ram down the highway. "What?"

"Somebody tried to kill my...a friend of mine. In Key West." Pilate said, returning the call.

"Whoa," Ryder said.

Val answered immediately. "John, it's some kind of nutjob. Maybe the same guy who locked you in that storage container."

"Slow down, Val. Are you okay?"

"Well, not gonna lie. Asshole sucker-punched, well, sucker-kicked me. Cracked my head and my ribs are bruised. I gave him a little back, though, before he ran out."

"Val, I'm driving with the sheriff here in Cross, would you mind me putting you on the speakerphone and telling us everything?"

"Okay," she said. "I'm getting good at retelling this already. Key West P.D. and Officer A have interviewed me."

"Okay, good," Pilate turned on the speakerphone option. "Okay, Val, this is Sheriff Ryder. Sheriff, this is my...good friend Val."

"Ma'am," Ryder said.

"Okay, Val, tell us everything, from the top."

Val gave a pretty good play-by-play to the men.

Ryder slipped a cinnamon toothpick in his mouth as she spoke. When she finished, he leaned a little closer to Pilate's phone. "Have they run the serial numbers on the gun?"

"Yes. Well, no. Actually. The numbers were burned off with acid and a file," she sighed. "And he wore gloves so the only prints on it are mine, I'm afraid."

Ryder winced at the information. "Okay, that's unfortunate. So, one more time, the assailant was wearing a mask?"

"Yes, it was like the devil, sort of. Or maybe one of those masks the anarchy weirdos always have? Like in the movie about the vendetta?"

"Oh, the Guy Fawkes mask," Pilate said. "He kind of looks like a devil if you're not seeing it in the light, I bet."

"Well, it was either that or he's the canned ham spread devil," Val said. "Take your pick."

Ryder chuckled dryly, his wheels turning. "Okay, Val. So you said the guy mentioned John by name?"

Val was silent for a second. "Well, not exactly."

"Okay, then, so what's the connection to John?" Ryder said, steely eyes behind his aviators, trained on the road ahead.

"Well, he said something. He said, 'Your boyfriend's wife is about to get hers,' and, well—"

"Oh, okay, Val," Pilate stammered. "You don't have to say any—"

Ryder offered Pilate a blank expression that somehow spoke volumes, then focused his eye on the road. "Excuse me, John. So, Miss, he said threatened to kill the wife of your boyfriend, is that right?"

"Yes," Val said, resigned.

"So this guy thinks you're John Pilate's girlfriend, then?"

Pilate grabbed at the verbal lifeline Ryder threw. "Yes, that's right, he knows we are friends and calls me your boyfriend. He did that when I was his prisoner. Remember?"

"Yes," Val said, her voice brightening. "This devil weirdo thinks John and I are having a…a thing. But anyway, the important thing is, he said he wants to kill John's wife."

"That's very concerning," Ryder said. "Ma'am, I appreciate your giving us a head's up. We're going to look into this. Is there anything else you can think of that might be helpful?"

"I think that's it," she said.

"You've done more than enough, Val," Pilate said. "I mean, I'm so glad you're okay. Can I call you back a little later?"

"Sure," she said.

"Okay, thanks my…friend. Bye."

Pilate terminated the call. "I can't believe this."

"Yeah, it's a pickle, Mr. Pilate," he said. "There seems to be a connection to what's happening here and the guy who tried to kill your gal."

Pilate let the gal remark slide. "So, you think Mister Nice-Nice is back in Key West, and shooting random people here in Cross?"

Ryder grunted, activating his turn signal. "All I know is there have now been three attempted murders and the common denominator is creeps with guns wearing goofy masks, and you."

"What do we do now?"

"Well, I'm dropping you off at your wife's place, then I'm going to call the Key West police and see what else they know."

"What do I tell Kate?" Pilate asked.

"Tell her what your friend told us. Tell her we are on the case, and to be sure to keep that shotgun of hers handy."

"All things considered, John," Simon sniggered. *"You may not want her to have the shotgun handy when you're around."*

* * *

Pilate caught Kate on her way back from her Pilates class at the college. Hot and sweaty from the workout, her manner cold.

"I remember when the student association asked me to run a Pilates class," Pilate said, forcing a smile. "Wanted to call it 'Pilate's Pilates' or something. Remember? Quite a knee slapper."

Kate brushed past him on the porch and went inside.

"Chilly out here," Simon said.

Pilate's chest tightened. He took a deep breath and marshaled his resolve, stepping through the door into the cozy living room.

"Where's kids?"

"Aftercare," she said. "I'll go get them in an hour or so."

"Oh," Pilate said.

"What?"

"Well, it's just that…"

"Or you can go get them," she said, shrugging as she picked up Peter's toys and put them in a basket beside the loveseat.

"Okay, but I have something to tell you," he said.

She moved to a basket of laundry on the loveseat and started folding towels and kids clothes.

"Kate?"

"I'm listening," she said.

"Can you please stop that and hear me out?"

She finished folding a towel and sat beside the basket, impassive.

Pilate told her about the situation.

"So, this gym owner guy? He knows you?" Kate said.

"Well, yes, she does."

"So *she* called you to warn you about this guy—who is probably the same guy who tried to kill you before?" She said, sounding a bit like an attorney.

Pilate's guts churned. "Yes, because this guy in the mask mentioned me."

"This is at the boxing gym?" Kate said. "Her boxing gym?"

"Yes, like I said," Pilate said.

"Makes sense," she said, standing up and walking to the small desk in the corner of the room. She opened the center drawer and lifted out an envelope.

"Aw jeez? Divorce papers? Have you been listening to what I'm saying?"

She raised an eyebrow and walked the envelope over to him, proffering it. "Here."

Pilate took the slender envelope, too light to be divorce papers. He silently cursed himself for using the word.

"Open it," she said, arms folded.

The envelope revealed a photo of him and Val having sex.

"She has a great body," Kate said, her eyes tearing. "And nice boxing gloves hanging on the bedpost."

Pilate's vision blurred, his heart hammered.

"Where did you get this?" Pilate stammered.

"Special delivery," Kate said. Her arms were not merely folded; her fingers dug into her biceps, as if she were holding on to herself for dear life. "I can only assume your nice-nice friend is not only a nutjob, but also a peeper."

"Oh God," Pilate said. "I'm so sorry. This is…" his voice trailed off as he slid the photo back in the envelope. "A nightmare."

Kate nodded, then backed away from him.

"I don't know what to say."

Kate looked at him, eyes watery, face impassive, her hands still gripping her biceps.

Pilate stepped toward her a few steps. She backed into the doorway of the kitchen.

Pilate stopped. "Kate, I...I have nothing, except I'm sorry, and I can explain so much of this. But we have to deal with it. This crazy guy is shooting people."

Kate continued to look at him, her eyes darkening.

"Kate?" Pilate pleaded. "Don't you have anything to say?"

She glanced floor a moment, her hands falling to her sides.

"How could you be so selfish?" her voice monotone.

"I don't know," he said, his voice cracking. "It's complicated."

"Then you can get your complicated ass out of my house," she said. "And take that fucking picture with you."

It crossed his mind to argue, but he had seen this look on her face before. No getting around it. Busted. No matter what Kate did with Grant, she held the high ground.

Pilate muttered another apology as he walked out the door.

"Looks like Mister Complicated gets to walk his ass back to the B&B," Simon said.

Chapter Ten

"Yeah, well, it's like this Taters. I had a situation," Pilate said.

"You? You had a situation?" Taters scoffed. "There's a shock."

Pilate heard the sounds of the harbor.

"Seriously. Listen man, about this shit that happened with Val, and what's going down here? The police are concerned for just about anybody who's close to me. I think you need to, you know, be extra careful."

"Well you know I'm always extra careful. And that's why I only drink certain kinds of beer."

"Seriously, Taters, that's not all that funny, right now. I'm not joking around."

"Well I surely do know that John, but I don't know what else I can do other than live my life without getting a neck sprain from looking over my shoulder. And it kind of helps that I can always get in my boat and sail away."

Pilate sighed.

"Let's go back to Vegas. You need to meet me there. Get your ass away from all that drama in Iowa."

"Nebraska."

"Close enough," he chuckled dryly. "All right, well I've got my gun handy. I will keep a weather eye on the horizon, and hopefully you guys can catch this sumbitch."

"Yeah, I mean, it's a small town, and they're bound to get tripped up. I hope it happens before somebody gets killed."

"Fair enough, my brother. Weather the storm. Hang in there, keep your pants zipped. I'd tell you to say hi to Kate for me, but I assume you're not going to be speaking to the missus much."

"It's probably best that there's going to be a deputy sheriff nearby to at least keep tabs on her because I'm not sure I can deal with that withering glare of hers."

Taters' words were drowned out by the sound of a boat horn for a second. "You know, I know you're beating yourself up about this," Taters offered, "But you did tell me she seemed to have a boyfriend or something going on, too."

"Yeah, but that doesn't excuse it on either front," Pilate said.

Taters pondered.

"You still there?" Pilate asked.

"I need to tell you something you don't want to hear," he said.

"I get told things I don't want to hear every day. Sometimes even by other people. Shoot."

"This may be a temporary rough patch for both of you and you can work it out."

"Shit, Taters, why wouldn't I want to hear that?"

"Because I think you're starting to talk yourself out of your marriage, and I don't know if that's a good idea. I think you love her, I think you've always loved her. So here's what you won't want to hear: you're selfish, John. I hate to say it, but it's true. You're selfish, and

God knows you've got every right to be selfish after what you've been through in your life."

"Okay, well," Pilate said, stunned.

"I'm not finished, so shut it," Taters cleared his throat noisily. "I understand you had situations when you were young that made you the way you are. Shit, man, we all do, but I think it made you selfish."

Pilate felt his face redden as Taters spoke, softly, yet stern, like a big brother or even a father would.

"I think you're selfish, but mainly as a means of protecting yourself. And I wonder if you can fully give yourself to her."

"Oh my God man, have you been like watching Oprah a lot lately, or what?" Pilate said, chuckling ruefully.

"I'm serious, man. Nearly dying focuses the mind, let me tell you. You need to give it a hard think. Let's talk it over soon with some fine booze."

"Okay, if I can get away," Pilate said.

"The skinny sheriff down there, what's his name? Strider?"

"Ryder," Pilate said.

"He's a guy who has his shit nailed down. Not sure if that works to your advantage."

"All right, man," Pilate said, surrendering. "Thanks for what you said. I appreciate it. Please keep an eye on things. And do me a favor, check in with me every once in a while, let me know you're all right."

"Will do, mildew. Hang in there." Taters hung up.

Pilate put the phone in his pocket and cast around the festively decorated dining room at the Cross and Cork. Cusack appeared behind the bar. Pilate went over and filled him in.

As Cusack absorbed the information, Pilate looked behind him at the bottle of Jameson. "I'm sorry for getting hammered the other night. Not my finest hour."

"Not at all. Not at all. No, not a thing to worry about. We'll keep an eye out, Marcy and I, for any strange people." Cusack stopped for a moment and looked down at the bar top, then back up at Pilate. "I gotta tell you, I thought that this place would be a great place to retire. You know, this quiet little village in the middle of nowhere. Silly me. It's certainly had its share of surprises over the years for me, I'll tell you that, my friend."

"You're telling me."

* * *

"I think I need to get out of town for a few days," Val said.

"Good idea," Pilate said.

"Let me come see you."

"Oh."

"Is that a no?"

"Val, I don't know if that's a good idea."

"Why?"

Pilate started to explain about the photo.

"Fucking creepy. That fuck took pictures of us screwing?" she shouted into the phone.

"And sent the photos to my wife."

"Holy shit. Are you joking?"

Pilate did not answer.

"Okay, well," she exhaled noisily. "That's even more reason for me to get out of town. If those creeps are staking out my house? Not to mention trying to kill me at the gym."

"Did I mention they sent the photo to my wife? The wife who lives here in Cross, the smallest town in the world?"

Val went silent a moment. "Oh, yeah, and I guess you have a wife who would probably like to help them kill me."

"I'm not saying that, but, yes."

"Let me come see you. I won't make a hairy deal out of it. I'll be discreet. I already checked and that little B&B you're staying in has plenty of open rooms."

"Yeah, I know Val. But is it really a good idea? I mean, isn't there any place else in the whole world you could hide out?"

"There's not any place in the whole world that I want to be other than near you. I'm worried. I'm not asking for anything else, but I'm coming, John, and you're gonna have to deal with it."

"You just love trouble, don't you?" Simon said.

* * *

The next day, Pilate called Kate to talk about the kids.

"I am moving forward on the legal separation," she said, eerily businesslike.

He surprised himself by not arguing with her. In fact, he welcomed it.

Maybe a distinct separation is what we both need right now.

They worked out a loose custody agreement they could both live with, especially in light of the security concerns.

"And I need you to not talk about any of this with the kids," he said. "We'll explain to them that I'm working."

"Noted," she said, again all business. "So I need you to call before you drop by the house from here on out."

"Ouch," Simon muttered.

"Noted," he said, the syllables tinged with acid. "And what about Grant? Is he going to be coming over?"

"Yes." She let out a ragged breath. "Sometimes."

"Kate, I truly am sorry," Pilate said.

"Noted," and she ended the call.

* * *

Pilate smelled a delicious aroma wafting from downstairs. Marcy had promised she would make her famous Irish stew. The night before, she drew a stew pot on the chalkboard that announced the next day's lunch menu.

"So what makes it Irish?" Pilate asked as he dragged past her on the way to his room.

"Well, I make it the way Cusack's Mum does—which is the only way he will eat it," she said, looking up from the chalkboard and blowing an errant lock of hair out of her eyes. "Truly traditional Irish stew has only a few ingredients. Your mutton, your onions, your potatoes, of course, and sometimes carrots. No beef. Irish stew is also thickened with mashed potatoes, instead of a roux. I'll be cooking it all morning to serve at lunch. It's a favorite of everybody except Toni at the diner. She says it kills her lunch rush every time I make it."

"I'm sorry you asked," Simon said.

"Sounds delicious," Pilate said. "Looking forward to it."

He needed coffee. Maybe an egg or two.

Pilate skipped the shower and shrugged into his wrinkled shirt, some jeans and Red Wing work boots. He noted with pleasure that lacing his boots were not as much an ordeal as they were before Val started training him; his belly no longer pressing into his ribs when he bent over.

"Training you," Simon said. *"That's quaint."*

Pilate opened the door and slipped on his first step. He righted himself and looked down at a large manila envelope marked "Pilate" in black marker he had stepped on.

He scooped it up as he glanced up and down the empty hallway. He opened the envelope and shook out several photographs.

"Not again," he groaned inwardly. He flicked through each photo of shadowy shapes engaged in sex.

"Not exactly," Simon said. *"I know that ass anywhere. That ain't Val. And that dude..."*

"Fuck," he rasped, sagging against the wall. "Aw, damn it, Kate."

Downstairs, he found Marcy flitting between taking the breakfast buffet and the kitchen.

"Marcy," he said.

"Good morning," she said. "What do you think?" She asked, her eyebrows raised expectantly.

"Think?" he said, puzzled. "You mean about this?" He said, holding up the envelope.

"Umm, no. I mean the stew. Can you smell it?"

"Oh," he said. "Yes. It smells incredible. Umm, Marcy, did you...see anybody head upstairs?"

"When?"

"This morning? Or last night?"

She shook her head slowly. "No, not that I can recall. You're the only one here right now. The Walkers from Oklahoma checked out last night, and we don't have another check in until tomorrow."

"Not even a delivery-type person?" He said, holding up the envelope.

"No, sorry, John. I've been on my own today. Been in the kitchen all morning, except for when I put out the scrambled eggs and coffee and such. I can ask Cusack when he gets back from the store if you'd like," she scrutinized his face. "Do you mind telling me what's wrong?"

Pilate shook his head, forcing a smile. "Nothing, Marcy. Probably a prank. Gotta go, thanks." He brushed past her and headed for the door.

"Don't forget lunch. Irish stew," she called after him. "Everybody loves it!"

* * *

The Guy Fawkes mask leered from the floorboard until she jumped in and threw her purse on top of it. She slipped the key into the ignition, cranking it and revving the engine to life. After a quick glance in the rearview, she pulled out of her space near Mostek's store and crept up to the Cross and Cork, parking across the street. Slumping down in her seat, she rubbed lotion on her hands as she watched the door of the B&B.

In a moment, John Pilate burst through the door, slamming the screen door behind him. Grasping the envelope, his face a mask of its own.

Sadness, she thought. That's what registered. *Angry, yes. But sad, too.*

Pilate threw the envelope in the passenger seat and slid behind the wheel, slamming the door. He gripped the steering wheel for a moment, his forehead on his knuckles, before starting the engine and speeding down the street, nearly hitting a beat-up Chevy Cobalt, drawing a middle finger and a horn blast from the driver.

She harumphed, smiling, as she followed Pilate.

* * *

182

"This is out of hand," Ryder said, carefully slipping the photos back into the envelope. "I appreciate you letting me look at these. I know it's not anything a husband wants to show another man, but I must verify the evidence."

Pilate nodded, pacing in front of Ryder's desk. "So what do we do?"

Ryder picked up the other envelope. "So, by the looks of these photos, both were printed off a computer. Looks about the same. Same kind of paper. You can see here—" he pointed to a small line on the lower right of the photo of Val and Pilate. "Same as the shots of, of Kate. So the printer is messed up a bit and doesn't print clean."

"Is there any doubt this isn't the same person spying on us?"

Ryder replaced the photo in the envelope and dropped it on his desk, leaning back in his creaky wooden chair. "Nope, but I need to be sure."

"Who the fuck is doing this to us?"

"Well," Ryder said, slipping a toothpick into his mouth. "I'd say you and Kate have made a mess of your marriage on your own."

"That's a fucking cheap shot, man," Pilate said, pointing at Ryder.

"Just saying, you two have problems, and this guy is doing whatever he can to make them worse." He sighed, impassive.

"No shit, sheriff."

"Who is it? That's the question."

"I have no idea," Pilate said. "I mean, I even thought for a second that Dead Jack is back. But he's gone. I saw him die."

Ryder nodded. "Let's think on that. Did Jack have any family? I mean, he had a wife. Any kids?"

"I think a daughter?" Pilate said. "She's grown. Don't know much about her. He wasn't close to her, from what I gleaned."

Ryder leaned forward, resting his elbows on the desk. "Hmm. That is interesting."

"Oh come on, Ryder. This is not her. I mean, it's Mister Nice-Nice. Not Miss."

"Yes, but the person who shot Reverend Falley? A woman. A young woman."

"Yeah, but I mean, if it is Jack Lindstrom's daughter, people would've probably recognized her. Wouldn't they?"

He threw up his hands.

"True. Just a thought. But what is clear is that this Mister Nice fella has accomplices, is willing to travel, and is either a piss poor shot, or is actually a really good shot. Managing to wound but not kill a couple of dudes."

Pilate fell heavily in the chair opposite Ryder. "Where does that leave us?"

"I don't know. I think we're dealing with at least two people here. This nice guy and the chick. I truly don't understand the motive other than they're nutjobs. What I do know is that you and your wife need to be very careful."

"No kidding," Pilate said.

"One of these characters slipped into the Cross and Cork and delivered this envelope without anyone noticing. Never you mind taking the photos without getting seen in the first place."

"They aren't bad at shooting people and escaping, either. So, what do I do about those?" Pilate's eyes flicked to the envelope on Ryder's desk.

"Let me handle it," Ryder said. "I will call her. It's best you don't confront her right now. Can you handle that?"

"Yeah, I think that is…wise."

"Good man," Ryder said. "In the meantime, I have a BOLO out for the gal who shot Falley and your Mister Nice Guy."

"And that's it?"

"Well," Ryder said, clasping his fingers together. "What else do you suggest?"

"Let's go find them. I mean, you know damn well Hilmer Thurman hired these people."

Ryder's face contorted with incomprehension. "What?"

"Well, I mean, who else? You saw how he acted the other day. He's behind this. Who else?"

"Go home. Or to the B&B, sorry. Stay frosty and let me handle this," he said. "Keep your head on a swivel, and I'll make sure we keep eyes on Kate and she's fully aware. Kids too. Will put the school on stranger danger alert. Okay?"

Pilate grunted, nodding. "One more thing, sheriff."

"What's that?" Ryder asked, bringing his coffee mug to his lips, sipping.

"That gal in the photo with me? She's ummm…coming to visit me here."

Ryder spat coffee all over the envelopes on his desk.

* * *

Hilmer Thurman grunted and spasmed a few seconds. In a moment, he rolled off of Nelda.

"Thanks, honey," he whispered.

"My pleasure," she said, flicking her lighter and inhaling her cigarette.

"It was nice?" he asked, slipping into his pants and tucking in his shirt.

She blew smoke aside, rolling onto her side. Cigarette dangling from her lips, her right breast flopped loosely over her left. She rested her head on her left hand, festooned with hot pink fake fingernails.

"Beats getting fucked on the poker table again. Thanks for bringing me out to the cabin. Whose is it, again? I mean, it's a shitty bed, but still."

He shrugged. "I figure we're both too old to screw on the green felt. Besides, the damn table darn near broke last time."

She chuckled, lifting herself up and leaning against the headboard, her breasts were bright as neon in the small areas her bikini covered.

"It was once owned by Jack Lindstrom's toady, Dick Shefler. But when he went into the penitentiary he sold it to Perry Mostek, who is…"

"Missing," she said, eyebrows arched, a chiclet-toothed smile, cigarette smoke snaking through her teeth.

"You can say it," he said.

"Say what?"

"No, it's okay. We're…closer now. You should know."

"You killed Perry?"

"I sure as hell didn't give him a one-way ticket to Rio," he said, taking the cigarette from her hand and puffing it.

"I wondered," she said as she took the cigarette back, flattered by being let in on the gruesome secret. "Well, the fuck was nice," she said. "All this and the Rib Shack, too."

He nodded, tying his boots.

"I mean, it's like all my prayers have been answered lately," she said, chuckling in satisfaction. "It's too good to be true."

"Yeah, and I'm really sorry," he said.

"What do you mean?" She said, pulling the sheet up over her breasts, suddenly chilly.

"So's you know, I'm sorry about all this," he said, facing away from her.

"All what?"

"All…well," he slid into his jacket and turned to her, his face covered by a strange mask. The absurd sight so jarred her she barely registered the gun in his hand. "The fact you couldn't keep your mouth shut to Ryder, mainly."

Nelda shrieked, the cigarette falling from her mouth, hands raised in pitiful defense.

Chapter Eleven

Ryder looked out across the pond on his acreage, the sound of quail cooing past the mist rising off the water. The sun peeked a few inches over the horizon as he mourned his night of fitful, unrestful sleep. The coffee tasted good this morning, though, and that cheered him a moment. He loved this place and hoped to hand it down to his son one day.

He hoped.

He kicked gently at the dirt beside his Lab mix, Searcher, rousing him from fitful sleep. "Come on, boy," he whispered, heading to the house.

Searcher and Ryder welcomed the smell of bacon cooking. He patted the dog's head, then his wife's behind as he slid past her to sit at the table.

"You still thinkin' what you were thinkin' last night?" she asked, eyes on the bacon and scrambled eggs she multitasked on the range.

Ryder sighed and put his coffee mug on the table, eyeing the busy Delft pattern on the blue china plate before him. "Hmm?"

"Your theory," she said, over her shoulder as she turned the bacon, dodging the painful pops of hot grease it fired at her.

"Was drinking last night," he said, sipping coffee.

"You weren't drunk," she said, forking strips of cooked bacon on a plate lined with a folded paper towel,

"True. I just don't know," he said. "I mean, nobody ever really saw that Mister Nice Guy who kidnapped him in Key West. And this gal? From the gym? Who's to say she's the real deal?"

She scooped up scrambled eggs and laid them on his plate, then slid the bacon onto the table. Searcher whined for a piece, which Ryder gave him without missing a beat. The dog wolfed it down and looked up expectantly for more. Ryder waved the dog off, pointing at his bed in the corner of the kitchen. Dejected, Searcher went over and laid down.

"Well, you did hear her on the phone," she said, warming up his coffee and filling her own plate before sitting down.

Ryder ate a piece of bacon. It had just enough crunch, but plenty of chew to it. She always got breakfast right. "Yeah. But who's to say she's not a confederate of some sort? There's a woman who shot Falley in a church full of witnesses. The one who shot Bob at the air strip? Coulda been a woman or a man."

She sipped her coffee, eyeing him over the rim. "People in town say he talks to himself."

Ryder looked at her, raising an eyebrow. "Yeah, I heard about that. He's definitely an odd duck. Moody as an old steer. But he seems decent. What if this gal is real? The one from the phone who said she got attacked. What if she's real, but not who he thinks she is?"

"Oh my," she said, eyes widening. "You didn't mention that last night."

"It came to me in a dream," he said, chuckling. "Actually not kidding, it did. What if she's the one who kidnapped him?"

"This is so strange, Jer," she said.

"It is that," he said, dipping a piece of toast in his coffee.

"So what are you going to do?"

"Watch him real careful," he said, shrugging. "Nothing else I can do."

* * *

Val bounded across the dining room of the Cross and Cork, hugging Pilate and kissing his neck as Marcy and Cusack looked on, jaws dropping.

Pilate gently pushed her away. "Hello, so good to see you."

Val's smile faded as Pilate turned to introduce his friends to Val. "Marcy, Cusack, this is my friend. My friend Val. From Key West. Where we are friends."

Marcy's smile turned down at the edges. Cusack's eyes laughed in a way the rest of him was afraid to, lest he kindle Marcy's secondhand wrath.

"Oh, nice to meet you," Val said. "I'm, uh, checking in."

Marcy nodded. "Check in's at three."

Cusack tutted and picked up Val's bag by the door. "But we can get you into your room early, not a problem."

"Great," she said. "So, John. You want to show me around town?"

* * *

Kate dropped the kids off at the school, reassuring them they would see their dad again soon. She drove away, heading back towards the college, listening to the radio. Checking the presets and finding all crap she didn't recognize or much care for, so she flipped to the CD player. It had been so long since she had used it, she had no idea what would play.

A familiar old Colin Hay song played. He wailed the chorus, saying his babe gives him everything he needs. John loved Hay, and this song often ended up burned on CDs, back when they were in love. And when people burned CDs for each other.

She reached to punch the eject button, but stopped, instead allowing herself to listen to the warmth of Hay's vocals. Remembering sweet Johnny, Kate pulled off to the side of the road, tears streaming down her face.

* * *

"Oh my God, I don't think that lady likes me," Val said with a nervous chuckle as they got into the car.

"Yeah, that's because she knows Kate, and she's putting it all together, I guess," he said. "Don't worry about it. It's something we'll have to deal with here."

Val nodded, detecting the slight dig from Pilate about her coming to Cross.

"So, how was your flight?"

"Oh, fine."

Pilate started the car, noting the bandage on her forehead. "How's the noggin?"

"Hmm? Oh. It hurts a little bit but much better now."

"Yeah, Officer A was not too happy to hear my plans to come down here."

"Officer Asshole? Why just A?"

"Well, he did help save your life, you remember. I guess that buys him a bit of a rollback from Asshole."

"Fair enough. But why did you tell him?"

"Because he said that they needed to keep me under observation after what happened and I said, 'don't worry about it I'll be out of your jurisdiction for a while.' And it went on from there. Anyway, he's not real happy. He feels like I should stay in Key West so he can, you know, protect me because you know that's what he does, protect people."

"Protect and serve," Pilate added meditatively. "It's kind of a thing, isn't it?"

"Yeah, right, protect and serve. My ass."

He nodded, glancing furtively at every car that passed them to see if he was recognized with a strange woman in the passenger seat.

"So, this is the big town," Val said.

"Yeah. Contain your excitement while I give you the grand tour. Then when those ten minutes are expired we can figure out something else to do."

"Man, this is… wow." Val said, looking around as they cruised slowly towards Main Street. "This is freaking small."

"I warned you this is probably not what you would expect," he said.

"Yeah, I thought it would be, you know, maybe a little bucolic. But this is positively, something, you know, trapped in time from the *Andy Griffith Show*."

"And what's wrong with that?" He said in mock disbelief. "It's okay. Cross has its charms and the college is nice."

"What charms?" She asked.

"Umm, well, you know, it's a great place to grow vegetables."

"That's funny," she said.

"Well, you know, Key West isn't exactly a burgeoning metropolis."

"It does have some interesting people coming through," she said.

"Yeah, that's true. Lot of people. And a lot of weirdos, apparently. I feel bad, about what happened to you. I feel like it's my fault."

Val squeezed his thigh. "It's not your fault. I mean, the nuts rolled downhill to Florida, am I right? That said, thanks for saying that. But I'm fine, John. I'm just worried about you. That's why I'm here. And I also think that maybe you should think real seriously about something."

"Oh?" he said, pointing. "That's the college president's home. And over there, that's the campus."

"Great, love to check that out later. I'm kind of hungry. Are you hungry?"

"Yeah I'm hungry too."

"How about we go eat on campus," she said. "They have good cafeteria food?"

"Is there such a thing? No, let's not eat on campus," Pilate said. "That's probably not a good idea."

"That bad, huh?"

"Let's just say we're in a tiny town and we're very likely to turn a few heads and get tongues wagging."

Val chewed her lower lip. "And maybe run into somebody, hmm?"

"That's a very real possibility, Val. She works there. And again, it may seem rather gauche of me, considering."

Val looked at him. "Considering?"

"She's seen the pictures."

"But from what you told me, you've seen the pictures of her and her friend."

"Yes," he said.

"It's not keeping score, Val. I just think it best if we don't tempt the fates. We'll go somewhere else. In fact, there's a good place over in Goss City."

"How long will it take?"

"It's about a twenty-minute drive, he said.

"John, I'm starving. I didn't get anything to eat on the way down, I was so excited to see you. Isn't there some other place here in town?"

He said, "Well there's the convenience store, which does a good job on pizza."

She shook her head.

"We have a little diner in downtown Cross."

"Oh my god, like a greasy spoon?" she said, excited.

"I haven't checked the grease quotient of the flatware, but I guess for all intents and purposes it is."

"Do they have anything incredibly small town diner-ish? Like, I don't know, like chicken fried chicken or some kind of beef steak or something?"

He laughed. "Yeah, they've got chicken fried steak and other stuff. You sure you want to break training with that kind of crap?"

"Let's go there," she said. "Life's too short and this recent little brush with death has me rethinking drinking green juice and never enjoying a good piece of meat when I get a chance."

"All right, let's get you fed."

* * *

The lunch rush bustled. Toni motioned to Pilate to pick whatever table he'd like. They sat down and Val instantly picked up her flatware, making an exaggerated show of checking its cleanliness.

"See? There's, there's no grease."

"You know I'm a little disappointed," she said.

Toni brought over two ice waters.

"Hi Toni," Pilate said.

"Hi yourself," she said. "You and your niece know what you want?"

Pilate restrained himself from rolling his eyes. "Umm, give us a minute, okay?"

Toni flashed a look of disapproval. "Special's chicken fried steak," she said over her shoulder as she went to the next table.

"Local character," Pilate said, making a dismissive gesture.

"So how have things been here?" Val said.

"Good, if you, you know, like heartbreak and guilt and shouting and things like that."

"No, okay, not so good," she said, "I'm sorry I had anything to do with that."

He said, "Well you know it's evident that both of us have our issues."

Val looked up from the menu.

"I mean Kate and me. And you unfortunately got pulled in."

"Wait a minute. Let's get this straight. I kind of pulled you in too, and that's another reason I'm here. I wanted to look you in the eye and tell you I'm sorry about that."

"Very kind of you to come all this way."

"Well, I'm here to tell you I'm sorry caused you pain but I'm also here to tell you I'm not at all sorry I did it."

"Oh," he said. "Let's look at the menus before Toni comes back and gives me another silent lecture."

"I want the special. It's amazing it's exactly what I wanted. I can't believe this. I've actually never had chicken fried steak."

"It's the coin of the realm here," Pilate said, getting Toni's attention. "Two specials, please."

"So, I'm trying to say that I care about you, John. I always have. And I think we could do some things to get us both to a good place. If you're interested in me," she said.

He leaned forward, his voice above a whisper. "You do realize as flattering as that is, I have a wife and a family, and I'm trying to save my marriage."

"I don't get that impression. I don't think anybody gets that impression."

"All right, let's put that aside for a moment. What I am fighting to do most, right now, is to find out who this whack job is who is taking shots at people I care about here in this town and who could very well be connected to the, the asshole who put me in that goddamn oven back in Key West. The one who attacked you."

"That's another reason I'm here. I want to help you with that."

"I don't know what you could do, Val," he said. "You obviously can handle yourself well enough, but I don't know how you being here is going to help."

"Do you want me to leave?" she said, downcast.

"Yes, well, no. Strike that. No, I don't. I don't want you to leave."

"Exactly," she said.

Pilate sighed, leaning back in his chair. "Val, this is such a mess." The bell on the diner door rang. Grant held the door for Kate to enter.

"Oh, this is just fucking great," Simon said.

* * *

"Really, John?" Kate said, folding her arms across her chest. Grant's eyes widened as he took in the scene.

"Hi," Pilate said, though it sounded like a question.

"Yeah hi," she said. "Are you going to introduce me to your friend?" Her face was hard but her eyes gave her away.

"Yeah. Well yeah. Okay, my wife," he cleared his throat, which suddenly felt dry and tight. "Okay. This is my—"

Val set up straight in her chair, turning to look at Kate.

Pilate continued. "This is my friend Val."

"How do you do?" Val said.

Kate ignored Val; her eyes boring into Pilate.

"So, who's he? Your doorman or chauffeur?"

Grant moved forward, coughing nervously into his fist.

"Hi, I'm Grant. I have heard a lot about you."

"Oh? From who? My kids or through pillow talk with my wife?" Pilate's voice vibrated with adrenaline.

"Not nice, John. Not nice at all," Simon said, barely registering in Pilate's brain, awash as it suddenly was in anger.

"Fuck, John, what are you doing?" Kate said.

"We were attempting to try the special. Care to join us?"

Toni, who was making no attempt to hide her fascination with this scene as she stood behind the counter, dropped her pen into a diner's iced tea, her mouth slack.

"No I don't think we will," Kate said. "But I will take your advice on the special. Toni, two."

Toni nodded, mouth still agape. The diner had fallen as silent as a graveyard at midnight. Nobody wanted to miss a syllable.

"So," Kate said, turning back to Val. "You're the trainer, right?"

Val nodded.

"So you came all the way to Nebraska to give my husband a training session?"

"Well, no. John is my friend. I've been concerned about him. You know, kinda like the way Grant seems to be real concerned about you just about now."

Kate took a step closer to Val, who tensed slightly in her seat, slowly swinging her legs from underneath the table as if in preparation to rise and go toe to toe.

"I think I know you're more than friends because frankly I've seen a lot more of you than you think, missy. All the way down to the way you shave your twat."

Now, Val's mouth fell open.

Pilate raised his voice and his hands. "All right, I think that's about enough of this shit."

Grant took a halting step forward.

"Hey, elbow patches," Pilate growled. "I don't think this is the place for you to say a word. Back up."

Grant took a step back as directed. "Look, I don't want any trouble, guys, I..."

"And you'll have no trouble if you shut the fuck up right now, professor."

Kate shot Pilate a filthy glare.

"This is obviously something we have to work on between ourselves," he said, looking at Kate. "In private."

Kate nodded, her eyes fixed on his.

"Yeah that's definitely what we need to talk about," her voice hoarse.

"All right, fine. I'd like to see you tonight. You and me. Drop the kids at the babysitters and you and I will talk like grown-ups. Can we all agree to that?"

"Sure, do you know where I live?" Kate said.

"I should, considering I paid off the mortgage. Six o'clock."

Kate nodded, looking at Val. "Okay, see you there then."

Pilate nodded. "Come on Val, we're leaving."

Petulantly, Val turned back to her plate. "I didn't finish my lunch."

"Val? Let's go."

The pair moved past Kate and Grant, Kate discreetly checking out Val's muscular build. Val nodded, smiling at Kate.

Outside, Val groaned. "Oh my God, that was the worst."

"Yeah I know. I'm sorry you had to go through that."

"I'm sorry too, that you felt the need to schedule a date with her tonight," Val said.

"Date?"

"What the fuck, man?" Val said.

"Look I need an hour or two to talk to her and get some things ironed out. I will see you right after. We can have a late dinner. Whatever you like."

"Fine," she said, walking away.

"What are you doing?"

"I'm going to the bed-and-breakfast and see if they have anything to eat."

"I'll go with you," Pilate said. "They have stew."

"No, that's okay," she said. "I'll see you tonight when you get back."

Pilate stood on the sidewalk watching Val trundle up the hill towards Cusack's. He desperately wanted to turn and look inside the diner to see if Kate and Grant were watching but resisted the urge.

"John, if you're getting hard watching two women fight over you..." Simon said.

The quick whoop of a police siren made him jump. He turned to see Ryder's Dodge ram pickup roll up.

"Get in, John. Looks like we've got another shooting," Ryder said.

"Shit," Pilate said.

"This is becoming a thing," Pilate said, sliding into the passenger seat, happy to make a getaway.

* * *

"So, who's the latest victim of my fan club?"

"Hard to say."

"Okay, I assume you'll tell me. Destination?"

"Spy Bluff," Ryder said, doing a u-turn on Main Street.

"Spy Bluff? What's that?"

"Just about the only profitable enterprise Hilmer Thurman's got left," he said.

"Meth?"

"Nope," Ryder said. "There's not much meth production going on up there anymore. We cleared out the last of the toothless and ruthless a while back, and you helped when they shot up the jail with us inside it. Old Hilmer borrowed some Minnesota muscle to take over the Grayson clan's good old fashion marijuana operation."

"Pot? I thought it was legal most places or getting there?"

"Legalization has done nothing to diminish the black market. In fact, violence is a lot worse now," he said.

"So what happened?"

"Got a call from Trooper Hulsey saying there were some ruckus up near Spy Bluff," he said as they passed the town limits and onto the state highway. "Tell you more in a minute." He reached for his radio and told the dispatcher to alert Hulsey he was enroute. "Actually, let's hold off chatting until we get to the scene. Sorry. I need to think."

"Fine by me," Simon said. Pilate nodded in agreement, and Ryder accepted the gesture as if it were meant for him.

Fifteen silent minutes later, they pulled off the highway and ventured down a series of direct roads. Soon they pulled off the road and onto tracks worn down by four wheelers. A mile in, they parked next to Hulsey's state trooper patrol vehicle, a crime scene van and an ambulance.

"Here's where we get out," Ryder said. "We're going to hook up in about a quarter mile. Can't go any further in my truck."

"Jeez, this is some uncharted territory," Pilate said. "I can't believe I've lived here this long and didn't even know about it."

"Well, that's the way they want it. In fact, people who know about it generally know well enough to stay the hell out of here. This is not a place where a badge carries a lot of weight, to be honest."

"I see," Pilate said as they walked in the trail made by four-wheeler ruts.

"As a former constable, you know damn well we're understaffed countywide. Sheriffs and local PDs stretched thin. So it's an area we tend to stay away from now that all that money they set aside back in the eighties to root out pot dried up. Something we look the other way on. Except this." He spat out his toothpick. "Can't look away from this."

"Dang, don't you have a four-wheeler or something?"

"Like I said. Budgets."

The area was thick with pine, oaks, and assorted scrub vegetation. Pilate decided it was definitely where he would put a clandestine pot grow if alcoholism ever lost its allure. Remote, rough terrain, and anybody on Spy Bluff can see lowlanders coming for miles.

"Was that gal walking down the street a friend of yours?"

"I have learned after knowing you a while that you rarely ask a question without already knowing the answer, sheriff."

"Fair."

About fifteen minutes later they arrived on the scene. Hulsey, another trooper, a crime scene tech with a large camera and two paramedics—Burl and Story, as Pilate remembered— looked down at the scene.

"Hi Mr. Pilate," Story said. "Long time no see."

Pilate nodded at her. "You full-fledged now?"

"Yup," she beamed, "Training is over. I'm full time."

Burl nodded. "She's running rings around me."

Pilate mustered a weak smile, turning to the body.

The body of a young woman lay face down underneath a pine tree, tattooed arms tied behind her back. She had blonde hair and was clad in shorts and a tank top. A flowery purse lay beside her. A red, round hole stained her tank top.

"Shot in the back, execution style," Hulsey said, batting at some flies that descended around the body.

"Oh God," Pilate said, stomach churning.

"Rigor?"

Hulsey nodded at Ryder. "Yeah, Burl and Story checked her over. Been dead a few hours. Got an anonymous call telling us to have somebody to come up here because there's something nice being served to the bobcats."

"Ugh," Pilate said. "How long has she been out here, you think?"

"Looks to me she couldn't be any more than ten hours dead so that indicates to me somebody got her last night. Poor thing is starting to smell, as you can tell. We were getting ready to turn her over."

Ryder nodded. "Do it."

Burl and Story slipped latex gloves on.

"You okay?" Burl asked his young counterpart.

"You know better than that," she said.

"Okay, okay," he said. "Just checking."

The pair gently turned the woman's corpse on her back, gasping when her upturned face revealed a demonic visage.

"Holy shit," Hulsey said. "Is that a mask?"

"It appears so," Ryder said.

* * *

"Well, the Halloween getup's not all," Hulsey said.

"Oh?" Pilate said. Vacantly staring at the mask and gore.

"It's what we found in her purse," he nodded at a spot a few feet away. "It was laying over there, about ten feet away. Looks like she dropped it before they executed her."

Ryder whistled through his teeth. "I'll be damned. That looks an awful lot like the gun that shot Falley."

"That it does, sheriff," Hulsey said, holding the gun, bagged and tagged, up for inspection. "It had two rounds in it. Um, there's more."

"What?" Ryder said.

"There's also your book about the murders here in Cross," Hulsey said, holding up a well-worn, plastic-bagged paperback. Pilate's author photo beamed from the back cover.

"So much younger then," Simon said.

"Oh, nice," Pilate said. "That's wicked nice."

"Nice?" Ryder said, cocking an eye at Pilate.

"Nice-nice."

"Uh huh," Ryder said, looking back at the body. "So I guess you could say I wasn't lying to you when I said it wasn't somebody killed by a member of your fan club. It was actually a member of your fan club who got killed."

"I'm sorry," Pilate said, softly, crouching by the body. Hulsey looked confused. Ryder shot him a *he's not talking to us* look.

"Any ideas?"

"Always. I'll tell you about them but I wanted you to see this. I want you to understand what our stakes are now because what we had before were some nuisances and strangeness. That's annoying. We also see some shootings. That's bad. But this here? What we got now is murder and we have no idea who did it. Only thing I got to go on is this is the area where all the illicit pot growing occurs."

"I see," Pilate said, glancing at the mask.

"The only person is Thurman."

"Shit," Hulsey said. "Since when is he stupid enough to arouse suspicion like this?"

Ryder shrugged.

"Well, I mean, sheriff, he's kept a pretty low profile recently," Hulsey added.

Pilate looked up at the men. "Are we going to…you know?"

"Look under the mask?" Ryder said. "Yup. Story," he said, a hand behind him. She quickly put a pair of latex gloves in his hand. He snapped them on and crouched on the other side of the body.

Pilate started to rise.

"Where you going?" Ryder asked.

"Nowhere," Pilate said, settling back on his haunches.

Ryder reached under the chin of the mask and gently lifted it off her face. The blonde hair came off with it.

'Oh," Ryder said, whistling again. "Sorry, honey."

"A wig," Pilate whispered.

Ryder lifted the mask and wig off, and handed them to Hulsey, who dropped them into a brown paper bag. Her true hair color was dark brown.

The woman's face was contorted in a sickening grimace, a red bandanna tied around her eyes.

"Oh Jesus," Pilate gasped. "Blindfolded."

Ryder leaned back as the crime scene photographer took several photos of the face. When he stepped back, Ryder raised a hand over his shoulder. "Story?"

She wordlessly slipped a pair of rounded-tip trauma scissors into his hand. Ryder slid the scissors between the woman's temple and the bandana, shearing it in two. He handed the scissors back to Story, his eyes fixed on the body.

"In the late 19th and early 20th centuries, it was widely believed that the eye recorded the last image seen before death," Ryder said. "It was a popular plot device in fiction of the time, to the extent that police photographed the victims' eyes in several real-life murder investigations, in case the theory was true."

Ryder's drawing out of the examination of the decaying body with his oddly timed commentary made Pilate's chest tighten. Sweat rivulets raced down his side into the material of his shirt.

"The concept has been thoroughly debunked as a forensic method. All the same, we are going to take a look." He pulled the red bandana away from the cold face, revealing glassy eyes, open wide. Pilate could only conjure the word *astonishment.*

"Her last moments had to be sheer terror," Hulsey said.

"She knew," Ryder said. "As soon as they tied her up and put the blindfold on her. She had a horrible ride out here. I imagine she was begging for her life by the time they put this sick fucking mask on her, pushed her to her knees and shot her."

"Oh God," Pilate said, words strangling in his throat.

"John, don't you dare vomit here," Ryder said. "Go over there."

"No, you don't understand. I know this girl. *She* saw *me* vomit."

Ryder's head snapped to Pilate. He grasped him by the shoulders and brought them both to their feet.

"What in the hell are you saying?"

"The vomit. She works at the grocery store in Cross," Pilate said, trembling. "Oh god, the last time I saw her was when I vomited all over the sidewalk outside the store."

* * *

Pilate cradled a paper cup of water Burl had wordlessly slipped into his hand.

"I made some calls," Ryder said, looking at his notebook. "That gal's name is Nora Potter. She blew into town about a month ago with her boyfriend, and she started working part time at the store. Boyfriend is MIA. That's all we know. Stew, the manager, said she showed up one day, all spacey and strange and asking for her smock and name tag. He told her she was nuts, then she said the owner hired her."

"Holy shit," Hulsey said, snapping his fingers. "Greg Bartley? The owner of the store."

"Bartley? The community theater guy over in Goss City? He's the straightest arrow in the county." Ryder said, one boot on the chrome bumper of the ambulance. "Well, at least for a community theater guy."

"This doesn't make sense," Pilate said, looking over his shoulder at the crime scene investigator packing up his gear.

"Well, wait. Maybe Bartley is involved, look at the evidence," Hulsey said.

"I don't follow," Ryder said, helping himself to an ambulance paper towel to wipe sweat from the inner band of his hat.

Hulsey, nonplussed, raised his arms skyward in exasperation. "The mask."

Pilate and Ryder stared wordlessly.

"Theater guy. Masks," Hulsey said excited. "This gal and her missing boyfriend were weirdoes, right? Like actors? Kinda flaky?"

Ryder put a hand on his shoulder. "Okay, Lestrade, we'll look into that."

"Just saying," Hulsey said, checking his phone. "I gotta roll in a minute."

"Well, there's also the possibility somebody's yanking Bartley's chain. Bartley's a total civilian. Wouldn't know how to handle the right kind of pressure from unsavory types."

"And there it is," Pilate said. "Okay, so let's assume that's the case. Thurman is pressuring him to put this poor girl in his employ. But if she's one of Thurman's crew, why would he do this to her?"

"Maybe she got mouthy," Ryder said. "Or once she dutifully took some pot shots at people around town he decided she was a loose end."

"Wait a minute, Thurman's not the pot baron around here, is he?" Hulsey asked.

"Well, no," Ryder said. "He *was* the meth king, but that's been wiped out since Mr. Pilate here stumbled in and knocked over his operation."

Pilate shrugged. "I have a way of doing that."

"Our local pot lord is an old boy named Jerome Halt. He's not your stereotypical hippie pot guy. No sir. This guy has a dark streak in him. Acts like Colonel Kurtz. Now, most places, meth and pot production go together like peanut butter and chocolate. And I can tell you what, back in the day when Ollie Olafson and his buddies tried to take over Jerome's pot operation, they got their snouts swatted. They backed off and focused on the meth stuff. Gave Jerome a wide berth."

"Maybe that's changed, since our recent shotgun diplomacy," Pilate said.

"Thurman's been struggling for relevance since," Ryder said. "His Minnesota mafia friends are bleeding him dry, I suspect. Taking their meth losses outta Thurman's more legit business interests."

"The Brown Betty," Pilate said. "The Tin Roof Rib Shack."

"Don't forget the No-Tell Motel on Highway 9," Hulsey chimed in.

"True," Ryder said.

"So," Pilate downed the water and crumpled up the cone-shaped paper cup, tossing it in a small trash bin in the ambulance. "Maybe he's making a play for the pot trade, to get that cash flow."

"Go on," Ryder said.

"Well, you said the meth operation got burned out. Maybe Thurman decided that it's a lot easier to steal a profitable going concern than to rebuild one that got burned to the ground."

"That's not a crazy idea," Hulsey said. "It's widely believed he owes a pretty penny to Minnesota, after all."

"Yup. This is interesting. He'd have to be pretty desperate to go toe to toe with Jerome, though." Ryder said. "And I don't understand why he would do this."

He gestured at the paramedics picking up the corpse, ensconced in a white body bag, they had carried down to the ambulance. "Or to be more precise, I don't understand coming up here, especially if he wanted to take over the pot trade."

"Well, what if Thurman was the guy who sent Mister Nice-Nice to see me, and in turn, ordered this gal to shoot people all over town?" Pilate said.

Ryder scratched under his hat. "I don't know, you may be grasping at smoke here."

"Think about it," Pilate said. "Destabilizing the situation? Drawing attention to the pot operation to bring the heat? Maybe he's putting pressure on Halt like he did Bartley, and plenty of other folks prior? Maybe he's telling Halt he can make this heat go away if he sells out."

"Okay," Ryder said. "That makes sense, in a circuitous sorta way."

"But why go to the trouble to kill me? To make these people act like they have some kind of Jack Lindstrom cult revenge thing going?"

"Hmm," Ryder stroked his chin and flipped a thoroughly chewed toothpick in the bin. "Well, he hates your guts, for one thing. Guess he wanted you in the grave to keep your Scooby Doo curiosity from getting involved somehow. I dunno."

"I tend to do that," Pilate said. The men were quiet a moment, looking at their feet, lost in thought.

"And maybe, just maybe, there really is a weird cult thing and Thurman's using it to his advantage."

Hulsey nodded. "Seems more likely. I mean the 'net has all kinds of weird shit going on. People who are either deluded or stupid enough to think elections are controlled by the Illuminati, or that Satanists and Hollywood movie stars run a worldwide child sex ring."

"It's a truly messed up, dumbed down world," Ryder said. "Personally, I blame the Democrats."

Pilate ignored the remark. "So how far from here is the illicit pot growing?" Pilate asked.

Ryder slipped a fresh cinnamon toothpick into his mouth. "Spy Bluff is right over that ridge there, about another mile. Whole operation's up there. Not saying that this is as bad as northern California, but it's certainly plenty heavy enough for people to make a living around here. And a ton of people, mostly migrants, come work the harvest for quick cash."

"Plenty of them disappear, too," Hulsey said. "Sad. We all too often get frantic calls at the barracks from folks in Central American countries looking for lost relatives and such. Most of them are working in the meat packing industry, but more than a few have been found dead around here over the years."

"Why?"

"People get mouthy. Or greedy. Or see too much. Beyond that," Ryder said, moving aside as Story and Burl pushed the gurney carting the remains of Nora Potter into the ambulance. "John, you know this as well as I do. Some people will kill you for the gold in your teeth."

* * *

Twenty minutes after departing the murder scene, Ryder broke the silence. "I need to know where your lady friend was last night," he said, eyes on the road.

"That's not very damn funny," Pilate said.

"You see me laughing? I'm asking you a serious question. When did she get in and where is she now?"

"Is she really a person of interest?" Pilate said, mouth slack, looking at Ryder's hawkish profile.

"Yeah, she is. So are you. So is everybody in this town. But it does seem kind of interesting that your lady friend who had a run-in with these very same thugs is here in town and at the same time— almost simultaneously, mind you, somebody's turned up dead."

"That is unvarnished horseshit," Pilate said.

"I'm not finished. And that certain somebody is almost certainly the person who was part of this little fan club of yours going around shooting the good people of this town. So I got to wonder if there might be some kind of connection."

"Well, yeah I think there is a connection," Pilate scoffed, his pulse quickening, his vision tunneling. "I think the connection is me and I don't know what to tell you. All I know is everything in my world is the god damn encyclopedia entry for the word entropy."

"That does seem to be the state of affairs Mr. Pilate," Ryder said. "Getting late. You think she's over at the B&B, waiting on you?"

"Yeah, but I…have to be somewhere else," Pilate said, heart sinking.

"Drop you somewhere?"

"Just the B&B. My car's there."

"I'll give you a little head start before I go see your friend."

"Most kind. You going to arrest her?"

Ryder snorted. "Should I?"

"I am the recipient of the legendary Chinese curse," Pilate muttered.

"Interesting times, indeed," Ryder said, shifting the toothpick to the other side of his mouth.

* * *

"Hi," Pilate said after standing on the porch a moment, psyching himself up.

"You knocked," she said, partly a question.

"Well, I uh, figured," he started to say.

She nodded. "Probably wise. It's strange is all," Kate said, standing aside to let him in.

"Kids?"

"At Mrs. Molloy's. I'll get them later," she said, running a hand through her hair. She wore a denim shirt with pearl buttons and Levis.

"I didn't know it was John Mellencamp day," he said.

"What?"

"Never mind," he said. "You look good. How are you?"

She sat on the couch. "Thanks. I've been better. How about you?"

Pilate felt eerie, wary formality hanging over them, as if they were people who met at a fender bender, waiting for the police.

"Honestly, I'm tired," he said, sitting in the overstuffed chair across form the couch. "Just got back from Spy Rock."

"Spy Rock? You mean Spy Bluff," she said, her left eyebrow raised in mild surprise.

"Right," he said.

"Why were you up there? That's not a good place to go, John."

"Murder. Someone who is tangled up in this whole mess with me and the guy who tried to cook me like a Swanson dinner."

"Are you serious? He was murdered at Spy Bluff?" She said, leaning forward.

"Not exactly," Pilate said. "It was a woman, the same woman who shot Reverend Falley and probably Bob Hayes. Execution style, out in a field not far from Spy Rock, er Bluff."

"Jesus, and you had to go why?"

Pilate looked at her as if she knew the answer.

She nodded. "Ryder?"

"Yeah."

"That's awful. You saw the body?"

"Yes."

"You need a drink."

"Not sure I need one, but I sure as hell want one," he said.

"Well, your backyard bar fell over, but I have some vodka in the freezer."

"I'm surprised. You're not much of a vodka drinker."

She looked down.

"Oh," Pilate said. "I see. He likes vodka."

Without looking up, she said "Do you want some or not?"

"Yes, please."

Pilate followed her into the kitchen. She took two glasses from the cabinet and pulled a bottle of Stoli from the freezer.

"Half empty," Pilate said. "He has good taste."

She poured them both a double. "Maybe it's half full, John." She slugged back the vodka and set the glass down on the counter.

Pilate cocked his head in surprise, looking at her dark brown eyes, which were leveled at his. He downed the vodka and put the glass down.

"I'm not sorry," she said.

Pilate pushed her against the fridge, his lips on hers. He felt her stiffen, then she kissed him back, her tongue teasing his. Pilate ran his hands over her breasts, seizing the shirt on either side of the pearl buttons. He pulled them apart, the snaps giving little resistance. She grunted, her hands fumbling with his belt. Their breath came in heavy, loud gasps between kisses and moans. Pilate maneuvered Kate to the kitchen table, stripping the shirt off her. He was surprised to see she wore no bra, and when her jeans came off she had no underwear either. He stopped a second and looked at her.

"It's laundry day, you fucker," she said, kissing him again.

"Are we doing this here?"

His belt unfastened, she made quick work of unbuttoning his pants and pulling down his underwear. She stroked him a moment, her eyes on his.

"I'll take that as a yes," he said, breathless, as she pulled him into herself.

Chapter Twelve

"So," Pilate said, lying beside Kate in their bed. "Got anything to eat?"

"You're not staying for dinner. You had enough anyway," Kate said, leaning up on her elbow to look at the time. "Shit, I'm going to be late picking up the kids."

Pilate pulled her closer. "Well, we can pay the overtime."

She gently pulled away from him and got out of bed. "This wasn't supposed to happen, you rat."

"You're the one who had no underwear on."

"No, I mean us."

"What? Separating?"

"No, John. Marrying. We were supposed to move on after we got through the mess with Jack Lindstrom and Ollie Olafson. You were going to move on with your life, but…" she sat back on the bed, at the footboard, out of reach.

"But, Peter," Pilate said. "Are you saying if you hadn't got pregnant?"

"Please don't say it like you're accusing me. You helped in the situation, as I recall."

He nodded, hands raised in contrition. "True. Sorry."

"We moved too fast," she said. "We got thrown together in a life and death situation. It was a crazy roller coaster and we clung to each other for dear life."

"My god, Kate," Pilate said, almost a gasp. "I do love you."

"John, do you think for one minute I don't love you? You are the kindest, bravest man I know."

"Don't forget sexy," Pilate said.

"Yeah, you're kind of sexy. But that's not enough. You want to live on an island. For me it's the farm. Teaching and raising my kids in a safe place."

"A safe place where we have both nearly been killed at least a half dozen times in the past few years?"

"You know what I mean."

"What do you mean?"

She crawled back into bed, her lips touching his chest, then his mouth. She was gentle this time, less the frenzy of passion, more an expression of tenderness. "I love you, and I always will, but I think we both know we want different things out of life."

Pilate felt his chest tighten, the brief beginnings of renewed tumescence beneath Kate's body faded.

"Please don't take my kids away from me, Kate."

Her eyes welled with tears. "I will, never, ever do that to you," she said. "No matter what."

He kissed her tears and pulled her gently to him. They made love again, both wondering if it were the last time.

* * *

As Pilate and Kate dressed, they agreed to revisit the subject of their separation when things were calmer. He filled her in on the need for Ryder's reserve deputies to keep track of her and the kids for a while. Kate nodded to the gun safe in the corner.

"I guess the shotgun will get a little air again," she said.

"Be careful," he said, pulling her in for an embrace.

"I think that's my line," she said. Kate stepped back and looked at his face, touching her hand to his cheek. "This is not your fault."

"I know," he scoffed. "I mean, really? How can I control what weirdoes and hillbilly crime lords do?"

"I mean us," she said. "It's not my fault, either. It's what happened."

"Do you think we can ever be friends? After this?"

"No. Not just friends. Devoted friends," she kissed his cheek. "I love this face."

* * *

Val slapped Pilate, hard.

It was actually very close to a punch, he thought, as he reeled from the energy of the blow.

"You went over there and fucked her?" she said. "I can't even believe this." She paced around her room in the B&B. "After that goddamn wannabe cowboy sheriff practically accused me of murder?"

"Who said I fucked her?" Pilate said.

She closed the distance between them, theatrically sniffing the air. "You smell like sex, John. You stink of that woman."

"Yup, you probably shoulda had some shower sex at the end with ol' Kate, there, Johnny," Simon said.

He exhaled, biting his lip. "It's complicated, Val."

"Why did I fly all the way out to this hellhole?" She shouted. "You fucker. I am so stupid. I actually cared about you. I was trying to be your friend."

"Okay, okay, please keep your voice down," he said.

"Wrong answer, shitheel," she shouted. "John Pilate, the shitheel, is in this room after fucking around on his girlfriend!"

"Val," he said, raising his voice to the rung on the ladder below shouting himself. "Stop this right now. Let's talk like adults."

Her face was as crimson as her most intense training session, chest heaving, hands on hips. Val inhaled deeply, looking at the ceiling, trying to regain her composure.

"Okay," she said, continuing to breathe deeply.

"Thank you. Now, what do you want to talk about first, the murder or the woman who just asked me for a divorce?"

"If true, she asked for a divorce in the absolute nicest way possible," she said, folding her arms.

"I know, but," he searched his mind for analogy. "It's like the energy left over in one of those tops you had when you were a kid, you know? The kind with the plunger on top? It stores up energy in the shaft and keeps going a while, even after you stop working it?"

"What the fuck does that even mean?" her voice rising again. "And it sounds like she worked your shaft pretty good."

"That's what the kids call a sick burn, John," Simon said.

"Okay. Let's switch to the easier topic, the police inquiry."

"You mean the interrogation?" she looked at her phone. "Can I get a flight out tonight?"

"Probably not. Omaha's not exactly Chicago, or Dallas," Pilate said.

"That's academic, anyway," she said, putting her phone down. "Sheriff Red Rider told me not to leave town."

"Oh, shit," Pilate said, sitting heavily on the bed.

"Yeah, as in deep shit, which I apparently flew into by trying to help a shitheel friend. Get out of my room, John. I've had enough of you."

"Val, I am sorry about all of this, but you must understand, it's not," he started.

"If you say this is not your fault, I'll kick you in the crotch so hard you'll have fuzzy new eyes," she said, her finger poking his chest. "Get the fuck out of my room. I need you out of here."

"Okay. Can I check on you later?" He ducked, the TV remote narrowly missing his head and clattering against the wall.

"Message received. A definite maybe," he said, hand on the doorknob. "Nothing good on, anyway," he muttered, in retreat.

* * *

"I don't think she had anything to do with it," Pilate said.

Ryder nodded, hands at ten and two in the Ram, eyes forward, hidden by aviator sunglasses, heading back out to Spy Bluff.

"Val," Pilate added. "I think she's just a little…"

"Obsessed with you?" he said.

"No, not at all," Pilate scoffed.

"Though she may have had a more serious concussion than we thought," Simon said.

"So it's normal for a casual acquaintance to fly out to the sticks just to see how he's doing?"

"Well," Pilate folded his arms. "It's complicated."

"Uh-huh," Ryder said. "Well, she was defensive in our little discussion, but yeah, I'm not thinking she had a hand in the murder."

"Good."

"However," Ryder said, holding up his hand, index finger pointing at the Ram's headliner. "I have not completely crossed her off my list."

"And...neither have you, John," Simon said.

"Why?"

"See previous portion of this conversation. She's acting unusual, and there is nobody who can corroborate that she was at the B&B when the murder occurred."

"Oh come on, as if Val, who has never even been to the state of Nebraska before, would know her way around, never mind be a stone killer?"

Ryder chuckled. "You got me there. So tell me, what's your wife think of this friend of yours?"

Pilate's mind switched back to last night, with Kate in the kitchen. "No comment."

"Fair enough," Ryder said. "Okay, listen, we are going into the heart of darkness in about another twenty minutes."

He had explained when he got in the truck that they were going to pay a visit to Jerome Halt, putative head of the Cross area illegal pot growers association.

"Anything I should know?"

"Just that we are not actually going to the grow, which suits me fine. Rough terrain trying to pay him an unannounced visit."

"I don't follow?" Pilate said.

"Well, I have no interest in stumbling over his various booby traps."

"Seriously?"

"Yup. Fishhooks on fishing line strewn between trees, trip wires connected to camouflaged twelve-gauge shotgun shells—kind of a poor man's Claymore."

"Charming."

"Yeah, and then there's the garden variety rat and bear traps. Those'll ruin your whole day. So, ol' Jerome is meeting us down near the trail head."

"Over by where the body was?"

"Not very far off, yes sir," Ryder said.

"Okay, so what are we looking for this guy to tell us?"

"I want to look in his eye and see if he's already part of Hilmer Thurman's operation or merely an interested party. Keep in mind, he's paranoid."

"So I should?"

"Keep quiet," he said. "Unless."

"Unless what?"

"Unless you have something worthwhile to say," Ryder said, chuckling again.

"Do I ever?"

"I don't know. What did your wife say last night?"

* * *

The Army surplus Humvee dominated the paltry width of the dirt road. It was dead center, its wheels practically in the ditches on either side of the narrow road that it blocked completely.

"Think we can get around that thing?" Pilate asked.

"I'm pretty sure there's no need," Ryder said. "Look."

On closer inspection, the Humvee had a roof but no doors. A bald, bearded man of about sixty stepped out, clad in green army pants, black boots, and a sleeveless t-shirt. He walked to the front of the Humvee, resting one hand on his hip, the other on the butt of a holstered handgun.

"Colonel Kurtz, I presume?" Pilate whispered.

Ryder nodded wordlessly, stopping the Ram about five feet from Jerome Halt.

"That guy is huge."

"He is a substantial man. Let's say hello," Ryder said, exiting the Ram and walking to the front, one hand on the truck's Ram hood ornament, the other resting on the butt of his Colt.

Pilate leaned back on the hood of the Ram, instantaneously jerking away from it.

"That hood's hot," Ryder said out of the side of his mouth.

"No shit," Pilate muttered.

"Sheriff," Halt said.

"Hey there, Jerome," Ryder said. "How you be?"

He gestured with his head, bobbing it side to side. "You know, same old, same old."

"I hear ya."

"Who's your friend?" Halt said, cocking an eyebrow at Pilate.

"This here's one of my departmental consultants. John Pilate."

"Pilate?" Halt said. "Wait a minute. I know you. You're that crazy town constable in Cross, ain't you? You wrote that book?"

Pilate held up his hands in surrender. "You got me. Though I'm retired."

"Just consulting, huh?" Halt said, stroking his lengthy gray beard.

"Yeah, whatever I can do to help."

Halt's gaze shifted to Ryder. "So he consulting on dead bodies up here in my zone? You thinking I know something about it?"

Ryder shrugged. "Do you?"

He snorted. "Shit no. And I think you know that," he pointed at Ryder.

"You telling me what I know?" Ryder said.

"Well, no," Halt said, shaking his head. "But I don't know what this has to do with me."

"You said a body was dumped in your…um…zone, so here I am. This is me," he jerked a thumb at himself, then pointed a finger at Halt. "The county sheriff, asking you questions. I think that's reasonable."

He shook his head. "I don't know shit about it, sheriff."

"What do you know?" Ryder said.

"I just said I don't know shit."

"Tell me what you do know, Jerome," Ryder said, slipping a toothpick in his mouth. "And do me the courtesy of taking your hand off the butt of that pistol."

Halt looked at Ryder blankly a moment before his face broke into a smile. "Alrighty," he said, lifting his hand off the gun with exaggerated care and folding his arms under the end of his voluminous beard. "I know somebody dumped a body not far from here the other night. Some gal."

"You know her? She a trimmigrant?" Ryder asked, rolling the toothpick from one side of his mouth to the other with his tongue.

"No. Ain't nobody I ever heard of."

"Didn't work for you?"

"Nuh-uh."

Ryder adjusted his aviator sunglasses. "How's business been lately?"

Halt spat into the dust. "Ditchweed ain't nearly the cash crop the ignorant dickheads in Lincoln promised. But we're getting by."

"Supplementing your hemp income with some of the high dollar stuff?" Ryder said.

"Nebraska nonsense pays the bills," he shrugged. "Just ain't been all that, and the medical cannabis business is so corporatized—don't get me started."

"So, you don't grow cannabis?" Pilate asked. "Seems like it would be pretty easy to do if you're already selling hemp."

He harrumphed and looked at Ryder. "Sheriff, is there anything else?"

"So who do you think the girl was?"

"Shit, probably a college student. You know they get out here and run into the wrong people."

"Your people?" Ryder said.

"No," he said. "Not my people."

"Well, it is your zone, Jerome, and I know for a fact not one damn thing occurs up here without you knowing about it."

"I heard about the gal 'cause I heard you and the ambulance folks all on the police radio."

"And you heard what?"

Halt tsked, rubbing his bald head with both hands, then folded his arms again.

"That you guys had a dead girl out here."

"And you didn't come out to see?"

"No, not my business somebody shot some college girl in the back."

"In the back?" Ryder said. "We never said that on the radio."

Halt leaned back on the Humvee, a small smile peeking out of his beard. "Sheriff, can we talk turkey now? I think we are done dancing."

Ryder nodded.

Halt shifted his gaze to Pilate. "Mister, most people who smoke weed, even that fancy legal shit you probably enjoy from them dispensaries? They got no idea how much blood is fertilizing those plants."

"Meaning?"

"Meaning we kept the peace for a whole lotta years until you and yours wiped out Hilmer Thurman's meth operation."

"Well, that's a good thing, isn't it? I mean, for somebody who is competing."

"You read history, constable?"

"Retired. Yes," Pilate said.

"So you heard of the Molotov–Ribbentrop Pact?"

"Of course. Early in World War Two. The nonaggression pact between Stalin and Hitler. They agreed to stay out of each other's affairs."

"And how did that work out?" Halt asked.

"Hitler got stupid and attacked Russia."

"Operation Barbarossa," he said. "I believe that bit of genius— and letting the Brits escape at Dunkirk—cost him the war. I got satellite. Watch a lot of History Channel."

"Fair enough," Pilate said. "So Hilmer Thurman broke your pact?"

"Let's say he's suddenly desperate to get ahold of my little…hemp operation, and he's starting to make trouble. Executing gals who used to work for me—and yeah, I lied. She worked for me a while. Her and that crazy tweaker boyfriend. Anyway, they got in hock with Thurman, far as I can see, and became spies for him."

"So," Pilate said, searching for the right words. "He co-opted these two and for that you are no longer keeping an uneasy peace?"

"In a manner of speakin'," he said.

"Sure doesn't look good for you, Jerome," Ryder said. "I mean, I'm thinking maybe you coulda killed this gal. Did you?"

"I never laid a hand on Nora Potter," he said. "She gave me the creeps. Her and her weirdo boyfriend Nick—but his real name's Hal. They did their work okay but got sloppy. She was always going on about this whole conspiracy with that dead college president fella, Jack Lindstrom. In fact, I think she was reading your book."

"You didn't answer my question," Ryder said. "And again, keep your arms folded away from that hog leg or I will ask former Constable Pilate to disarm you."

Halt nodded. Pilate felt his chest tighten up; his stomach rolled.

"No sir. They bailed outta here a few weeks ago. I said good riddance. My other trimmers didn't like 'em around. They were acting like they were part of some satanic cult or some shit—had these funny masks and made the satanic hand gestures. Not the best thing for morale, especially with my Catholic folks from south of the border. They have no truck with that Satan shit. And I'm pretty sure Hal got meth on the regular from somewhere."

"Masks?" Pilate asked.

"Yeah, like some kind of Guy Fawkes mask. But it looks kinda devilish."

"Hal got a last name?" Ryder asked.

Halt bit his lip, thinking. "Olson, might have been. No, Owen. Hal Owen. That sounds right, I think. I mean, I didn't exactly get his social security number."

"So when did you last see them?" Ryder asked.

"I haven't seen him in a month or more, but one of trimmers saw her about two or three weeks ago, workin' at old Perry Mostek's store at the check-out. Lord only knows how much money she pulled outta that till."

"Where did they live?"

"When they weren't staying with me at my camp, I think they lived in a van. Rusty old Econoline piece of shit. Parked it at the church parking lot in town."

"Didn't drive it to Spy Bluff?" Pilate asked.

"That sort of thing is simply not done," Halt said.

"Blindfold Express?" Ryder asked.

"I provided transport to work." Halt shrugged. "Ain't no reason anybody works for me needs to know exactly where we be."

"Let's get down to it," Pilate said. "Why is this Potter girl dead?"

Halt shrugged. "She crossed Hilmer is my guess. Maybe she and her boyfriend were playing both sides and got crossways."

"Did you or any of your crew kill her?" Ryder said.

"No," Halt said. "I was as surprised as you. Like I said, she's been working in town for a while now. I had no quarrel with them but didn't want them around. Why hurt her? That brings me heat I don't need," he finished with a meaningful look towards Ryder's badge.

"Then why was she dumped up here?" Pilate asked.

"Well, I think this poor girl was Hilmer's first salvo at me," Halt said. "Our pact is apparently at an end."

"Don't leave town, Jerome," Ryder said. "I mean, don't leave your zone."

"Where would I go?" he said, laughing, climbing back in the Humvee.

* * *

"Tangled web, huh?' Pilate asked Ryder in the Ram, watching Halt reverse the Humvee out of sight in the dust cloud thrown up by its massive tires.

"If it's like I think, I'm pretty sure this is all on Hilmer Thurman," Ryder said. "Though Jerome's fingernails ain't exactly pristine."

"Why do you let him keep operating?"

"Well, to continue the war metaphor, there's a balance of power out here," he said. "And for a long time the meth folks and the pot folks kept an uneasy peace. I knew we'd eventually have to deal with all of this. In fact, we've been planning a little operation on Jerome's crops. But priorities change, budgets go to hell, and nosy types from out of town get in the way."

"As in, John Pilate types?"

"Yup."

"But why the shooting? Bob Hayes at the airport. Rev. Falley at the church," Pilate said.

"Yes, it's quite the two-pipe problem," Ryder said, starting the engine.

"Next moves?"

"Gonna see if I can find this Hal Owen guy. See if his story shakes out with Jerome's," he turned the Ram around, pointing it towards town. "Counting on him being dumb as a dial tone."

Pilate turned the conversation over in his head. "So what was the 'blindfold express' thing you guys were talking about?"

"The more traffic back and forth to your patch, the higher your threat profile for getting busted. Growers want their folks to stay put and process the harvested weed. So, anytime the people came and went—and I assure you it would not be often—they'd be blindfolded. SOP."

"I see," Pilate said.

"Yeah, you don't want to get on Jerome's bad side at harvest time. Or ever. I've heard stories. Nothing I can prove, but not pleasant. One guy who we pulled in on public drunk was a trimmer up there a few years ago. We offered him a deal if he could give us anything on Jerome, a recent disappearance in particular. This kid started shaking, real bad."

"Oh?"

"Yeah, we got him some Oreos and a Coke. Eventually he calmed down and told us one day that one of Jerome's dogs—he has Dobermans and pit bulls up there, as you can imagine. Anyway, this kid said a dog dug up our missing man's tennis shoe and brought it back to the compound where they process weed."

"How did they know it was from the guy? Was it distinctive somehow?"

Ryder navigated the Ram down a wider dirt road. "Smelled like piss."

"The shoe?"

"Yeah."

"I don't follow."

"That's how the dog found the shoe. Apparently one of Jerome's— ahem—managers started laughing and said it was Jose's shoe. Because Jose had pissed himself before they shot him."

"Jesus," Pilate said.

"Yeah. We were pretty close to setting up a bump line search out there, but after that I canceled the search for Jose and gave the public drunk kid a bus ticket. Don't let Jerome's faux erudition and the fineries of conversation fool you, Mr. Pilate. He's a damn killer."

"I get you. So, what's this connection with me, though?"

"You always this narcissistic?" Ryder drawled. "Just busting your balls. I don't know. If this is Hilmer's doing, he coulda encouraged that. Or it could be independent of the whole thing. We're gonna find out."

"This is so weird. I never would've thought anybody could even grow pot of any serious scale around here."

"The state of Nebraska has two major climate zones. Both are ideally suited to seasonal marijuana cultivation. This county is on the ragged edge of both zones. And don't kid yourself. Even if you could only grow pot on one square acre in the entire state, there'd be people killing each other to control it."

* * *

Pilate checked in with Kate and the kids as he stood on Cusack's wraparound porch. He asked her to put both kids on the phone to chat a minute, though Kara was engrossed in her TV show, which he heard in between her silences. Peter was a little distracted but asked when he was coming home more than once.

After he said goodbye, he sat heavily in the porch swing, picking at chipped pink paint.

"What's the matter, John?" Simon said. *"You putting off going inside for some reason?"*

Pilate mentally flipped him off, sighed, and watched a truck loaded with corn go by.

Reluctantly, he got to his feet and went inside. He smelled dinner, though Marcy and Cusack were not in the dining room. He padded up the stairs to his room, a pink stickie note on his door impossible to miss. **Come to my room. — V.**

He thought about ignoring it but knew that was a non-starter. He stepped down the hall to her room and knocked.

"It's open," she called.

He opened the door and walked in the darkened room; Val had every blind and curtain closed.

"Be right out," she called from the bathroom.

"You worried about another peeping Tom or something?" he said. He noted that her suitcase was nowhere in sight.

Pilate didn't hear her walk from the bathroom; she slid her muscular arms around his waist and pressed herself against him.

"Hi?"

"I'm sorry about what I said," Val whispered.

He patted her hands, which were locked together, moving up over his belly.

"It's...okay?" he said, bewildered.

"I need you to make it up to me," she said.

"Okay, how?"

"Ride to the airport?" Simon said.

"Take off your clothes," she whispered, her hands moving back to his waist, unbuckling his belt.

"Val, maybe we should talk," he started to say as she furiously unbuckled his belt and unbuttoned his jeans with a smooth, strong pulling motion. She whirled him around and pushed him on the bed. Even in the darkness Pilate could see she was nude. Val yanked off his shoes and tugged off his pants. Quickly, she did the same with his underwear, then his shirt.

"That's it, don't fight me," she said, climbing over his legs and straddling him, grinding. In a matter of seconds she pulled him inside her, riding on him cowgirl style.

As her gyrations picked up pace she moaned in synch with him a moment more, then leaned in close, biting his lip gently. She rose back up, making a fist and punching him in the jaw.

"Ow! What the fuck are you doing?" he said.

She said nothing, continuing to grind.

"I said," but his sentence was cut short by another right hook, this one with a little more mustard on it.

His eyes acclimated to the darkness. She smiled and started to backhand him with her left. He intercepted it and pushed her off him, she landed on her belly beside him. He wasted no time gathering her arms and pinning them behind her.

"Yes, that. More of that," she muttered. "Slap my ass."

Pilate pondered the request for half a second, then complied, eliciting yelps of pain and pleasure.

Val struggled a few seconds, breaking his hold on her and rolling over. "Now hit me."

"John, we need to get you some help in the women department," Simon said. *"Maybe somebody…normal?"*

Pilate decided the mere fact Val wasn't wearing a Guy Fawkes mask made her more than normal enough.

He curled his fist.

Chapter Thirteen

"Mister Pilate?" The voice on the hotel line to his room was familiar, yet he could not place it.

"Yeah?"

"They killed Nora," he said in an odd cadence. "They killed her, and I'm next."

"Who are you?"

"You gotta come up here. I let you live before. You owe me."

"Jesus," Pilate said. Her head under the sheets, Val reached out and put her hand on his shoulder.

"It would be so nice-nice if you could help me."

Pilate felt his chest tighten. He sat up in Val's bed. "You sick fuck. Where are you?"

"I'm up at Spy Bluff. But you have to hurry. He's going to kill me."

"Who? Jerome?"

"You have an hour before this plays out. If you come up."

"So you can kill me? What will you do this time? Bury me alive?" Pilate felt Val twitch under the covers, then jerk them off her head as she looked at him. "Fuck you, man. Turn yourself in."

"Come up here and you'll know why I trapped you in Key West," his voice sounded more...normal. "Or don't, and you'll never know. And you and your wife may be next after he kills me."

"You're nuts. He has no reason to kill me."

"Ticking ticking ticking. Spy Bluff. One hour. He'll be here then, and I have nowhere left to hide."

"Where on Spy Bluff?"

"Come up to where you were yesterday. I'm hiding not too far down the hill. You'll find me and you can get me out of here. He won't dare kill me if you're here."

"How can I trust you?"

"Hurry Mister Pilate. Be my friend. Help me out of here. It would be so nice-nice if you could." The call ended.

"What the hell?" Val said, running a hand through her bedhead.

Pilate ignored her, calling Ryder's number. "Sheriff, I just got a not-so-nice call from an old friend."

* * *

"Will you be here when I get back?" he asked, dressing hurriedly after telling her very little about the caller, and that she could not come with him and Ryder.

She reclined on her side, head propped up on her hand. "Yes."

"Why are you smiling?"

"Because you finally figured it out."

"What?"

"The real reason I'm into boxing."

"You must have some pretty intense workouts," he said, kissing her forehead.

"I come about ten times a day, yeah," she said, laughing. "See you when you get back, John."

"I'll be sure to keep my left up."

* * *

Ryder's Ram rolled up just as Pilate burst onto the porch. Pilate jumped in.

"Backup coming with us?"

"Oh yeah," Ryder said. "Plenty."

"So what's the plan?"

"We're gonna go up there and find out why he thinks Jerome's going to kill him."

"In the dark? The sun goes down in a few."

"We're going to get up there and count on Jerome not being stupid about this."

"When will the deputies be there? We meeting up before we get to Spy Bluff?"

"We have backup. No worries," Ryder said. "Just follow my lead."

Pilate felt queasy. "Have you called Trooper Hulsey? I can do that if you haven't yet," Pilate said, taking his phone from his pocket.

"No need," Ryder said. "Got it covered. Follow my lead. And stop talking. I'm thinking."

* * *

The sun dipped below the horizon as the Ram pulled up to the same spot from before. Parked on the side of the narrow road was a beat-up, rusted-out Econoline van.

"He's punctual," Ryder drawled as he slowed, parking thirty yards away on the opposite side of the road. "He turned off the engine. John, follow…"

"Your lead?"

"Good man," he said. "Here." He pulled a semi-auto pistol from underneath his seat.

"Oh, hell no," he said. "I'm a civilian."

"No, John, you're not. You're backup. Round's already chambered."

"Jesus," Pilate said, accepting the gun. "No deputies? Why?"

"Move very carefully. Don't shoot unless I do." Ryder tucked two speed loaders in his jacket pocket and stepped out.

Pilate's heart raced, the queasiness now a full-fledged gorge rising. He swallowed, hard, willing his heart to slow down. He paused in the truck a moment, swallowing back adrenaline, then joined Ryder.

Grasping a large flashlight in one hand and his Colt in the other, Ryder shone the light on the van, slowly surveying the illuminated area.

"Maybe he's hiding somewhere else?" Pilate whispered.

"Maybe," Ryder said, turning in a quiet three-sixty, the light illuminating trees as he went. "I'll cover you. Go look in the van."

"John, this isn't right," Simon hissed.

"No shit?" Pilate muttered to himself.

Pilate switched the pistol from his right hand to his left as he wiped his sweaty hand on his jeans, then switched back. He crept to the van, the gun in his outstretched hand. "You going to shine that light over here or what?"

Ryder wordlessly shone the light on the van's cracked windshield as Pilate grasped the door handle, yanking it open with the warped protest of rusted metal. Ryder appeared over Pilate's shoulder, shining the light inside. The van smelled of unwashed bodies, weed, and rust. There was nothing inside but a fetid sleeping bag, a few cardboard boxes, some trash bags, and dozens of fast-food wrappers.

"Maybe he's taking a leak," Ryder said.

"Van smells like he already did, right here in the back," Pilate said. "And maybe a shit."

"That's not nice-nice."

Ryder wheeled around, leveling the Colt and aiming the flashlight across the road. "Freeze," he growled.

Pilate turned, shuddering as he took in the shambolic skinny man who had abducted him and left him to die. It seemed long ago and yesterday. He raised his gun.

He slowly put up his hands, a crooked-tooth tweaker smile glistening brown in the flashlight beam.

"Where's Jerome?" Ryder said. "On your knees, fingers laced, hands on your head."

"Yes, of course, remember to please be nice-nice," he cackled.

Pilate realized the voice was a put-on all along.

"You fucker," Pilate said. "Who put you up to it? Why did you kidnap me?"

"Figure it out, smartass," he said, laughing again, his voice deeper than before. "You think on it real hard to see who the man behind the mask is."

"So you're not a Jack Lindstrom fan, I take it?" Pilate said.

The man laughed again. "Oh please, get over yourself. I got no idea who that even is. The boss thought it might be hilarious."

"Jerome?"

The man smiled, shaking his head. "Sheriff, where did you get this guy?"

"Shut up," Ryder snapped. "Where is he?"

"I told him sundown," he shrugged.

"Ryder, what the hell?"

"Quiet, John. It will all make sense in—"

"A minute or so," Pilate heard the unmistakable sound of a torch lighter. The smell of strong cigar smoke wafted up from behind the van. "Howdy, sheriff. Constable."

"Thurman?" Pilate said.

Thurman chuckled, stepping out, puffing on his cigar. "Oh Mister Pilate, a day late and a dollar short as usual." He puffed again, the orange cherry of the cigar brightening a second. "So sheriff, we good here? The stage all set?"

As if in reply, a four-wheeler crested the hill, the unmistakable shape of Jerome Halt riding.

"What the hell?" Pilate muttered, his hand grasping the grip of the pistol harder, but keeping the barrel pointing at the ground between him and Thurman.

Jerome cut the engine, stepping off the four-wheeler. "Gents," he said, hand resting on the butt of his gun.

"So, Jerry, how you been?"

"Doing all right, but I'd be doing a whole lot better if you stayed in your lane, Hilmer."

Thurman scoffed. "Not sure what you mean, Jerry. You're the one who decided to get into my line of work. I thought we agreed a long time ago that you were into plants, not powder."

Jerome snorted. "Bullshit. You know full well I agreed to Sheriff Ryder's detente, and then you got your meth business shot out from under you. Now you want in on my product line."

"Our skinny friend here," Thurman said, gesturing with his cigar. "Reported you were getting into meth."

"That's funny," Jerome said. "He told me you were getting into pot."

"Who is that little shit, anyway? And why the fuck did you send him after me?" Pilate said.

"Just a run of the mill tweaker willing to do odd jobs for a bag of dope. Some odder than others," Thurman said.

The man snorted. "Well, I'm not sure how run of the mill I am. I fooled both of you. Mr. Pilate, I'll tell you who sent me and why. I'll even make you another martini," he looked at Ryder. "But I want immunity and safe passage out of here."

"People in hell want ice water," Thurman said, flicking his cigar at Pilate and Ryder, embers flying as it hit Pilate's pistol. Thurman pulled a pistol from behind his back, leveling it at the man on his knees.

The flash of the muzzle came curiously ahead of the sound from Ryder's gun.

Pilate swung his gun at Thurman as the old gangster fell to his knees, gun hand dropping uselessly to his side, mouth moving as he gaped at the sizeable new hole in his chest.

"Son of a bitch, Ryder. You double-crossing son of a…" Thurman's jaw slackened as he collapsed.

Jerome, who had crouched defensively as the shot was fired, slowly rose to his feet, whistling low and slow. "Well, that was easier than I thought."

Ryder nodded. "Pilate? Give me the gun. We're all good here."

Pilate cocked his head and looked at Ryder questioningly. "You sure?"

"Yup, all good," and he held out his hand. Pilate put the gun in his palm. Ryder holstered the Colt, looking at the Glock. "You had the safety on, John."

"Oops," Pilate said, looking at Thurman lying dead in the twilight.

"So, we all good? No more issues with you about my product line?"

Ryder nodded. "As long as you keep outta the meth business." He stepped behind Mister Nice-Nice.

Jerome clicked his tongue. "Now you know damn well we agreed I get to run everything once we got rid of Thurman."

"Fuck," Pilate said.

Ryder shrugged. "I lied," he said, turning off the safety and pointing the Glock at Jerome.

Jerome's hands went up. "Whoa whoa whoa, sheriff. Think it through man," he said. "You know I got people."

"You mean *I* got people, don't you?" He fired two shots into Jerome, sending his bulky body sailing back over the four-wheeler.

Nick screamed as Ryder kicked him in the back, knocking him face-first into the dirt. Ryder stepped over to Jerome's body, lifting the dead man's Luger pistol from his holster. As Nick raised himself up, Ryder dispatched him with three bullets, center mass.

"Oh god," Pilate said, leaning against the van, ears ringing.

"Don't worry, John," Ryder said, wiping the butt of Jerome's Luger pistol with a handkerchief and putting it into the fallen man's hand as he lay gurgling in the dirt. "You're one of the good guys." He wiped the Glock and put it in Nick's lifeless hand.

"Good guy?" Pilate said. "Then what's that make you?"

"The guy who picks up the trash," Ryder said. "And I have purely had enough of these guys shitting all over my county. Haven't you?" His voice was strangely cracked.

"Shit. He desperately needs to be seen as the good guy. I mean, even more than you do." Simon said.

A siren echoed in the distance.

"That's Hulsey, I expect," he said, sliding a toothpick in his mouth.

"You...you murdered these men," Pilate said, voice quavering.

"Nope, you saw the whole thing. They got in a little gunfight as I was trying to broker a truce, to keep the peace and preserve public order. I did all I could to stop the violence, but you saw."

"You're not pulling me into this, Ryder," Pilate said.

"You're already in, John," he said. "And your life will get far less complicated if you stay in your lane."

"Did you have something to do with that freak locking me up to die?" Pilate said, pointing at the body.

Ryder shook his head. "No, I didn't. He was square about that. Thurman was stirring up trouble down here and I guess he figured it would be fun to fuck with you while he was at it. Get a little revenge. This guy went along purely to curry favor with his boss."

"And what about the girl, Nora? And the shootings?"

"Tweaker. Thurman had her shoot Bob to destabilize things at the airport. So they could get in and out without being seen for a while. Saved a shit ton of time hauling out meth and pot by plane."

"And Reverend Falley?"

Ryder bit his lip in thought. "That one perplexes me, to be honest. But I think he screwed her when she came to him for help, and she gave him a little payback. Meth's a helluva drug."

"So what are you going to do now? You going to shut all this down? How long do you think it will take for somebody else to start doing the same shit Thurman and Jerome were?"

Ryder flicked the brim of his hat up, the last light of the day reflected in his eyes as he leaned in close enough for Pilate to smell the cinnamon toothpick in his mouth. "I think you know the answer already. You remember all the drug people you shut down. We arrest, what, a thousand dopers a day in this country? Ten thousand? Who knows? Who cares?" His voice grew more urgent.

"We arrest at noon, by two someone else is running the same route, using the same tools, selling to the same people. No. *We* control things, and that way at least the problem is managed. Management is the key, John."

"By the way, I do have a thought for you," Ryder said. "Seems there's gonna be a management change at the Tin Roof. I know you're looking for something to do, and you love the BBQ."

"What are you saying?"

"Nobody's seen Nelda for a few days. Wasn't me in case you're wondering."

Two cruisers appeared at the end of the road, dust flying, sirens wailing. They still had a fair distance to cover.

"You son of a bitch," Pilate said.

"Go home, John Pilate. Cheer up. Get your house in order," Ryder said. "After you give your corroborating statement, of course. You really don't have any choice."

Pilate stood locked in thought. His mind raced across the miles of cotton and river valley and beaches lining the golden Gulf of Mexico, across the water to a tarnished jewel of an island. He could hear Dr. Sandberg chuckling at him. That was the day he had claimed to the psychologist that he sometimes just had to drink; he had no choice. Sandberg had looked at him, face beaming with kindness, before explaining how this was the least true thing that Pilate had ever said.

"The human brain, John," he said through his continuing grin, "is the ultimate decisionmaker. It's so good at making decisions, making choices, that it has learned to persuade itself that there was only ever one option. Saves on guilt and probably cuts the therapy bill, but it leaves us with a false assumption about the world. 'I didn't have a choice'. You have nothing but choices."

He thought about Kate, bound to this tiny town so tightly that no matter what he might do, she would likely never make the choice to leave. What would life be for her? Intelligent, perceptive, wanting nothing but safety and happiness for her children, watching the law and the courts and the money and the drugs and the crime all slowly merging into one monstrous compromise with evil? What would happen to Peter, to Kara? Would Peter work for his old man, slowly learning the appalling secrets of Cross County? He thought of Kara sitting afraid by a creek at night, asking a four-year-old to reassure her that their father did care, that her father did love her, that her father would never walk away. Never leave her to be used and hurt by worse men than himself because that was the easy path.

Pilate knelt on his haunches, feeling sick. He asked himself a question; and not for the first time, was a little surprised by where Simon came down on the issues.

'Fuck this guy, John. He doesn't have any baseballs to steal, but. Fuck. This. Guy.'

"You're right, Sheriff Ryder."

"What's that, John?" Ryder looked up from the incident report form he was already filling with lies and distortions, while his murder victims cooled off in the dirt at his feet.

"I have had enough of drug lords shitting on this county. I've had enough of bad men shitting on this country to make a dollar or to keep themselves safe for another year. It's got to stop. Someone has to stop it."

"I knew you'd hear me, John. With you watching my back, we..."

"No, Sheriff." The nine-millimeter flew from the ankle holster so smoothly and quickly John had to admire himself for a split-second. The barrel pointed at Ryder's head like a laser beam, safety definitely off this time.

"Sheriff Ryder, I am placing you under citizen's arrest for the murders of these three men and criminal conspiracy." He looked at Ryder, who was clearly pondering his odds with the Colt. "Don't try it. Sheriff."

Hulsey was still a hundred yards off, probably starting to wonder what was going on.

"Why not? I'm pretty fast."

"You are. But then you have to explain my death."

He shrugged. "No biggie. You were caught in the crossfire."

"Look at the dash of the truck," Pilate said. "Slowly."

Ryder turned his eyes slowly to the truck and registered dismay as he saw, beneath the litter of paper on the Ram's dash, the tiny blinking light of a cellphone recording video.

"Surrender. You have no choice."

"Shit," Ryder exhaled, the sound of a man making his peace. "I know, John. I really don't." He went for the holstered Colt. His hand was a blur.

'Jesus, he's fast as a fucking sna....'

The shot rang out sharply. It caught Ryder in the temple, and he went down heavily like a dam collapsing in a tsunami. Pilate followed his fall with the nine-millimeter, ready to put more rounds into Ryder if necessary.

Ryder moaned, writhing in the ground, his head bleeding profusely. The shot had gashed the side of his head but hadn't killed him.

"You know, John, maybe I should cut you a little more slack sometimes. You seem wound up. Maybe go to decaf?"

Chapter Fourteen

"So he's a fucking criminal?" Kate said after Pilate recounted the evening's events to her, pacing back and forth on their porch. Hulsey, after a very bad and confusing few minutes, had watched the cellphone video and made a call to Lincoln. Burl and Story transported an unconscious Ryder to the hospital under the watchful eye of a state trooper, riding along.

Sentiment had been strong for locking Pilate up on general principle, but Hulsey had persuaded his superiors that at the moment, the law enforcement resources of Cross Township consisted of one very tired John Pilate, and at least for the moment, he was walking free.

"I think in his own mind he is all law and order," Pilate said. "But I also think he got his eye on making a fortune. Seems he owed a fair amount of money on his acreage. Probably a botched land deal, so he mortgaged the farm to hold off creditors. He needed cash. And I mean, what better way? County commissioner, acting sheriff, controlling all the drugs, all the cops, everything? Who could touch him?"

"There has to be somebody in law enforcement who could have helped," she said, shaking her head. "FBI?"

He shrugged. "I suppose. They would have gotten out there, when, six months from now? By then Ryder's rigged every report and every witness to match his narrative," Pilate sighed. "You know what's funny? The only person who tried to warn me was Scoville. Over beers the other day. He hinted I should watch Ryder. I didn't understand at the time. Shit, the crooked sheriff sure knew one of his own kind, didn't he?"

"Yes," she said thoughtfully. "Or maybe he needed to make one thing right. One thing."

"Could be. Could be," Pilate said, looking in her eyes he sat beside her. "Let me ask you something."

She looked back, expectantly, wine glass in hand.

"Are you ready to leave Cross? I mean, truly leave? Because out of all the people we've had narrow brushes with, Jeremy Ryder is the last one I want to point at and say *j'accuse*."

"Shit," she said, downing the wine. "You're talking about cutting and running."

"An intelligent strategic retreat. I have friends here, but also enemies. It never would end, Kate. If I stay here...with you...there's only one way I see to make it work. And there'd be one man with a badge. He's me. Or we can go and build from a clean beginning somewhere new."

"We couldn't though, could we? Someone would always know. Someone would always come."

He nodded, somberly.

"Okay," she said, softly. "Then we stay here in the home we built, and we make it work right, make it work the way it's supposed to. What about Val?"

"All three of us have some serious talking to do."

She hesitated, then decided to never lie to him again. "John...all four of us."

He laughed. "Seriously? Elbow patches?"

"He's kind, John. He's decent and takes care of our children when they need him better than anyone I've ever met, other than one man."

"It's huge, isn't it? Like an anaconda that swallowed a pig."

"Oh my God, you are so insecure."

"That isn't a no."

"No. It isn't a no."

"Damn it."

"You started flinging the dung, monkey," she said. "Don't complain about how it tastes."

"Fair enough. Tomorrow, I want to be with my kids, before I'm in court and in and out of trials for a year. And then, take all of us to the Keys. One more time. The kids need to know that oceans are not primarily made up of corn. "

She nodded, smiling. "Going to have Taters teach us all to sail?"

"Why not. Why the hell not?"

She looked at her wine glass. "So are we going to stay married?"

"I don't know, kid." Sobriety was starting to weigh heavily on him in the wake of yet another violent episode, but he knew that opening a bottle now might start a cycle without an end. "But I'm always up for an adventure."

"With me?'

"With you."

She slipped her hand into his. Both looked up at the inky night, eyes feasting on the brilliance of a multitude of stars.

"But I have to go somewhere else first," he said.

"Where?"

"Home. Need to see my folks. I need to get things right."

"Oh my God. That's huge," she said. "What is it Dr. Sandberg said you were working towards?"

"Regeneration. Reconnection. Moving past all the bad and connecting with the good."

"I'm glad you are. Want to take the kids?"

"They'd like that, I think," he said.

The pair sat still, neither wishing to unclasp hands.

"Mommy?" Peter said through the screen door, holding his favorite stuffed animal. "Is that Daddy?"

"It sure is, little guy," Pilate said. "Want to come sit with us?"

He nodded vigorously and burst through the screen door, climbing onto the swing between them, his head leaning on his mother's side.

"Where's your sister?" she said.

"I'm here," Kara said, appearing at the door.

"Plenty of room for you, Kara," Pilate said. Their eyes met, hers shy, his exhausted and strained, but never happier than he was in the moment. She opened the door, her face a mask of confusion and concern.

"Dad, are you going somewhere else soon?"

"I might have to take care of some business, honey. But I will always come back here, for as long as I can climb up those porch steps. After that I might have to live in the backyard with the turtles."

She approached them on the swing, then crawled up into his mother's lap. "Do you promise?"

"I promise. This is where I belong, Kara. This is my family."

Satisfied, she lay her head on his chest, sighed, and quickly fell asleep.

END.

Afterword

What can I say?

There isn't much left but thank you for reading. After all, "The John Pilate Mysteries" were originally supposed to be "A John Pilate Mystery," but here we are, nearly twelve years later, on book eight. This is solely because readers love John, Taters, Kate, Simon, and Co., and asked for more. What a compliment!

I worked very hard on this book, and it took a lot longer than I expected. Sorry about that. I owe so much to my longtime editor, Robert Hayes, Jr., who rescued this one from the depths of my insecurities. Readers generally never know how much work an editor puts into the books they read, but let me assure you, Robert dug deep. Thank you, my friend.

I also want to thank my cover artist, Jason McIntyre, for another wonderful visual. He knew what I wanted for this book before I even told him. Such is the way with talented designers. Thanks heaps, pal. I look forward to future collaborations!

So, as we come to the end, I want you to know I think the team left it all on the field. I hope you agree, and that this series has entertained you as much as it did me writing it.

Bless you, faithful readers.

J. Alexander Greenwood
Kansas City, Missouri
2021

Acknowledgments

Sincere gratitude to my faithful beta readers and supporters! Your thoughts and eagle eyes on typos, mistakes, and just plain weird stuff helped make this book better.

Pete Dulin

Stephanie Greenwood

Lori Hanson

Mike Hulsey

Brian Hutton

Tammy Hutton

Sharon Lochman

A.I. Marlowe

Jason McIntyre

Mary McKenna

Michelle Stinson Ross

Deb Trivitt

And extra-special thanks to Miss Toni, for calling often to ask when the next book was coming.